T0271661

The Three Deaths of Justice Godfrey

L. C. Tyler

CONSTABLE

CONSTABLE

First published in Great Britain in 2024 by Constable

1 3 5 7 9 10 8 6 4 2

Copyright © L. C. Tyler, 2024

The moral right of the author has been asserted.

A CIP catalogue record for this book
is available from the British Library.

ISBN: 978-1-40871-873-5

Typeset in Adobe Caslon Pro by SX Composing DTP, Rayleigh, Essex
Printed and bound in Great Britain by Clays Ltd, Elcograf S.p.A.

Papers used by Constable are from well-managed forests
and other responsible sources.

Constable
An imprint of
Little, Brown Book Group
Carmelite House
50 Victoria Embankment
London EC4Y 0DZ

An Hachette UK Company

www.hachette.co.uk

www.littlebrown.co.uk

For Trystan

Some persons in this book

John Grey – or, to put it another way, me, the teller of this tale, former spy, now magistrate and lord of the manor of Clavershall West in the famous if somewhat flat county of Essex, the fortunate husband of

Aminta, Lady Grey – a talented writer of stage comedies and lady of the manor of Clavershall West, daughter of

Sir Felix Clifford – aged cavalier, who doesn't feature much in the story, thus raising the tone of things more than you could ever imagine, but who is happily still making the hearts of one or two widows in the village flutter, much as he did in the days when he served in the royalist cavalry, fighting gallantly for the late father of our current monarch,

His Gracious Majesty, King Charles the Second – whose diverse and extensive collection of mistresses my father-in-law greatly covets, and who continues to rule his subjects wisely and well, when he is not doing more important things such as horse racing or sailing or carousing with courtiers such as

Philip Herbert, Earl of Pembroke – an inebriate brute of impeccable lineage, or

Lord Chief Justice Sir William Scroggs – who can drink even Herbert under the table and still misdirect a jury afterwards, or

Thomas Osborne, Earl of Danby – Lord Treasurer and head of an administration that is rapidly becoming as famous for its instability as it is for its corruption (no mean feat), but who is nevertheless determined to remain in office for as long as possible by any means available and not to be cruelly discarded by the King, as was

Henry Bennet, Lord Arlington – once my employer, in the days when he was Secretary of State, now demoted to Lord Chamberlain, a post that entitles him to strut round the court with a white wand of office but not much else, having been replaced as Secretary by

Sir Joseph Williamson – in happier times Arlington's loyal deputy, but now currently struggling to placate Parliament, mollify the King and protect the state from villains such as

Sir Robert Peyton – an extreme Protestant, Green Ribbon man and leader of the so-called Peyton Gang, whose dangerous views are shared, at least in part, by

Titus Oates – graduate (he says) of Cambridge University and doctor of divinity (he says) of the University of Salamanca and bearer (he says) of details of a Popish Plot to overthrow the rightful King (see above) and replace him with an evil tyrant papist upstart (currently better known as **His Royal Highness the Duke of York**), whose secretary, the good-looking, well-connected and gossipy

Mister Edward Coleman – is beginning to prove less circumspect than he ought to be, laying him open to the machinations of villains such as

'Captain' William Bedloe – a rogue, horse thief and knight of the post, sometimes briefly known to his victims as Lord Cornwallis, a man wholly without a conscience of any sort, unlike

Miles Prance – a silversmith, who does in fact have a conscience for a few days towards the end of 1678 and again in 1685, but not much of one in between, which could be inconvenient for

Father Kelly and Father Gerald – but only if those are their real names and if they really exist, matters that might be clarified for us by

Henry Berry, Robert Green and Lawrence Hill – who definitely do exist and work as loyal but humble servants of various descriptions at Somerset House, though not as humble as

Elizabeth Curtis – who is employed as a maid servant at Hartshorne Lane in Westminster, and to whom nobody much listens, though she would wish to inform you that's simply how things are these days, if you do all the hard work they never notice, up from before dawn till almost midnight, slaving away in the kitchen for a pittance and it's shocking, sir, and you'll scarcely believe it when I tell you, but, *even then*, most of the tips round here go to

Judith Pamphlin – housekeeper at the same establishment in Hartshorne Lane in Westminster, who gives herself airs in Elizabeth's opinion, though nothing like the airs appropriated by

Henry Moor – the sole manservant at the same etc. etc., who is most certainly being generously bribed to keep quiet about something by

Mister Michael Godfrey and Mister Benjamin Godfrey – prosperous City merchants, and brothers to

Sir Edmund Berry Godfrey – who is famous mainly for getting murdered. Possibly by one of the above. But, of that notorious incident, more very shortly.

Actually, just turn the page and you can start to read about it now.

The Journey Begins

Saturday 12 October 1678

He's cautious leaving the house this morning. He has to be. The yard is a maze of carefully stacked, sweet-smelling firewood. Anyone willing to risk a splinter or two could be hiding there. Anyone at all. And today is as good for murder as it is for anything else. Cold. Opaque. Unobliging.

Narrow, muddy Hartshorne Lane is a thin rivulet of mist that has flowed up from the sleek mudflats of the River Thames. Smoke has been spiralling from thousands of London chimneys since just before dawn. The damp air is already becoming yellow with acidly corrosive coal smoke. He takes a deep breath of it and nods approvingly. After all, he sells sea coal as well as wood.

At the gate leading from the yard to the lane, he pauses, uncertain whether what he is doing is as wise as he thought. From the nearby tower of Saint Martin-in-the-Fields, a heavy bronze bell begins to chime ten o'clock. He checks his pockets just one more time. Four broad pieces of gold wrapped up in paper. Four pounds in heavy silver coins that make his coat pocket bulge. And three small gold ones, added in at the last moment. Quite a lot there now, come to think of it, but whether it's going to be enough depends on how things turn out. He pats his pockets again – good, he didn't forget the notebook. He'll need that too.

He turns back to see his clerk standing on the doorstep watching him. The old man looks cold and worried. Best be getting along then. He's already told Moor that he's not taking him with him. Being accompanied by a servant is, as he observed recently to a colleague, a great clog to a man. Whatever's waiting for him out there, he'll deal better with it on his own, unencumbered by domestic staff.

He's going to die. You've worked that out already. Of course you have. The question is how. And when. And where. And why. And, most important, who's already waiting to kill him. After he's found, dead in a ditch on Primrose Hill, none of those things will be quite as clear as you'd like them to be. I'm warning you now, it's not going to be the most straightforward of cases.

But at ten o'clock on this gloomy morning of Saturday the twelfth of October 1678, he still thinks he's in with a chance. However bleak things might look, however many bad choices he's made over the past month – and, God knows, he's made a few – he's actually going to get away with it. He pulls his broad-brimmed hat more firmly on to his periwig. He checks that his sword is hanging properly from its emerald-green sash, turns confidently on a newly polished heel and is gone through the gate into the wide, wide world. He'll never be seen alive in this woodyard again.

Others will see him, though, in more places than you could ever believe. They'll say so in the evidence they will shortly give at his inquest. Get yourself murdered and all sorts of people will want to share a little of your glory. It's only natural, isn't it?

Mister Parsons, coach maker and church warden, will swear he saw him in Saint Martin's Lane at nine o'clock, which is a good hour before he'd even left home. He'd asked Parsons the way to Primrose Hill. Parsons had jokingly enquired if he planned to buy it, Primrose Hill being well-wooded. Parsons had smiled, waiting for the wood-monger's answering chuckle. 'What is that to you?' came the gruff reply. 'I have business there or else I should not have asked you.'

At exactly the same hour, William Collins saw him talking to a milk woman at Marylebone Conduit, no more than a mile from Primrose Hill.

Around ten o'clock, Thomas Mason of Marylebone saw him going towards the fields between Marylebone Pound and Marylebone Street. The two of them passed the time of day briefly. Mason was an old customer of the wood-monger. No question of mistaken identity there.

At eleven he was seen back in Saint Martin's Lane again, and also in the Strand and also close to Lady Cook's lodgings at the Cockpit in Whitehall Palace. Some of those who saw him thought he seemed a bit melancholy.

At twelve, Thomas Snell, who looked after the Holborn Turnstile, saw him on his way to Red Lyon Fields.

At one o'clock fellow vestryman Joseph Radcliffe saw him in the Strand and urged him in vain to stop and take a glass of something warming. He shook his head and pressed on from wherever he'd been to wherever he was going.

Between two and three o'clock he, or somebody a bit like him, was observed at Lincoln's Inn and also several miles away back at Primrose Hill. He definitely looked melancholy in both places.

Just as it was getting dark, and identification more difficult, John Oakley saw him walking near the Watergate at Somerset House in the Strand. There was a man or two near him, though whether they were murderers was unclear at the time. With hindsight Oakley felt he should have said something, but he didn't. Well, you don't like to, do you?

After that, nobody (except possibly his killer) saw him alive again. He'd gone from being everywhere at once to being nowhere at all.

Much later, his clerk, Henry Moor, will say that the really odd thing about that Saturday was the coat. 'Bring me my new camlet coat,' my master said to me. So I did bring it and I helped him put it on. Very smart. You could visit anyone in a coat like that. But no sooner was it buttoned up to his linen cravat than he changed his mind. No, he said, his old camlet coat would serve the day well enough. Shame really. He might at least have been killed in a nice coat.'

'What's that old fool Moor been telling you about coats?' asks Judith Pamphlin, housekeeper. She narrows her eyes, leans back in her chair and folds her arms. 'Why shouldn't my master go out in his old camlet if he wanted to? Still had a lot of wear in it, that coat did. The strangest thing was actually the message he received the night before – Friday night, that would be. A man came to the door with a letter. He gives it to my master and says he'll wait for a reply. Well, master sits there in front of the fire and he reads it once and he reads it twice and he reads it again – that's three times. The messenger's getting impatient by now. Not used to being kept waiting. What answer shall I take back? he wants to know. Master gives a great sigh. "Tell him

I don't know what to make of it", he says. Then he threw the
letter into the fire. I mean, if that's not odd, what is? Don't bother
to ask Elizabeth what she saw. She doesn't know anything about
anything. Shit for brains, that one.'

'They think I don't notice things, but I do,' says Elizabeth Curtis,
maidservant. 'Oh, yes. And I'll tell you something: burning that
letter was the least of it. The master's burnt all sorts of papers
lately. I've tried to read some, when I've cleaned the grate, but,
God bless you sir, they just crumble in your fingers and get on
your apron. You don't want ash on a clean white apron. One paper
was a letter from the master's friend, Mister Edward Coleman,
I do know that. The bit with his signature didn't burn. He's the
Duke of York's secretary, I think. Catholic, but very nice with
it. Plenty of money, that Mister Coleman, I will say that in his
favour. Always dressed in the latest fashion. Fine, glossy periwig.
Well-fitting breeches. Lots of lace and ribbon. Silver buckles.
But *thin*. So thin it worries me sometimes, sir, it really does.
Don't they ever feed him at home? A proper gentleman, anyway,
whereas the master was just a common wood-monger when all's
said and done. I'm sorry but he did sell wood and coal, so what else
does that make him? He didn't have a lot of friends, so I always
thought he was very lucky to have one like Mister Coleman. And
did they tell you about the strange man who visited the master
the morning he died, just before he went out? I don't mean
the one who came on Friday night – a different one on Saturday
morning? No? Well, there you are then. Two unexpected visitors,
not one. Moor and Pamphlin don't know everything. Or, if they
do, they're not telling *you*. I think I heard the Friday one say who
he was sent by. Common enough name. I'll tell you in a second.
It's on the tip of my tongue. No, it's not. It's gone. Anyway, after

that visit the master seemed ... well ... melancholy. Yes, that's the word, now I think about it. He was sore melancholy, the poor man.'

The name of the dead man? I'm so sorry. I thought you knew. He's really famous after all. He's Sir Edmund Berry Godfrey. Noted in the parish of Saint Martin-in-the-Fields as a canny businessman, magistrate and member of the vestry. Knighted for remaining courageously at his post during the Plague year. An upright member of the community, albeit that he overcharges for his wood and coal. But all the wood-mongers do that. They're known for it.

You will have already noticed that his name is an anagram of 'dy'd by Rome's reveng'd fury'. At least, it is if you misspell his name as 'Edmundbury' and are happy to interchange Vs and Us as necessary. And spell 'Sir' as 'Syr', which I suppose you could at a pinch. When people start to look for proof that he perished as the result of a Catholic plot, that anagram will be one of the most convincing pieces of evidence they come up with.

Yes, he's almost as famous as Doctor Titus Oates (anagram 'testis ovat', as I scarcely need to tell you), with whom Sir Edmund's name will ever be connected. Don't tell me you can't remember Doctor Oates either? Dame Fame is a fickle jade indeed. You'd better meet the reverend doctor next then. I mean, he's quite central to the story too. But, if you've no objection, we'll go back a couple of months to a time when nobody had yet heard of Oates or the celebrated Popish Plot, and Primrose Hill was just a pleasant spot, a short way from London, where you could ride or walk or hunt entirely as you chose. You could stroll there all morning with your wife or mistress and never find a single corpse. Happy days, eh?

Chapter One

In which, two months prior to the famous murder of Sir Edmund Berry Godfrey, I meet an honest clergyman, a little down on his luck

The early peace of a fine summer morning is broken by a commotion in the hallway outside the dining room. My wife, Aminta, is fully occupied in feeding a spoonful of egg to the youngest of our three children and I sense, in a way that husbands occasionally can, that she feels commotions are my responsibility. I am therefore about to rise from my seat to deal with it, when I hear our village constable say: 'Just stay where you are, you rogue, or I'll fetch you another clip round the ear.'

I consider for a moment whether Ben is issuing an instruction to me from the far side of the door. I can think of nothing I've done lately that would cause him to address me as a rogue. There is, on the other hand, enough in my more distant past that would justify it only too well. Before I can make up my mind one way or the other, the gleaming brass door handle is turned with some violence and Ben enters, scowling but respectfully removing his battered leather hat as he does so. I wonder if Ben realises he's starting to go bald? Probably not.

'I've caught a thief, Sir John,' he announces to me. 'And I've brought him here for you to deal with. Fairly but harshly. As the King's law demands. Shall I take him to the library, since it's a legal matter? You might prefer not to have the filthy cur in your dining room, with a clean linen cloth and food to the table. Good morning, Lady Grey. I hope you are well?'

'We are all very well, thank you, Ben,' says Aminta. 'I hope you are too? And Nell and little Beth?'

'Wife and daughter very well indeed, my Lady,' says Ben. 'And all the better for your having asked. Though Beth's growing up faster than a bean sprout and not so little as she was.'

'True,' says Aminta. 'I saw her yesterday and remarked on the same thing myself. How they all grow! And she spoke to me so intelligently and politely, Ben. Nicely brought up, I thought. She really is a credit to you and Nell.'

'Excellent,' I say. 'We are all in good health and our children are getting bigger rather than smaller. I assume you have the thief outside, Ben?'

'Ready to be committed for trial at the next assizes or put in the stocks straight away, entirely as you prefer, Sir John.'

'Your devotion to duty does you much credit, Ben. The villagers should be grateful for your efficiency in protecting them from evildoers. Who has he stolen from?'

'Me,' says Ben.

Well, that would explain Ben's zeal. Still, a thief is a thief.

'What did he steal?' I ask.

'Food and a bed for the night,' says Ben with great indignation. 'Arrived yesterday and asked for a room at the inn. Had a very good supper indeed and retired to sleep with a whole bed to hisself. Then, this morning, I caught him sneaking off, without any attempt to pay me what he still owes.'

'I have been trying to explain,' says a rich, deep voice from the hallway. 'But this officious fellow declines to listen to me.'

'I know what you did,' Ben snarls back. 'And Sir John here is going to make sure you receive the appropriate punishment.'

'What's the thief's name?' I ask.

'He calls hisself Oates,' says Ben. 'Tight Arse Oates.'

'*Titus*,' intones the still invisible man in the passage. 'A Roman name of some distinction. An emperor's name, forsooth! The Reverend Doctor Titus Oates. MA. DD. At your service, Sir John, if I might possibly just enter your dining room and explain? Here in the hallway I do feel at a certain disadvantage.'

A head pokes round the door frame. But somehow it does not belong to the voice.

'Why does that man have his mouth in the middle of his face?' asks our son Charles.

'Shh!' says Aminta.

'But he does, Mummy. They've put his mouth in the wrong place.'

'That's enough, darling,' says Aminta.

But Charles is right, they definitely have. Oates has such an enormous chin that it disrupts the whole balance of his features. His cheeks are round and his neck is remarkably short. His lips are plump and moist. It is an unfortunate head to possess, unless you are a blowfish or something of the sort. Which he isn't. His legs are short and bandy, but you don't notice that until you have completely finished with his face.

'But Mummy . . .'

'Why don't you take your sisters out into the garden to play?' says Aminta.

'Do I have to?'

'Yes.'

'They'll have to play soldiers then.'

'No harm at all in suggesting it to them.'

'Mummy says you've got to play soldiers,' Charles informs his sisters.

'No, I don't,' says Aminta. 'Off you all go, out into the sunshine. Play nicely.'

Three members of my family depart reluctantly. They feel they are about to miss something good. Aminta stays. It's her dining room. Anyway, a playwright turns down no opportunity to observe the absurdities of human nature.

'So, Doctor Oates,' I say. 'Why don't you tell me what happened? No, there's no need for you to sit in one of my chairs. You can stand until we've dealt with the matter.'

'Yes,' says Ben. 'You mind your manners in front of a magistrate and remember you're a prisoner. My prisoner.'

Oates takes his meaty hands off the back of the chair. 'Of course, Sir John. I am willing to do whatever you wish. Stand. Sit. Kneel. Ha! I am content to be guided by you, unaccustomed as I am to treatment of this sort and thus happily ignorant of the correct posture I should adopt. As to what happened, I am simply making my way to London from Lowestoft, as any gentleman might. Unfortunately I find myself short of funds and so am obliged to do so on foot, rather than by carriage as you might expect for a person of my rank.'

'What took you to Lowestoft, Doctor Oates?'

'Private business.'

'Could you kindly elaborate on that?'

'It would not be appropriate.'

'I am a magistrate, Doctor Oates, and am entitled to know why you are travelling. Obfuscation will delay things rather than speed them up. Unless what you have been doing embarrasses you very much indeed, I would suggest you tell me, quickly and briefly.'

'Very well, I landed there. I was sailing from foreign parts.'

'Which parts?'

Oates pauses for a long time. 'Saint Omers,' he says at last.

'Saint Omers?' I say. 'You mean the Catholic college?'

I look him up and down. He claims to be a clergyman, but his dress is a simple black coat and black breeches, threadbare at the cuffs and knees and much travel stained. All respectable enough, but not obviously clerical. Yet the voice is one designed for the pulpit and little else. Is he saying he's a Catholic priest entering the country illegally and in disguise? If so, he's made a mistake in telling a magistrate.

'Yes,' he says. 'I have come from that notorious papist school. But, were it not for your good wife's presence, I would spit on its name, sir! I must assure you I am a loyal member of the Church of England – formerly vicar of Bobbing in Kent and lately a naval chaplain. I simply had business at Saint Omers. Business that must for the moment remain confidential, and I would ask you to respect that.'

'But Saint Omers is just on the other side of the Channel. You've come a very long way round to find yourself in Lowestoft.'

'My ship was blown off course by the recent gales. Blown onwards into the ever restless and wine-dark northern seas.'

'We've had no gales here,' I say.

'Then the Good Lord has been most merciful to you. Beyond your low, marshy Essex coast, the winds were grievous and arbitrary.'

Ben raises his eyebrows at me, just in case I can no longer spot pretentious nonsense in my own dining room. Of course, there are sometimes gales at sea that scarcely trouble the church weathercock this far inland. But it is neither the weather nor Doctor Oates's attempt to quote Homer that puzzles me most.

'Your shortest route to London from Lowestoft lies some-what to the east of this village,' I say. 'You are still many miles out of your way. For a man forced by circumstances to travel on foot, that must be inconvenient. Are you lost?'

'Since I had fortuitously arrived in this charming part of the world, I decided to make a short detour to visit a friend of mine, whose advice I wished to seek. A very important man. A minister of His Majesty's. He lives near Thetford.'

This statement is clearly intended to overawe me and I am doubtless expected to ask with immense respect who that friend can possibly be, so that he can inform me that it's none of my business. But I think I already have the answer to my unasked question. This friend is almost certainly my old employer, Lord Arlington, who lives at Euston Hall, near Thetford and not too far away from here. I know of no other ministers, past or current, who fit the bill. Arlington has come down much in the past four years. The formerly all-powerful Secretary of State has been driven from office and replaced in the King's esteem by Lord Danby and in his old post by his former deputy, Joseph Williamson. I could therefore, if I wished, say to Oates that I know exactly who he has been with. I am in fact mildly interested to know how Arlington fares these days. But I doubt any of that will be relevant to the question of payment for a bed, to which we must return very soon if I am to finish my breakfast.

I therefore simply smile at him. 'Very well. I'm sure it is all as you say. We could always write to Saint Omers in the unlikely event of your presence there proving to be material to the matter in hand.'

Oates smiles smugly. 'They would not know me as Doctor Oates. I went by the name of Samson Lucy.'

'Why?' I ask, though obviously I am invited to deduce he was bravely engaged in some secret and dangerous project.

'That is also something I cannot disclose to you at present,' says Oates smugly. 'Let me merely say that it was necessary and of great advantage to the King. Look, Sir John, I think we should simply forget the ridiculous charges that this person is trying to bring against me, don't you? They are unimportant and my journey to London must not be impeded, not for one solitary hour. Why? you ask. Very well, I am prepared to reveal this much to you and no more. I am carrying to the King information about a plot that, even now, the papists in London are attempting to hatch. A plot to bring down His Majesty and all his Parliament and place the King's popish brother on the throne. A plot that strikes at the heart of everything you and I hold dear. A plot so terrifying, Sir John, that I could not decently describe it in front of your good lady.'

'Don't mind me,' says Aminta. 'I've probably written worse. And do spit on the name of Saint Omers if it helps in any way.'

Oates looks at her then gives what I can only describe as a theatrical gasp. 'But of course!' he exclaims. '*Lady Grey* . . . You are the celebrated playwright, whose name is on the lips of everyone in town – I mean every person of taste and discernment. I bow, my Lady, to your genius.'

He does so, a little awkwardly since he is, frankly, corpulent of body as well as round of face and short of leg.

Aminta receives enough genuine praise from people she respects not to need Oates's greasy flattery. Still, she gives him a thin smile. A compliment is a compliment, just as a thief is a thief, and no writer ever gets quite enough of them.

'I do, of course, yield to nobody in my admiration of my wife's talent,' I say, 'but what exactly is this plot? Do you have any proof that the Duke of York is involved? You would be unwise to say it if you haven't. I tell you that as a lawyer.'

Oates suddenly appears concerned. Slander? *Scandalum Magnatum*, to be precise. He'd overlooked this aspect of things. 'You misunderstand me, Sir John. I did not say that the Duke was part of the plot. Not at all.'

'You implied it.'

'I merely meant that the aim of the plotters would be to make him king. Nothing more than that. I do not accuse the Duke of complicity. The whole scheme will doubtless be of great distress to His Royal Highness when he learns of it.'

'And who are these plotters?'

'That, Sir John, must be for the ears of the King, and the King alone.'

'But you nevertheless told Lord Arlington?'

Oates's mouth now opens very wide indeed. He'd clearly forgotten boasting about his important friend and is disconcerted to discover I know who it is and that he may have given away more than he intended. But he quickly recovers his composure.

'I did not say I had revealed anything to him. Merely that I wished to seek his wise counsel. If it would be of assistance to you in the current matter, I can swear an affidavit that I do carry such information. Afterwards you can let me go on my way and then box the ears of this officious so-called constable so that he does not harass his betters in future.'

Ben coughs meaningfully. 'Sir John,' he says, 'does not wish to listen to any more of your lies, Tight Arse. You're a common thief, even if you are a doctor of religiosity.'

'A doctor of *divinity*,' says Oates with immense condescension. 'Of the University of Salamanca. And a graduate, *baccalaureus artium*, of the ancient and famous University of Cambridge. Of which even you and your bedbugs must have heard.'

Oates turns from his contempt of Ben and smiles, defying me, a fellow *baccalaureus artium*, not to side with him. Sadly he is about to suffer another disappointment.

'I think,' I say, 'I've heard all I need to hear. To summarise, you say you are coming from a Catholic college but are not a Catholic yourself. You are walking to London by an unnecessarily long route for reasons I still only partially understand. You say you are carrying details of a plot that you cannot share even with my wife, hardened though she is to theatrical intrigue and deceit. The plot will bring the Duke of York to the throne, to his great personal annoyance. That seems to be that. Unless you still have something of relevance to tell me, it remains only for me to ask you one thing: did you in fact pay for your supper and bed, Doctor Oates?'

'I was fully *intending* to,' he says in the richest and most velvety tone he can manage. 'But I was simply not permitted to make the payment. The truth of the matter is that I went for a short walk early this morning, to revel in the glorious sight of the sun on the golden fields of grain. It is such a *joy* to be back in England, and in your own county of Essex especially – superior to Norfolk and Suffolk in every possible way, I always think. This ill-educated person mistook my intentions, pursued me and accused me of trying to avoid payment. Nothing, absolutely nothing, Sir John, could have been further from my mind. I swear this to you as a loyal subject of the King and a man of God.'

'The man of God took his pack and all his belongings with him on his morning walk,' says Ben. 'That much I know.'

'So that you couldn't pilfer from it!' says Oates, pointing a clerical but allegedly non-Catholic finger at Ben. 'Do you think I'd leave my luggage behind so you could do as you wished with it? For aught I know you are a recusant yourself. I have detailed notes on the plot that I intend to report to His Majesty. Names! Dates! Cyphers! I must guard them with my life, sir!'

'You could have taken your notes and left your shitty linen,' says Ben. 'Your gold would have been safe too. I've never stolen from a customer. Not ever. And Sir John knows it.'

I'm assuming that, as usual, Ben isn't counting giving short measure as theft. If so, I'd be happy to vouch for his honesty in any court in the land.

'Do you have the money to pay my constable in his role as innkeeper?' I ask Oates.

'Of course I do.'

'Then just pay him what you owe him now. And an extra two shillings for the trouble you have put him to by wandering off to admire the fields of golden corn. Otherwise, I'll have you in the stocks as a common thief.'

'I would have hoped, sir, that one gentleman would believe what another gentleman tells him. Perhaps you are less of a gentleman than you appear to be.'

'My tailor and my periwig maker,' I say, 'must take credit for my appearance. As for the rest, just pay Mister Bowman what I've said and be on your way.'

Ben isn't entirely happy. He'd been hoping he'd see Oates in the stocks for a day at the very least. On the other hand, just as a compliment is a compliment (and so on), two shillings are exactly four and twenty pence. Not a farthing more nor less. And they're going to him this time, not to the King.

Oates slowly takes a purse from his pocket and counts out the silver and copper coins as if they were sacred relics of impeccably Protestant origin. The purse is noticeably hungrier after that. The good doctor may be hard-pressed to pay for his bed tonight. I wonder what tricks he'll have to come up with. For a moment I almost feel sorry for him, but only for a moment.

'The King shall hear of this,' Oates adds as he pushes his remaining funds back into his pocket. 'That one of his magistrates has hindered and delayed the exposure of Catholic treason, doubtless because of his own clandestine romish sympathies. That one of his constables has failed to show due respect for a clergyman of the Church of England. I smell popery in this village, even above the stench of stale beer and horseshit.'

I think it is the remark about stale beer that really incenses Ben. But he accepts that the charge of treason against me is possibly more serious. 'What if Sir John does let papists off fines for not attending Sunday services?' he demands. 'Sir John's always said he won't penalise anybody just for what they believe. He's a fair man and a good one.'

I am sure Ben intends to be helpful, but I can already see what this may become in Oates's mouth on some future occasion. Well, let the learned doctor do with Ben's words whatever he wishes to do. If Oates does get to speak to the King and to describe the extent of the treason that flourishes in Clavershall West and the surrounding villages under my watch, then I can take comfort in the fact that the King knows me well enough. And we are very much of the same mind on the subject of fining Catholics for refusing to be nominal Protestants. Anyway, Oates will probably get nowhere near the King.

'If you fail to get an audience with His Majesty,' I say, 'and I warn you he is a very busy man, then I'd suggest that you take your information to the current Secretary of State, Sir Joseph Williamson. He'll be more use to you than Arlington. Or, if Williamson's absent, you could make a statement to a London magistrate.'

I expect Oates to tell me that the King will most certainly see him, but there proves to be a streak of realism in him that I had not anticipated.

'Which magistrate would you suggest?' he asks.

I try to remember who I've had dealings with lately.

'You could always try Sir Edmund Godfrey in the parish of Saint Martin-in-the-Fields,' I say. 'He's regarded highly. Honest and straightforward. And more to the point, he's the Court Justice, with responsibility for the precincts of Whitehall Palace. Now, if you've paid Ben all you owe him, I would suggest you get on your way.'

'Perhaps you could do me the service of putting me on the right road for London?'

'Ben will go with you and make sure you leave the village the proper way,' I say.

'It's what we always do with paupers and vagrants,' says Ben. 'Out of the village by the fastest route, with a kick up the backside if they're too slow.'

This, for Oates, is the last straw, but his anger is directed entirely at me. 'The day shall come, sir, when you will regret your shabby treatment of an honest man who desires only to serve his country. There will be a reckoning – mark my words.'

'Save your breath, Doctor Oates,' I say. 'You will need it for the long journey you have ahead of you.'

*

'Well, what did you make of that?' I ask Aminta.

'It's not Doctor Oates's fault that he looks as he does, but he's the biggest charlatan to visit this house for some years, and that includes your former master Lord Arlington.'

'Oates seemed dismayed when he realised I knew Arlington,' I say.

'I wonder why he went to him for help? It's years since your erstwhile employer was dismissed as Secretary of State. He has no influence with anyone.'

'I agree,' I say. 'Unless Oates was cloistered in some monastery while he gathered information about the plot, he must be aware how much Arlington has come down in the world. He's Lord Chamberlain, but that means very little. He's an old man that the young blades, like Philip Herbert, laugh at behind his back. There's nothing Arlington could do to assist Oates, except maybe lend him his coach fare.'

'Do you think Arlington is happy as Lord Chamberlain?' asks Aminta.

'I doubt it. He enjoyed being at the heart of things. Danby has eclipsed everyone, not just Arlington but Williamson too. Williamson is treated as a useful drudge, not as one of the King's close advisors and drinking companions.'

'And is Williamson happy as a useful drudge?'

'Oh yes, most definitely.'

'Still, it would seem Oates would prefer to be dealing with Arlington.'

'Perhaps Oates would have known that a man who desperately wanted to get back into power and revenge himself spitefully on his enemies, as Arlington does, would be willing to clutch at almost any straw. But surely even Arlington wouldn't have wasted his time on somebody like Oates?'

'I suspect you're right,' says Aminta. 'Arlington was always a shrewd judge of character if nothing else. He would have seen Oates for what he was and sent him packing. I also doubt the King will be enthusiastic to receive news of a new Catholic plot. His Majesty treads a very narrow line between being a loyal member of the Church of England himself and protecting his Catholic brother from Parliament. Anything that stirred up feelings against the Catholics would be inconvenient.'

'It will come to nothing. If the plot really existed, Oates could have revealed the details of it to me, as a magistrate.'

'Especially if he needed your help to get to London. He does give the impression of somebody making things up as he goes along and retracting his words as soon as he realises they come back and bite him. Let's hope his story is better rehearsed by the time he gets there or he could quickly find himself in Newgate for slandering the Duke of York.'

'It's a dangerous world that Doctor Oates is walking into,' I say.

'Only if somebody believes him,' says Aminta.

'I can't see Williamson doing that. Or Godfrey, for that matter. We've all heard the last of Tight Arse.'

Chapter Two

In which Aminta's aunt explains things

'What's the news from London?'

'Sorry?' Aminta looks up from her letter.

'That correspondence seems to require a great deal of concentration, whatever it is,' I say.

'My aunt is gleefully informing me of the latest scandals. You won't believe this, but – do you remember Titus Oates?'

'The man who tried to defraud Ben a few weeks ago?'

'Exactly. He has been well received at court. After some initial and fully justified doubts, Lord Treasurer Danby seems quite taken with him. He's allowed Oates to testify before the Privy Council. The good doctor is claiming that he pretended to convert to Catholicism in order to infiltrate the Jesuit order.'

'Did somebody ask him to do that?' I say.

'No, it was all his own idea, it would seem. That was clever of him, wasn't it? He has named a number of Catholic lords who are plotting to overthrow the King and replace him with his brother James. He stood there reeling off the list of traitors – no notes.'

'If you're making things up, you don't need notes.'

'Well, it's a very plausible list anyway: Arundel, Bellasis, Petre, Powis and Stafford. All people who might be plotting if there was actually a plot. Bellasis is to lead the invading papist troops as captain general it would seem.'

'Bellasis is over sixty. I can't see him marching at the head of an army.'

'I'm sure they will find him a Catholic horse when the time comes. There are a lot of other names too – priests mainly, I think, but my aunt doesn't specify.'

'And the King actually believes all this?'

'My aunt thinks not. The King caught Oates out telling a number of blatant untruths. Oates claimed to have met Don John of Austria, for example, but clearly had no idea what he looked like. He thought he was tall and dark, which he definitely isn't. The King has met Don John and put Oates right. Oates also said with great confidence that the Jesuits had a house near the Louvre, which they don't. The King told him he was a lying knave.'

'So, it's all over, then?'

'No. Having made his views clear, the King went off to do something more urgent, probably with the Duchess of Portsmouth, and left the Privy Council to make up its own mind what action to take. They decided, on reflection, they'd like to see a few Catholics in jail and told Oates they'd be willing to hear more, just as soon as he could come up with it.'

'The King will put a stop to this nonsense once he returns to Whitehall. I have no doubt we'll hear shortly that the good doctor has been thrown into the Tower,' I say. 'He'll be caught out by his lies soon enough. That sort always is.'

*

'Another letter from your aunt?'

'Yes, she's becoming a regular correspondent. Very pleased with herself that she knows things that we don't. She says they've given Oates his own rooms in the palace. And an armed guard in case any Jesuits should threaten his precious life.'

'The Privy Council has actually given credence to the nonsense that old fraud Oates was spouting?'

'That's the Reverend Doctor old fraud Oates to you. He's got himself up in a black silk gown and linen bands and is strutting around Whitehall as if he owns the place.'

'Is he entitled to be called either of those things?'

'Reverend and doctor? Ah well, my aunt shares your doubts. A friend of hers, who was at Cambridge at the same time as Doctor Oates, says that young Titus never completed his degree. Indeed, he was thrown out of Caius College for debauchery – my aunt didn't know what sort, though she had pressed her acquaintance most strongly for details – and Oates was obliged to transfer to Saint John's, where they were less fastidious. But he spent only two years at Cambridge, so it's unlikely he took a degree there. The doctorate is even less likely. According to a priest my aunt knows – she clearly gets out much more than I thought – Oates studied for no more than a few months at Jesuit College at Valladolid before being expelled yet again. He never seems to have gone near Salamanca University, which he claims actually awarded him his doctorate. In view of his previous record, maybe they agreed to give it to him in return for staying away from them?'

'He also claimed to have been vicar at Bobbing in Kent. Another fabrication?'

'No, that seems to be true, though the appointment lasted only a short time before scandalised parishioners demanded his removal. Debauchery again. And theft. And a lack of orthodoxy in religious matters. He could probably have got away with any two of those but not all three. He had to become a naval chaplain.'

'And?'

'Sacked en route to Tangier.'

'After which he finally realised he should become a Jesuit?'

'But not a real one.'

'Your aunt is well informed.'

'It is in no way to her credit. She has little else to do.'

'Oates has a remarkable talent for being able to pick himself up and start again.'

'He clearly has more friends than you might have thought. And he is very persuasive.'

'I would have thought that the Privy Council was not so easily fooled. And that some of the Counsellors would have stood up to him, even if others were deceived.'

'People are scared of him, John. I would be too, if I were at the court. He apparently has only to point his finger at you and say "there goes another papist traitor" and you're carted off to Newgate and thrown into an underground cell with a stone floor and no bed, while a very leisurely investigation is carried out. The King may call him a knave to his face, but the Privy Counsellors are with Oates to a man, it would seem, and they are happy to see him round up Catholic rivals at Westminster for the public hangman to deal with at his leisure.'

'The courts would never convict on such flimsy evidence.'

'They've arrested Edward Coleman anyway.'

'The Duke of York's secretary?'

'His unofficial secretary,' says Aminta, 'since Catholics are banned from any important position. Officially he works for the Duchess. Nobody minds much who works for a woman.'

'And the Duke – the King's own brother – couldn't protect his secretary from a man like Oates?'

'Unofficial secretary. But, no, apparently not. At least, according to my aunt. Oates swore that Coleman was part of the great Popish Plot and that he was in correspondence with the Jesuits. He was apparently to be Secretary of State in the new administration, after the present King was deposed. I'm not sure what would happen to Williamson. My aunt doesn't specify.'

'That's the same administration in which Bellasis is to command the army?'

'At least Coleman's appointment is plausible. I mean, he already is a secretary of some sort.'

'So Oates, not daring to strike at the Duke himself, has had his servant – his wife's servant – arrested.'

'You warned him that a direct attack on the Duke would be too risky. He's clearly taken your advice. Perhaps Oates isn't quite the fool he appeared to be.'

'They actually came and arrested Coleman?' I ask.

'He went and surrendered himself to Williamson rather than submit to rough handling by Oates's minions. They've seized Coleman's papers. The Privy Council hadn't thought of looking for treasonous correspondence, then Williamson helpfully suggested it might be relevant. Made a very good guess where the letters would be, apparently. The King should listen to him more often.'

'Finding incriminating papers is Williamson's job. He's overseen the government's spy network long enough. A schoolboy error on Coleman's part, though. He should have burnt them all before giving himself up. Let's hope he wasn't writing to the Jesuits.'

'He probably was. No, what we have to do is hope that Coleman was just reporting to Paris on the weather in Westminster.'

'Coleman is an honest and decent man,' I say.

'Very keen on fasting, though. I've always suspected him of self-flagellation during Lent. He looks the sort.'

'He's well off. And well connected. Keeps open house, they say, for ambassadors, bishops and the King's ministers.'

'My aunt says his cell at Newgate is quite small. And cold. Not good for entertaining friends. But he probably has fewer friends today than he had last week.'

'Post from London?' asks Aminta. 'Good news, this time, I hope. I've had enough of my aunt's gleeful tidings of arrests and imprisonments.'

I hold out the sheet of paper to her. 'It's from Williamson,' I say. 'They've murdered Sir Edmund Godfrey.'

'The man you sent Oates to?'

'Yes.'

'How?'

'He doesn't say – he says they're still looking for the body.'

'Still looking? Why is he so sure Godfrey's dead then? *A fortiori*, why is he so sure it's murder?'

'He doesn't say that either. Just that Godfrey has been missing a couple of days.'

'Absent just a couple of days, no corpse, and your faithful correspondent concludes that Godfrey has therefore been murdered?'

'I agree the Secretary of State appears to be making what is, for him, a very hasty judgement.'

'So, Williamson is kindly keeping you informed?' asks Aminta. 'Or – let me guess – does he want something?'

'He'd like me to go to London and find out who did it.'

'But only if Godfrey's actually dead, presumably.'

'Presumably,' I say.

'Is he offering to pay your expenses?'

'No.'

'The government's usual terms then.'

'Arlington sometimes remembered to pay me for work done.'

'Not often enough. I remain to be convinced this is an urgent matter.'

'Williamson's not like Arlington. He wouldn't waste my time.'

'He learned a lot as Arlington's deputy.'

'Even so, I ought to go to London.'

'Ought to or want to? Even if you did send Oates to Godfrey, it's not your responsibility. What you mean is you've found a mystery that intrigues you – I don't mean Godfrey's disappearance, but the rational Williamson's irrational reaction to it.'

'Doesn't it intrigue you?'

'Not as much as it does you, my dear husband, but I was thinking of going to London anyway. It's a while since I visited my aunt. And I think she is much better informed and distinctly more level headed than your good friend the Secretary of State.'

Chapter Three

In which we meet Sir Joseph Williamson

'You've missed the inquest,' says Williamson as if it were entirely my fault.

'Your letter merely said that Sir Edmund was missing – not that they'd found his body.'

'Well, they have now. He'd been crammed into a ditch on Primrose Hill.'

'A pleasant enough place to die. And had he in fact been murdered?'

'That's what the inquest eventually decided. But one whole morning, nearly, was taken up with Edmund Godfrey's brothers – I mean Michael and Benjamin – trying to get the Westminster coroner replaced with another of their choosing. So you lost little by not being there for that part.'

There remains in his voice a touch of his boyhood Cumbrian. A breath of clean mountain air in smoky, clever, tidewater Westminster. It's always more noticeable when he's being ironic. It's quite strong now.

'To what end would they wish to replace him?' I ask.

'They were afraid Cooper might bring in the wrong verdict.'

'Which would be . . . ?' I enquire.

'Suicide,' says Williamson. 'If that were the case, Edmund Godfrey's estate would revert to the Crown and not fall to them. To lose family money so carelessly would be an unforgivable dereliction of duty.'

'But a verdict of murder was acceptable to everyone?'

'Yes, the brothers need not have worried. Cooper obliged anyway. The jury were initially minded to go for *felo de se* but, once they were properly directed by the coroner, they saw it was murder by an unknown hand after all. They didn't waste time arguing about it. The main thing a jury wants is to get home in time for supper. Their verdict certainly did not conflict with the evidence. Rarely has a man been killed so comprehensively. He suffered three deaths, in fact. Beaten, strangled and stabbed.'

'A single death is the usual way of doing things. Is it significant that there are three possible causes?'

'Possibly, as I shall explain in a moment. He was found five days after he vanished. He left his house in Hartshorne Lane at about ten o'clock on Saturday the twelfth of October. He was noticed by a number of people as he criss-crossed London, from Westminster to Primrose Hill to Holborn to the Strand, but at least half of the sightings are very doubtful. He was last seen alive for certain by Joseph Radcliffe, a fellow vestryman who knew Godfrey well. That was in the Strand at about one o'clock. Towards evening, a Mister Oakley thinks he saw him outside Somerset House being followed by ruffians, but that is less conclusive and I am still making enquiries. Godfrey's body was eventually discovered on the following Thursday evening in an overgrown ditch back on Primrose Hill. From the dryness of his clothes and the fact that the area had been searched earlier in the week, it is almost certain it had lain there no more than twenty-four hours, but the coroner thought he'd died some time before that – on the Saturday he disappeared, probably.'

'So the body had been moved after he died?'

'Well, he was in no fit state to walk there. There were bruises on his chest, strangulation marks and a broken neck and, last but not least, he had been skewered with his own sword, the point of which protruded through the back of his camlet coat.'

'As you say, very comprehensive. Somebody wanted him dead. Presumably, in the end, it was only one of those things that killed him, though?'

'Not the sword,' says Williamson. 'That was the final blow, but there was almost no blood on his clothes, indicating that the weapon was inserted some time after his death.'

'And the beating?'

'Possibly enough to kill but, according to the surgeon who gave evidence, it was the attention to his neck that was fatal.'

'Suspects?'

'Everyone is assuming it was the Jesuits.'

'Why?'

'Oates says they're behind everything. Haven't you heard?'

Cumbrian irony again, though this time with more than a hint of bitterness.

'What is their motive supposed to be?' I ask.

'Godfrey had aided Oates in his campaign against them, primarily by taking Oates's deposition on the great Popish Plot, as it's becoming known.'

'I told Oates to go to you,' I say, 'and to Godfrey if you were unavailable.'

'You did exactly the right thing, John. And he did come to me – first anyway. I, like you, thought Godfrey was the man to deal with it. As the Court Justice, I mean. And because of Godfrey's reputation for attention to detail. He was the obvious choice. So, I passed Oates on. It was the right thing to do.'

'And the Catholics knew that?'

'It was no secret.'

'There may really be a connection, then?'

'We cannot rule it out. One of the many strangenesses about Godfrey's death is, however, that he had told a lot of people, in the days leading up to his disappearance, that he would be killed soon – and hanged specifically.'

'But he didn't say who might hang him?'

'Unfortunately not,' he says.

I look around the office. Everything is much as it was in the days when I was a frequent visitor, in the pay of my Lord Arlington. The cabinets full of papers are in their accustomed places. A bust of a Roman emperor still sits on top of each one, to help in the identification of what it contains. I do a quick inventory. Titus is there, where he should be, guarding documents relating to Holland and to the Foreign Committee. Oates was right to remind me that he disgraces the name of one of Rome's most capable and virtuous rulers. Yes, all is much as I remember, but the pile of papers on Williamson's desk is higher than it used to be and I think stoney-faced Titus needs a light dusting.

'The stabbing puzzles me most,' I say, turning back to Williamson.

'Exactly. You are an intelligent man. I hope that you in turn would not regard me as unintelligent. For us, the lack of blood from the stab wounds points clearly to one thing. He was dead when it happened. It served no possible purpose. And yet, for all that, somebody did stab him. Twice, actually, because the first time the sword hit a rib. The question is why?'

'You say the brothers wished to avoid a suicide verdict. Could they have found his hanged body somewhere and tried to disguise it as a murder, transferring their sibling to Primrose Hill and stabbing him to make it look like the result of a chance encounter with a footpad?'

'That was very much the initial thought of the jury. And the brothers do of course own carriages in which a body could have been carried. But Benjamin and Michael too are no fools. They must have realised that people would see at once that the true cause of death was strangulation. The stabbing just confirmed that the body had been tampered with after death. If avoiding a verdict of suicide was the brothers' true aim, better by far to leave the sword in its sheath and hope that a jury concluded that he had been beaten and brutally strangled by some footpad where he was found. Murder of that class is common enough.'

'So, if the killers weren't expecting us to believe he'd really been stabbed to death with his own sword, what other conclusion were they hoping that we would draw from it?'

Williamson gives a helpless shrug. 'Perhaps, John, they are just cleverer than we are – or we are simply more stupid than they imagined possible. They have sent us a message that we are incapable of decoding.' He sighs. He is the King's spymaster. Decoding things is his job. He ought to be better at it than anyone else in London. 'I should add that we cannot be certain when the bruising occurred, but we are assuming that it was at the same time as the strangulation or just before it. It was quite extensive. It would have been severe and painful.'

'To make him reveal something before they killed him?' I ask.

'Oates says the Jesuits teach that it is no sin to murder a Protestant – or to torture one, presumably. And Oates should know, having very kindly infiltrated the Jesuit order, at considerable risk to himself, so that he could find out precisely that sort of thing. I must warn you now that people who do not believe what Oates says are branded Catholic traitors, or sympathisers, who deserve to be hanged along with the murderers. Outside this room, you express your scepticism at your own risk.'

'But, inside this room, you are nevertheless sceptical?'

'I don't know what to believe any more about anything,' says Williamson. 'That's why I need your help.'

I look at Williamson. His face is greyer than it ideally should be. There are rings under his eyes. He's lived for so long in the shadow of Arlington, managing the state's agents and informers, while Arlington managed the King and Parliament. It was a good partnership as long as it lasted – balanced, efficient – even if the sun shone on Arlington more than it did on him. Now he's on his own. For a man used to deceit and betrayal, he has a strange aversion to court intrigue. He understands very little how Parliament works and how to get it to do what he wants. He's waited many years to succeed Arlington but I think he'd now like Arlington back. He rubs his eyes, but when he opens them again, all he has in front of him is me.

'So, you really have no idea who might have wanted to kill him?'

'Not at the moment,' he says with an honest Cumbrian smile. 'I'd have told you if I had.'

'Your predecessor didn't always tell me everything,' I say.

'I'm not my predecessor,' says Williamson.

'That's good,' I say.

'I want you to do what you do best, John – what you do better than anyone I know. Go through the evidence, of which there is a great deal. Sort out the relevant from the irrelevant, in a way that the inquest did not. Apply logic to an illogical death. Find me the killer.'

'Do you not have agents who could do the same thing?'

'Nobody I can trust to do this.'

'I'll do my best then. Are you planning to pay my expenses this time?'

'Do you expect to have any?'

'London isn't cheap and Londoners may expect payment for information.'

'Submit an account at the end. I'll consider it.'

'Thank you. Should I begin by talking to Doctor Oates?'

'It would be better if Oates knew as little as possible. He and the Privy Council are conducting their own investigation. But they have already made up their minds it was the Catholics.'

'Will they try to stop us reaching a different conclusion?'

'Only if they find out what we're doing.'

'He'll find out eventually.'

'Of course he will. It only has to be kept from them long enough for you to discover what we need to know. You will of course have unrestricted access to all of the witnesses at the inquest, and to anyone else who may be able to help you. I shall give you a list, together with a copy of the testimonies.'

'And the body?'

'It has been returned to Hartshorne Lane.'

'Then I assume I can view it there if I am quick. When is the funeral?'

'I have no idea. Sir Edmund Berry Godfrey lies in state down a narrow lane, a few dozen yards from his river wharf. Crowds of citizens snake through the wood stacks and coal heaps to view the body. They weep and vow vengeance on the Catholics. They would plunge their handkerchiefs into Godfrey's wounds to make them bloody relics of a holy Protestant martyr, if that were in any way possible.'

Ah yes, those non-bleeding wounds again. Very inconvenient for all concerned.

'The key to it,' I say, 'is why somebody thought it worth stabbing him. If we knew that, we'd be halfway to knowing who the killer was.'

'And if we knew why they beat him,' says Williamson. 'And why they hanged him. All three deaths, in fact.'

Chapter Four

In which my wife gives me some good advice

'I am much relieved,' says Aminta, 'that Williamson says that he is not planning to treat you as Arlington did.'

'Yes,' I say.

'And to what extent do you believe him?'

'He worked hand in glove with Arlington for many years. But I think Joseph Williamson has aways retained some distant memory of what constitutes the truth. Arlington always felt the weight of the King's wishes heavily on his shoulders. He would have done anything to please the King. Or to advance his own career – the two things were never entirely separate in Arlington's mind. But Williamson has a deeper loyalty to the state. For many people the state is a somewhat abstract concept – an invisible and capricious deity that sometimes demands taxes or jury service. But for Williamson it is a very real thing, made up of stacks of papers, code books and lists of names, all filed neatly in the appropriate cabinet. He can reach out and touch the state any time he wishes, just to reassure himself that all is well. He's loyal to the King, of course he is, but he also believes in something higher, something which isn't distracted all the time by its mistresses or race horses.'

'So, how much is he paying you?'

'I am to submit a list of expenses in due course for his consideration.'

'Though not necessarily for payment. Did he offer you any of his clerks or agents to assist you?'

'No.'

'Then it's as well you have me.'

'I fear this may be dangerous work.'

'Not all of it. Some simply involves drinking tea. I went to see my aunt while you were visiting Williamson.'

'What did she have to say?'

'To be fair, most of it was that everyone was convinced that the Jesuits had killed Godfrey.'

'Did she say why?'

'Godfrey had a secret that they didn't want him to disclose.'

'What secret?'

'He never got to disclose it.'

'So far, I'm not impressed.'

'I agree. She added, however, that Godfrey, though regarded as eccentric in many ways, was always noted for his even hand-edness. He had no particular grudge against the Catholics – quite the reverse if anything. He was a good friend of Edward Coleman, the now-arrested secretary of the Duke of York.'

'Yes, I'd heard that.'

'Well, you haven't heard the next bit. When do you think that rumours started to circulate about Godfrey's murder?'

'Williamson's letter said people were making assumptions a couple of days after he vanished.'

'True but misleading. My aunt tells me that she first heard he'd been killed on the evening of Saturday the twelfth of October.'

I think back to what Williamson has told me today. 'But Godfrey didn't vanish until Saturday afternoon.'

'Exactly. So, why did people know he was dead so quickly?'

'They were simply guessing.'

'It's strange that, out of all the people in London who might have been killed that day, they guessed the right one.'

'According to Williamson, Godfrey had been saying for some time that he was worried he'd be killed.'

'So he did. But there were no rumours of his death before Saturday. So, they also seem to have guessed the right time. Did Williamson tell you how early the rumours were current?'

'No,' I say.

'Still think Williamson is being honest with you?'

'It's perfectly possible,' I say. 'In theory.'

'I suppose that, every now and then, even Arlington told the plain unvarnished truth.'

'Not really,' I say. 'But I'll bear it all in mind when I go to Hartshorne Lane.'

'I'll come with you,' says Aminta.

'Examining a week-old corpse can be quite unpleasant,' I say.

'I never said it wasn't,' says Aminta. 'I'll get my cloak.'

Chapter Five

In which we meet Mister Michael and Mister Benjamin

For a short time, the pious tide of Godfrey pilgrims has been stemmed to allow me to examine the body. They wait outside in the yard, with greater or lesser patience. The weather today is icy and their legs must ache from standing in line. But a pilgrimage without suffering would be wrong in so many ways.

Michael and Benjamin Godfrey, who greet us at the door, are solid, unimaginative citizens. Bulky. Well fed. Well clothed. Black broadcloth coats on their broad backs. Black periwigs. Spotless linen. They might take an orange-seller as a mistress or donate money for new silver plate at their parish church, but they clearly see suicide as a ridiculous extravagance. A man has a duty to his family to die naturally or to be killed in a seemly manner. Everything they have said to me so far is designed to ensure that I report back to Williamson that their brother passed away violently and mindful of his family responsibilities.

'Does Williamson now doubt the coroner?' asks Michael, the more vocal of the two. 'He raised no objections at the time. A coroner's verdict is not something to change on a mere whim, sir.'

'We know how Sir Edmund died,' I say. 'That was the function of the inquest. He was strangled. We do not yet know who strangled him. Discovering that is, very properly, the next step.'

'And such an investigation is your job? To dig out the killer? But you are not even a London magistrate. You come from ...'

'Essex,' I say.

I sense they do not like my county but I also sense something else – fear.

'I thought the Privy Council was investigating this?' asks Michael. 'What's it got to do with Williamson anyway? Doesn't he have enough work of his own?'

It's a good question. Williamson seems overwhelmed at the moment. You'd think that he'd be happy to step back from this. Leave it to the Privy Council, who seem to be revelling in the task anyway. It's true that any plot against the King is his concern, but there's no good evidence at the moment that Godfrey's death relates in any way to Oates's accusations. It's clear that nobody would blame him if he said he was too busy. Quite the reverse, in fact.

I smile reassuringly.

'If you will permit me to examine the body?' I say. 'I promise I won't be long.'

Godfrey lies in a coffin on a bier. The perfume in the air cannot conceal the smell of death. He is no longer as fresh as he was at the inquest. But what is presented to us is clearly still a human being, not a heap of decaying flesh. His face is greyer even than Williamson's, but he is recognisable from when I last saw him alive. His head rests on a large, linen-covered pillow, the softness of which holds it steady, but, when I touch it, it moves easily as if the spine were snapped in two. That's probably because it is. On the face of it, the jury were right to be talked into murder rather than suicide. A judicial hanging will break a neck, if the condemned man is lucky, but it's rare with a suicide, where death is usually by slow strangulation. Let's look at the neck more closely, then.

I pull back the shirt collar – he's carelessly lost his cravat in the course of dying. There are still marks where a rope – no, more likely a twisted cloth, judging by the width of the indentation – was wound round it. His own cravat may have been the means of killing him, just as his own sword was used to make a point. The marks are at an angle but it is not clear, from that alone, whether this is a hanging or whether he was simply strangled where he stood. On balance, I'd say two men had done this, one holding one end of the cloth and the other pulling for all his life. Would that be enough to snap the neck in this way? Or three men? Or more? There are, after all, a lot of Catholics in London. The sword has been withdrawn from the body, not out of respect but as a practical necessity in order to carry Godfrey from the ditch in which he was found to a nearby inn, the White House, where he was first examined. There is, as Williamson said, almost no blood to be seen – just a smear or two of brown on the waistcoat, which has been pierced in two places. I unbutton the waistcoat and shirt to expose the chest a little more. The bruise is large and very black.

'The coroner thought the discolouration might just be a settling of blood after death,' says Michael Godfrey. He wants as few complications as possible – just a nice, clean strangulation. No prior torture.

'Yes,' I say. 'That's possible.'

'Though I think our brother had some fairly rough handling from the men who carried him back to the inn,' says Benjamin. 'Slipping and sliding in the mud and in the dark. They'll have dropped him at least once, I shouldn't wonder.'

'Dropping him wouldn't have caused bruising like that,' I say. 'Not so long after death.'

The shirt under the twice-pierced waistcoat is strangely not damaged at all. That's clever. That's very clever. The sword seems to have passed through it without disturbing a single thread.

'The shirt he was wearing when he died had to be cut off before the inquest,' says Benjamin, noticing my puzzlement.

Michael shoots another look at him.

'Everyone knows that,' says Benjamin irritably. 'There's no secret about it. It was mentioned before the coroner. They cut it off and threw it away.'

Benjamin observes Michael's still-raised eyebrow and swallows hard.

'Thank you,' I say. 'I couldn't work out why it was unmarked. Now I know. It's not the shirt he was killed in.'

'We are pleased to be able to clarify matters for you,' says Michael, before his brother can speak again. 'We have nothing to hide, Sir John.'

'Did you see much of your brother Edmund in the days before his death?' Aminta asks sympathetically.

'Of course,' says Benjamin. 'There was no falling out between us. None at all. No arguments. No animosity or ill feeling of any sort.'

Michael shakes his head. He would so much prefer to tell this story himself, unaided.

'Relations within the family,' says Michael firmly, 'were exactly as you would expect. Nothing more nor less.'

'There was, as you know, some suggestion at the inquest that your brother might have killed himself,' I say.

A loud sigh escapes Michael's lips. Why is everyone trying to complicate things for him? 'I'm sorry, Sir John, but I thought we had all agreed it was murder. By the Jesuits.'

'Why would they wish him dead?'

'I think everyone knows the answer to that. Edmund had given considerable assistance to Doctor Oates, who is doing so much to reveal their devilish plans. As you may know, Oates was directed, shortly after he arrived in London, to go to Edmund and make a declaration concerning the Catholic plot. Without Edmund's help and support, Oates would still be sitting in some antechamber in Whitehall Palace, waiting to see the King, while the Jesuits arranged for the Duke of York to seize the throne. This is a simple act of revenge, Sir John, against one of their most courageous enemies!'

'I thought that your brother was quite fair in his dealings with Catholics?' asks Aminta. 'And a friend of Edward Coleman.'

'Who says that?'

'My aunt,' says Aminta. 'Though my husband also claims he knew.'

Michael considers this carefully. 'Yes, he was fair with the papists. In the general way of things. Fairer than they deserved. But he was also a firm defender of the Church of England and of the King. He would not have allowed treason of any shape or form to flourish.'

'He was also a good friend and adherent of Sir Robert Peyton,' says Benjamin.

'The extreme Protestant Member of Parliament?' asks Aminta.

'Yes,' says Benjamin.

'I thought his party had been proscribed as dangerous fanatics?' says Aminta.

'Most of them were deprived of all public offices a couple of years ago,' I say. 'I'm surprised Sir Edmund remained a magistrate if that's the case, let alone being allowed to continue as the Court Justice with access to the King himself.'

Michael feels it is time to intervene again. 'He was *formerly* a friend of Sir Robert's,' he says firmly. 'He has not associated with that gang since the government took action against them. Benjamin is right that it shows our brother has always been the staunchest of Protestants – as far from being a Catholic as you could imagine – but it has no relevance at all to the matter in hand, other than that it might have marked Edmund out some time ago as a man that the Catholics needed to fear. The Jesuits have long memories, sir.'

'Thank you for clarifying that,' I say. 'There's one other thing that puzzles me. People seem to have realised very quickly that something had happened – there were rumours of Sir Edmund's death spreading through London by the Saturday evening.'

'Is that intelligence also from your wife's aunt?'

'I'm afraid so,' says Aminta. 'But she seems very sure of herself.'

'Let me be honest with you,' says Michael Godfrey. 'During the weeks that led up to our brother's death, many of Edmund's friends were quite worried by some of the things that he said. Several times he expressed fears that he might be killed – killed, please note, not that he would kill himself. On the Saturday he vanished, we paid a visit to Colonel Weldon's house, where we knew our brother was to dine at midday. Weldon told us Edmund had not come as planned, which was concerning because he was of the most regular habits. What was really worrying, though, was Weldon's report that, the previous evening, our brother had been at his house with some of the other vestrymen. Not only had Edmund been anxious to settle some old debts, but the way in which he did so was wild and frantic. Weldon said he had never known business done in such a manner before. It was almost as if Edmund knew that might be his last chance.'

'So, even by midday, you were worried enough to assume he could already be dead?' I say.

'No, not worried. Not really worried. But, equally, we were far from sure what to make of it. Then Edmund's clerk, Moor, came to see me first thing on Sunday morning. He's a doddery old man, Sir John, full of silly ideas. He told us Edmund had not yet come home. He also spoke to us of a last-minute change of coat that he found particularly significant. We told him not to concern himself. Still, it was clear that Edmund had been out all of the previous day and the whole night too.'

'That was unusual?'

'He often went out at night,' says Benjamin. 'He had a fancy for wandering the streets, seeking out law-breakers.'

'But, brother, he was always home at a decent hour,' says Michael. He turns back to me. 'To stay out all night was very unusual, Sir John. Our brother was a man of regular habits. Sober. God fearing. Respectful of the law.'

'But odd,' says Benjamin. 'People often found him abrupt. Conversation with him wasn't easy. Or I never found it was.'

'He was merely of a serious and sober disposition,' says Michael. 'He didn't waste his time on jests and idle chatter. I do not see that as a fault in any way.'

'So, what did you do on the Sunday morning, after his servant brought you the news?' I ask.

'Nothing. We thought that Edmund might have gone to church early without Moor noticing, then perhaps to the Gibbons' house – the Gibbons were good friends of Edmund's and distantly related to us.'

'And then?'

'When we heard nothing further by the Sunday afternoon, we came here to Hartshorne Lane. Mistress Pamphlin – that's my brother's housekeeper – was sent to the Gibbons' house to see if he was in fact there. Moor and Benjamin and I went and enquired of other acquaintances whether they had seen Edmund. In short, we carried out as thorough an investigation as we reasonably could.'

'And nobody had seen him?' I say.

'Obviously. By then he was dead. That's what the inquest, on the basis of a great deal of detailed evidence, concluded. Because he was murdered by Catholics on the evening of the twelfth of October. In revenge for his help to Oates.'

'Thank you. You make yourself very clear. What did you do next?'

'We continued to ask after him. On the Monday, Benjamin and I went to see Mistress Gibbon ourselves in case she had any further news. When she had not, we decided the disappearance had to be reported to the authorities. We went to the Lord Chancellor and he informed the Privy Council.'

'The Lord Chancellor? You thought it was worth troubling the Earl of Nottingham himself?'

'Yes.'

'And the Privy Council?'

'Yes.'

'Because your brother had gone out and not yet come home?'

'Precisely that,' says Michael.

'But they took no action?' I say.

'They were inclined to believe one of the many rumours that were flying around – that Edmund had eloped and married a lady of fortune, that he was lying dead drunk in a low tavern, that he had fled to the country to avoid his creditors. Of course, it was all nonsense. It was unthinkable that he'd done any of those things.'

'The first two anyway,' says Benjamin. He gives a nervous little laugh.

'You mean he might have fled because of his debts?' I say.

'No,' says Michael, shaking his head. 'Not at all. In the past, I must admit there were difficulties . . . no point in hiding it from you. Others will tell you the same, no doubt. It was Harrison, his former partner, who had the real business sense. I think Edmund never really understood the need to encourage customers to return.'

'Let's be honest,' says Benjamin. 'He never really understood customers.'

'Anyway,' says Michael, 'after Harrison retired, the wood- and coal-selling concern was never quite the same. But what was worse was that, a few years later, Edmund unwisely put the business into the hands of Godfrey Harrison, his former partner's son and his own godson, in order to deal with some other pressing matters. Godfrey Harrison was so incompetent that he managed to lose four thousand pounds in a few months. Just about everything Edmund had. That's why people thought . . . wrongly, as I say . . . that he might have fled, suddenly and without warning, cramming as much money as he could into his pockets . . .'

'Did he cram money into his pockets?'

'At the inquest it was established that he had a great deal of cash on him,' says Benjamin. 'Which is a very important point, Sir John. Nobody commits suicide with their pockets full of money.'

'Don't they?' I ask.

'It certainly proves that he had no immediate money problems,' says Michael. 'That was my brother's point, I believe. In summary, he had had problems in the past, but was now better off. Much better off. Everyone will tell you that too.'

'And the money he had with him was not stolen by his killer?'

'As far as we can tell it was all still there. Some broad gold pieces wrapped in paper. A lot of silver. Two small gold coins. Had it been a common thief who killed him, it would have gone. But the Pope is rich enough that he doesn't need to steal from corpses. Or to get priests to do it for him. They steal well enough from their poor parishioners, sir. So, there it is. You'll waste your time, and other people's, looking further than a Catholic plot.'

'Thank you. Again, that could not be clearer,' I say. 'Did anyone at the inquest put forward any theory as to why his killer might have stabbed him after death?'

'Some strange popish ritual, no doubt.'

'I hadn't realised they did that,' I say.

'Then I'm glad to be of assistance to you. Well, if that's all . . .'

'I don't think we need ask either of you any more questions but we would like to speak to the servants if we may. There were apparently two visitors to this house, one on Friday night and one on Saturday morning.'

'Pamphlin, Moor, Curtis – they are all away. Knowing we would have to be at the house to receive you, we gave them a holiday – they have after all been here taking care of Edmund's body for days. And taking care of the crowds who wish to view it. It seemed only fair to give them some respite from their labours. Which is why they are not here now.'

'I understand fully.'

'And now, I hope that really is all the questions you need to ask? There are many people waiting outside. So many devout

Protestant people. And the weather is cold. It would be selfish and inconsiderate of us to refuse them entry. With your permission ... ?'

'But of course,' I say. 'You must let them in.'

'So,' says Aminta as we make our way back through the crowded streets, 'we are to believe that it was murder by the Catholics.'

'That was, I think, the main point Michael was trying to get across.'

'And certainly not suicide.'

'That was his other point,' I say.

'There's a third point: the brothers were also anxious that we did not suspect Godfrey died as a result of a family quarrel.'

'They would naturally come under suspicion if there were no more likely perpetrators. But their concern on that score simply means that they understand how magistrates think – not that they are guilty of fratricide. They wish to keep his money in the family but nobody's suggested they need it badly enough to kill him. And, if they had killed him for some perfectly valid non-financial reason, then, rather than hang for it, it would be far better they allow the world to believe that it was suicide.'

'Why were they so concerned about the missing shirt?' asks Aminta. 'They didn't like you asking about it.'

'That puzzled me too. There was no reason at all why it should not have been removed for the inquest. It's normal enough. If it was, contrary to what we've been told, covered in blood, then the blood would have undoubtedly transferred to the waist-coat anyway. As evidence it had no possible value. Its loss is utterly unimportant.'

'They also didn't want you to question the domestic staff,' says Aminta.

'I thought their concern for the welfare of the servants was a little overdone. All three given a holiday together?'

'I doubt they'll get another day off in the next twelve months.'

'Unless the brothers think we might inconveniently return and try to interview them.'

'They won't be expecting us to return tomorrow,' says Aminta.

'No,' I say.

'The servants will tell the brothers we've been asking awkward questions, of course,' says Aminta.

I think of what Williamson told me about keeping this investigation secret from Oates.

'By the time they find out,' I say, 'we'll have got the information we need. Tomorrow it is, then.'

Chapter Six

In which we meet Mister Moor

'There's no need to listen to the women,' says Moor. 'None at all.' I think he is stating a general principle of life rather than advising us on this specific investigation. Still, for all practical purposes it is the same.

We are in Godfrey's dining room. Across the passageway, through the closed door, we can just make out the tread of many feet as citizens continue to file past the dead martyr in the parlour. The door to the kitchen on the other side of the room is partly open, but complete silence reigns there.

Godfrey was an imposing man in life, and death has been unable to diminish him. He was and is almost awkwardly tall. But his clerk fully compensates for that. Moor is small and wizened with no ambition to be anything else. At his age he must have been relieved to find employment of any sort. Dead though he undoubtedly is, Sir Edmund Berry Godfrey retains Moor's complete loyalty. The form that loyalty takes this morning is a dogged refusal to assist us in any way whatsoever.

'It would still be useful if you at least could tell us what you know,' I say.

'I gave sworn evidence to the inquest. Read it. It's all there.'

'There's a summary of the evidence given, but I can promise you that the clerk will not have managed to record every word spoken by every witness. Far from it. And he may have been directed to put some things in and to leave others out.'

'Seen it. It's as close to what I said as it needs to be.'

'And there was nothing you kept back?'

'I've nothing to hide,' says Moor.

Just like the brothers, then. It's good everyone is being so open with us.

'Then perhaps,' I say, 'you might begin by telling us about the two messengers who visited him on the Friday night and the Saturday morning.'

Moor shows neither surprise nor any inclination to be cooperative.

'Didn't notice them,' he says. 'Lots of people came to the house on business. All the time. All day long. It wasn't my job to run and open the door to every footman and lackey who cared to knock.'

'I appreciate that was women's work,' says Aminta. 'You were somewhat closer to Sir Edmund and your duties more confidential. In which case, maybe you can say whether your master expressed any fears for his life in the days leading up to his death?'

'You are right that I was closer. Anything he said was therefore private, between me and him.'

'Or perhaps he didn't trust you enough to share his most private feelings with you?' says Aminta. 'It would have been a shame if that were the case. I'm sure you'd have given him excellent advice.'

Moor grinds his teeth and says nothing.

'Possibly we should be speaking to Mistress Pamphlin after all?' she adds. 'Just in case he might have confided in her?'

'Sir Edmund had no trust in women. He knew their weaknesses. And their lusts.'

Aminta nods and smiles sympathetically. 'He didn't marry, I take it?'

'He was never inclined to do so, my Lady,' says Moor.

'There were rumours that he had found an heiress.'

Just for a moment, Moor seriously considers laughing, then he shakes his head.

'You needn't blame yourself in any way for what happened, Mister Moor,' says Aminta. 'There wouldn't have been much you could have done that would have made any difference.'

She waits patiently while Godfrey's sole manservant grinds his teeth down a little further. Then he says suddenly: 'He should have let me go with him.'

'When?' I ask.

'Saturday. The day he was killed. I offered to. He said no. He said he could deal with them on his own.'

'So, he did fear an attack?' asks Aminta. 'Some people have suggested he did.'

Moor shakes his head vigorously. 'No, not fear, my Lady. He expected an attack. But he didn't fear it. He never saw dangers the way folk normally do. Never afraid to tell people what he thought of them. Never afraid to defend the law. Walking the streets at night with just his sword to protect him. Walking into a trap in broad daylight – as he must have done. He thought he could manage. Without me.'

He turns and looks towards the passageway, beyond which his master now lies in his coffin. There's not much doubt who got it right. Not really.

Moor gives a gulp that is as close to a sob as he is going to permit himself. 'I'd have been some help. I'm not completely useless. It's just that sometimes he didn't know how much help he needed. I should have been at his side. Then it wouldn't have happened.'

Aminta gives him another sympathetic smile.

'Maybe, kind man that he was, he thought you wouldn't keep up with all of the walking?' she says.

'Well, he would have been wrong, my Lady. On the Sunday, when he hadn't come home, I went out to Sir Edmund's mother's house, then all the way back to the brothers in the City.'

'And what did they tell you?' I ask.

'His mother knew nothing about it. Wasted trip.'

'The brothers?'

'They hoped he'd gone to church. But he wouldn't have, not in that coat. It wasn't a church coat, see?'

'What coat?' I ask.

Moor pauses, wondering what, if anything, Michael and Benjamin told me about the Sunday morning. He shrugs. If they've changed the story without telling him, that's their problem.

'It's like this – first he asked for his new camlet coat. Then he thought about it and put on his old one – as if he didn't wish to appear to be too prosperous . . .'

'Why wouldn't he wish that?' I ask.

The servant gives a long sigh. 'I've thought about it a lot,' he says. 'In the end, I did wonder whether he wasn't going to meet with his creditors, in the morning at least.'

'Yes,' I say. 'Mister Michael said something about debts.'

Moor looks relieved that I already know about it.

'There you are, then. The old coat would have been better for business of that sort,' he says.

'Are you saying that the creditors could have killed him?' I say.

'Course not. What would they gain from that? They'd want to be first in line for payment – not waiting months for the executors to sell real estate and distribute the proceeds. I said maybe he went to a meeting with them in the morning. And that explains the coat. On the way there or on the way back, somebody killed him. Jesuits.'

This time, he doesn't need to look at me to check whether Michael and Benjamin have told me the same thing. Only a fool would doubt the Catholics were behind it.

'And you think the meeting with creditors could have been on Primrose Hill?' I ask. 'Everyone has agreed that he went there. Nobody has really explained why.'

'There's a tavern,' says Moor darkly. 'Seedy, run-down sort of place. Maybe he didn't want people he knew overhearing things. Not if money was involved. Primrose Hill is far enough from Hartshorne Lane. And it was a place he knew well.'

'His brothers thought he might have solved his financial problems,' I say.

'What would they know? He wouldn't have told his own family about things like that.'

'Did he often go to Primrose Hill, then?' I ask.

Moor pauses, as if he feels I am trying to lure him onto more dangerous ground. 'Depends what you call often,' he says. 'Once or twice, maybe. He often took a fancy to go places.'

'The same way that he'd walk the streets of Westminster?'

'Who says he did?'

'Mister Benjamin,' I say.

Again, Moor breathes a sigh of relief. 'Yes, as a magistrate, checking that all was well. He was a conscientious man. He liked to know what was going on.'

Just for a moment I have a vision of Godfrey, creeping speculatively along the damp, narrow lanes that run up from the Thames, his long fingers searching out wrongdoing of an as yet unknown kind. But on the Saturday in question, all of the witnesses seem to agree that he was striding purposefully towards Primrose Hill. He knew exactly where he was going. And didn't seem happy to be off there. Perhaps he was going to meet people to whom he owed money, to discuss in shadowy privacy how he might extricate himself. If so, he still had the money on him when he was found.

'Could he have met with his creditors, failed to reach an accommodation with them and hanged himself in despair?' I say.

'No,' says Moor suddenly and with great firmness. 'Never. It would have been a sin. It would have been against the law. Sir Edmund was a great lover of the law and no lover of sin. He was the greatest hater of sin that I ever met.'

'Thank you,' says Aminta. 'That's very helpful, Mister Moor. I suppose Mistress Pamphlin and Mistress Curtis aren't free to talk to us now? Of course, I'm not expecting the women to know much – certainly not as much as you do – but it would nevertheless be so helpful. If they could spare the time. And if you permitted the women to do it, of course.'

'They're very upset,' says Moor. 'In mourning for the loss of their master, my Lady. I'm not having you troubling them. Now Sir Edmund is no longer here, it falls to me to protect them and I shall not fail in that trust.'

'In that case, thank you, Mister Moor,' says Aminta, handing him a gold coin. 'Thank you for your most valuable evidence. Please accept that for the trouble you have taken.'

'That was generous of you,' I say, as we walk back to our lodgings. 'Bearing in mind you are merely a weak and lustful woman.'

'Mistress Pamphlin was listening to every word,' says Aminta. 'I saw her peeping out once or twice behind the kitchen door. It seemed important that she should know that money might be on offer. Now she just needs to come and collect her rightful share.'

Chapter Seven

In which we meet Mistress Pamphlin and Mistress Curtis

Mistress Pamphlin sips her tea and critically observes our lodgings. If she were our housekeeper, she'd make a few changes, whether we wanted them or not. Oh, yes. And our maid would feel the rough side of her tongue for the way in which she cheerfully banged down the tray of cups and saucers and skipped off back to the kitchen. Young girls these days! No respect. No gratitude. No gravity.

'As you may realise,' I say, 'we spoke to Mister Moor and—'

'I heard,' she says. 'Most of it anyway. Told you a few things that were harmless and you already knew from the brothers. Kept plenty back, though. That clerk knows more than you can imagine, but he's in the brothers' pay, isn't he? And they've promised a lot more than you gave him yesterday, my Lady, even if it was a guinea.'

She views Aminta through narrowed eyes, looking for confirmation that a guinea is the going rate. She's certainly hoping we'll do better than miserly silver.

'They're not paying you the same amount as Moor, then?' says Aminta. 'That's very unfair.'

'Be lucky to get the wages I'm entitled to, let alone proper bribe money. Tight-fisted pair, they are.'

'It is so hard on servants who have served their late master loyally. Especially the women. More tea, Mistress Pamphlin?'

My wife refills the proffered cup with great sympathy.

'I'm not saying Moor wasn't loyal too,' says the housekeeper. 'In his own way. Of course he was. Full of his own importance, being the only male servant in the house, as you'll have noticed for yourselves. But mostly he fussed around the master, while Elizabeth and I did the work. Answer the door to callers? Him? I don't think so!'

She pauses and looks at me significantly.

'So,' I say, 'since answering the door fell to you, did you recognise either of the messengers? I mean the one on Saturday and the one on Friday.'

'I answered the door to the one on *Friday* night. Respectable-looking gentleman. I've no idea about the one on Saturday morning. Elizabeth must have let him in. She says she overheard the one on Friday say who sent him but, since she claims she can't remember the name, it doesn't help us a lot, does it?'

'You didn't recognise the earlier messenger yourself?'

'No. He thought a lot of himself, though. I did wonder if he'd been sent by Mister Coleman.'

'The Duke's secretary?' I ask. 'I know he was Sir Edmund's friend, but he was already in prison by then. Or are you saying a message from him might have been smuggled out – presumably at some risk?'

'You'd be surprised what people will do for money,' she says significantly. 'If there's enough on offer. A guinea, just to give you one example. Coleman sent a lot of messages in the old days. I recall another the master received. "One Clark would speak with him", was all it said. And the master hurried off as fast as he could, though he was in the middle of a fine supper I'd made him. Always ready to help Mister Coleman, he was. Too willing, I always thought. People take advantage.'

'When was that – the message you just mentioned?' I ask.

'Back in September some time, I suppose. Before Mister Coleman was arrested, certainly. But the master was at Somerset House often enough anyway. That worried me. They're all papists there. The Duchess wouldn't have it otherwise, being one herself, born and bred. And Italian, as if being Catholic wasn't bad enough.'

'Sir Edmund wasn't a Catholic, though?'

'Sir Edmund a Catholic! Lawks, sir, what an idea! He had no objection to them. Not as such. But, in general, his views were quite the reverse of papist. You see, he was also a good friend of Sir Robert Peyton, the famous Green Ribbon man, of whom you will doubtless have heard. Master would often attend gatherings with Sir Robert and his supporters. Sometimes they met in a tavern that Sir Edmund owns in Hammersmith. But not so much lately. He saw more of his Catholic friends. I wondered at one stage if he was planning to go over to Rome, as the saying is, but I never saw any sign that he had. Of course, I did check his chamber for rosaries and the like. You wouldn't want to end up working for a papist by accident.'

'Mister Benjamin mentioned the Peyton Gang,' I say. 'It's only a thought, but could they have threatened him, if he seemed to abandon their friendship for that of Coleman?'

'He might have told Moor that sort of thing, but he wouldn't have told me. Most of the time he hardly seemed to know I was in the house. I'd put his food in front of him and he'd not even nod to acknowledge the plate was there.'

'His brothers sound as if they are cut from much the same cloth,' says Aminta. 'They take too little notice of you, Mistress Pamphlin. They undervalue you. Good housekeepers are worth their weight in gold.'

'They threatened me,' says Mistress Pamphlin indignantly. 'Mister Michael told me that, if questioned, I should just say the master had been murdered by papists. Told me I'd lose my position if I said anything else. Never get another one at my age, he said, and me scarcely five years older than he is himself.'

'So, the brothers want your silence?' asks Aminta.

'All they want from Moor is his silence too,' says Mistress Pamphlin. 'Then, when it all blows over, they'll not give him the time of day in the street. When the brothers came over that first Sunday – the day after the master disappeared – I heard them saying to Moor that he needed to keep quiet. That meant not tell us. Then they and Moor went off somewhere. They didn't say where. Not my place to ask, was it? I'm only the housekeeper, when all's said and done.'

'Did they not ask you to help look for him?' asks Aminta.

'I was sent over to his friend, Mistress Gibbon. But he wasn't there. Didn't think he would be. Waste of time. Except to keep me out of the way.'

She pauses and looks at us both. She's wondering if she's given us a guinea's worth of information yet. Maybe not.

'Primrose Hill,' she says suddenly.

'Yes?' I say.

'He was always going out that way,' she says. 'It didn't surprise me when they found his body there. Moor made it sound like just once or twice, but it was all the time lately.'

'Do you know what he did there?'

'No. Came back with mud on his shoes, though, and I'd be the one who had to clean them.'

I try to recall what witnesses said at the inquest. Did somebody report that somebody else had told them that he had been seen walking there? But the notes I have are, as I say, likely to be at best an uneven summary of what was actually said. And I don't recall Mistress Pamphlin's testimony on that or anything.

'Did you tell the coroner about your master's visits to Primrose Hill?' I ask.

'Wasn't allowed to go, was I? The brothers said I wasn't needed. Moor went. Of course Moor went. Moor goes everywhere. Still, they got the verdict they wanted, so that's all right then.'

'Could your master have killed himself?' I ask.

Mistress Pamphlin is silent for a long time. Eventually she says: 'It's what I thought myself when I heard. So did Moor. The master had been so miserable for weeks before he vanished. He was always a bit quiet. That was his way. This was something else. And the brothers were so convinced so quickly that he must be dead. How do you know that unless somebody's told you that's what they're planning? I think the problem was that the brothers thought he'd killed himself but didn't know *where*. So they had to find the body before anyone else did and make sure it looked like murder.'

'But they didn't find it straight away?'

'Maybe. Moor went over to Primrose Hill, on the Tuesday I think. Claimed he was looking for the body, but I reckon he was looking for a good place to leave one. Then, two days later, a body was found there. Coincidence? Not for me to say, is it? I'm only the housekeeper.'

'Perhaps Moor's got a lot to keep quiet about in that case,' I say.

'You're the lawyer,' says Mistress Pamphlin. 'But I do know suicide is a crime. Which would make Moor an accessory after the fact – if he helped cover it up. Wouldn't you say so?'

Yes, I would. So, that's probably worth a guinea then. Even though she's only the housekeeper.

Elizabeth Curtis is more used to serving than being served. She picks up the teacup nervously, as if she's broken a few in her time and doesn't want to reduce any possible reward by doing it again.

'It was easy enough to follow her,' she says, in answer to my question. 'I knew where Pamphlin must be going, as soon as she slipped out without telling me. Well, two can play at that game, my girl, I said to myself. So I told Moor I had to go to the market for garlic and grabbed my cloak. She never glanced behind once, sir, not all the way from Hartshorne Lane to your lodgings. I waited outside, a little way down the lane, until I saw her leave. She bit the coin she received to check it wasn't made of lead, before she was out of your front door, almost – I mean, as if you'd do a thing like that! She gives herself airs, that one, bearing in mind she served somebody who was in trade himself. The fact that he was a knight and a magistrate counts for nothing with me.'

I nod. As a knight and a magistrate myself, I can only agree with her. I have never thought otherwise. 'You have information for us then?' I say.

'I wouldn't tell you this if he was still alive,' she says. 'But the master was up to something. I can't say what exactly, but he was in too deep for comfort. You know he was friends with Mister Coleman, him who was arrested for treason?'

'Yes,' I say. 'Did they see each other often?'

'Often enough. Sometimes Mister Colman would send for him. Sometimes Mister Coleman would come to Hartshorne Lane – a fine gentleman like that, having to walk through a muddy yard full of stacked wood and coal dust. It wasn't right. They would sit in the master's study for hours with the door locked.'

'Doing what?'

'Talking. Reading through papers. Burning things sometimes. Once the master called for wine and when I brought it there was a fine old blaze going. I didn't say anything. Not that they'd have listened to me, of course, if I had. Some of it was letters Mister Coleman had written.'

'You mean copies of letters he'd sent other people?'

'Must be. Saw his signature amongst the ashes next day. Oh, and the word "chaise" on one. That's the French for chair. French? Well, if that's not suspicious, I don't know what is, I thought to myself.'

'When was the last time they met?'

'Maybe the week before the master died? Mister Coleman was arrested soon after. But I can tell you the longest time was just after Sir Edmund had taken evidence from that Mister Oates. The master wanted to show the deposition to him.'

'Sir Edmund discussed with a senior Catholic official what to do about a Catholic plot?'

'I hadn't thought of it that way, but since you say it, I suppose that's right.'

'He didn't go to Sir Joseph Williamson first?'

'He wouldn't have told me, but I don't think so. The first thing the master did, after Oates left, was to ask Mister Coleman to come over. I know because I carried the message to Somerset House.'

So, having learned of a Catholic plot that threatened the King's life, Godfrey's first act was not to report it to the proper authorities but to discuss it with his Catholic friends. That feels very much like misprision of treason, to give it its technical name. That one act would have had the magistrate in well over his head. It was an enormous risk to delay informing the Privy Council. If I'd been Godfrey, I too would have worried I'd hang for it.

'They all say the Catholics killed him, though,' says Elizabeth Curtis. 'Moor says it. But I can't see why they would do that. Not with a friend like Mister Coleman.'

A good point from Mistress Curtis. If Godfrey was keeping his Catholic contacts up to date with Oates's activities, why on earth would they kill him? He was too useful to them. The Court Justice himself. A spy at the very heart of the government. You don't give that up unless you have to.

'Did you recognise the messenger who came on Friday evening or the one on Saturday morning?' I ask.

'Not the one on Friday anyway. He was very sure of himself. Arrogant, almost. But I'd never seen him before in my life. The one on Saturday was nervous. He was being made to wait somewhere he didn't want to be.'

'And you did recognise him?'

'I thought I'd seen him before, but I couldn't say where.'

'Neither said where they were from?'

'I did overhear the Friday one say who sent him – the door was open a bit and the master asked him.'

'But you don't remember who?'

'He definitely said a secretary. Or maybe a clerk. One or the other. The master's study door was closed except for the very last little chink. It wasn't easy to make it out, even with my ear hard up against it. But, as for his name ... don't keep telling me to try to remember, like Mister Michael did. That's just stupid. If I could do it, I would. But I can't.'

'Not Coleman?'

'No, I'd remember if he'd said that. Doesn't mean it wasn't him, but that's not the name they said. It was a very common enough one, though.'

'Jones? Smith? Brown?'

She shakes her head.

'Could either of them have been sent by creditors?' I ask.

'The ones Moor mentioned? I don't think so. A couple of years back, I know the master was very short of money and we got all sorts of people visiting him. Bailiffs' men, I suppose. Polite enough to your face, but you wouldn't want to cross them. The master did mix with all sorts of people – people who were below him. But these were low *and* nasty. I've seen them less lately. The master's business must have picked up. No, if he killed himself it wasn't over money – I'm sure of that. But he feared somebody might hang him anyway.'

'You mean on the scaffold?'

'He was a very private man, the master was. A public death would not have suited him at all. He'd have taken matters into his own hands before they could try him and condemn him.'

'Thank you, Mistress Curtis,' I say, handing her half a guinea. 'If there's anything further we need to know, I'll send for you.'

'Half a guinea was a little mean,' says Aminta. 'Especially since I hope Williamson will refund it.'

'Arlington always paid according to the rank of the informant, not the value of the information. She is subordinate to the housekeeper. Anyway, there are other considerations. I'd like her to continue to look for ways to earn the other half.'

'I trust her word more than I trust Godfrey's clerk or his housekeeper.'

'So do I. But we've learnt something from all of them.'

'Moor didn't want us to talk to Judith Pamphlin in particular. And they clearly stopped her testifying at the inquest.'

'The brothers would do well to offer Mistress Pamphlin the same terms as they've offered Moor,' I say.

'She's only a woman,' says Aminta. 'It would go against their every instinct to pay her properly. With luck, her very natural resentment will continue to work in our favour.'

'In the meantime, I'd say Pamphlin and Curtis definitely believe he killed himself. Moor and the brothers fear he did and think they need to cover it up. That's almost everyone who really knew Godfrey. Godfrey does not seem to have been the most talkative or sociable of men, but this melancholy, as Mistress Pamphlin said, was something else again. Whether Godfrey had really solved his money problems completely is unclear – Moor, as his clerk, would have had a better idea than Curtis or Pamphlin or even the brothers. What was far more important, however, was that Godfrey had acted unwisely over Oates and let his friendship with Coleman take precedence over his duty to the King. He had good reason to fear he'd be hanged, drawn and quartered as a traitor. Better to commit suicide while he could.'

'So, where did Godfrey hang himself, then?' says Aminta. 'Not Primrose Hill, even though that's where he went on the Saturday morning and that's where he was found on the Thursday evening.'

'No, there are plenty of witnesses that he was back in Westminster, close to his own house, by early afternoon.'

'If it was in his own house, I think the servants would have noticed the preparations and stopped him. Except ... what about one of the sheds in his yard?'

'And Moor found him there?' I say. 'Excellent suggestion. Maybe late on the Saturday afternoon or early evening? That would explain better than anything why rumours spread almost at once. The servants – or Moor and Pamphlin at least – knew.'

'And they'd have told their friends.'

'That's perhaps a little unfair on them.'

'Well, my aunt heard of his death pretty quickly. And I think Williamson did too, bearing in mind when he wrote to you. Even if she saw nothing, Mistress Pamphlin may have worked out what had happened and decided that, if nobody was paying her to keep quiet, she might as well tell a few close acquaintances.'

'The brothers were quite right: I wouldn't have let her within a mile of the inquest either.'

'Nor me,' says Aminta.

'So what happened then?' I ask.

'I think we can make a reasonable guess,' says Aminta.

Godfrey's Journey

The fog-muffled bells of Saint Martin-in-the-Fields are chiming ten o'clock as a tall, stooped figure slips out of the gate into narrow Hartshorne Lane. Enough carts have passed along it this morning to churn up the filthy London mud, but thankfully he now has it all to himself. Keeping as close to the wall as he can, he picks his way carefully towards the Strand. With each step he takes, he becomes a little more anonymous. Just that bit safer. Perhaps he'll get away with it after all.

'Good day, Sir Edmund.'

He turns reluctantly to watch a blurred shape emerge slowly from the yellow haze. It resolves itself into Parsons, the church warden. Better speak to the man.

'You're off somewhere in a hurry, sir,' says Parsons brightly.

'That's right. I am. Well, I'd better get there then. Good day to you, Mister Parsons.'

'Easy to lose your way in this mist, Sir Edmund. One road looks much like another, eh? I hope you don't have far to go?'

'Primrose Hill,' he says.

'Are you planning to buy it up, then?' asks Parsons.

The wood-monger looks at him, puzzled. Why on earth does Parsons think he'd do that?

'I mean, plenty of timber there. And that's what you sell. Timber,' says Parsons with a knowing smile.

'More sea coal these days,' he says.

'Really? That's interesting. Won't find much of that at Primrose Hill, eh?'

'I wouldn't have thought so. It would be a very strange place to store it, away from the river.'

'I didn't really mean . . . Oh well, best take the left-hand fork just beyond the church anyway. Less likely to go wrong.'

'Thank you.'

'Or you could wait until later. The fog may clear. That's what I'd do.'

'I have urgent business there or I should not be going.'

'Sorry, Sir Edmund. No offence intended, I'm sure.'

The wood-monger sighs. He shouldn't have spoken to Parsons so sharply. He knows he sometimes adopts the wrong tone, or so his family tells him. What's the right tone, though? And how do other people seem to manage that sort of thing so easily? He raises his hat apologetically and is on his way again. A few yards further on, he pats his pockets for the third or fourth time. It's all there. The broad gold pieces wrapped in paper. The silver. The three small gold coins. Will it be enough, though? A part payment towards what he owes, they'd said. But what if that's not what they really meant? People so often seem to say one thing and mean another. What if they say they don't want the money? What if they say they really want to take the woodyard in place of the debt? Well, that's not his biggest problem any more.

He'd been a fool to show Oates's papers to Coleman. So, let's get this morning's meeting over with as quickly as possible. Then straight back to Somerset House to make sure Coleman hasn't been gossiping to his friends about the deposition. Because, if he has . . . But, one problem at a time. There'll be a way out. There always is. He just can't see it yet. What he needs is time for some calm rational thought. Away from other people. Then he'll know what it would be sensible and reasonable to do.

'Lord have mercy upon us,' says Benjamin.

'Quiet, you idiot,' says Michael. 'The last thing we want is Pamphlin and Curtis out here.'

'I've told them to stay where they are,' says Moor. 'They won't budge.'

'Thank you for coming to fetch us straight away,' says Michael.

'He should have taken me with him. However bad the news, I wouldn't have let him do this.'

'Not your fault, Moor,' says Benjamin. 'The problem with Edmund was that you never quite knew what he was thinking. I never did, anyway.'

'Well, we can't have the women finding him hanging there,' says Michael. 'I need time to think – what's best for everyone. There's the family reputation to consider.'

'And the money,' says Benjamin. 'There's the money too. The King will take the lot.'

'If there's any left,' says Michael.

'There's enough,' says Moor. 'I do the accounts for him, remember?'

'We'll need to cut him down,' says Michael. 'Maybe hide him behind that pile of timber there.'

Moor gives a short, bitter laugh. 'What then? It's cold out here, but he won't stay fresh for ever.'

'No, of course not. We'll have to find somewhere else. Tomorrow or the day after. As far from here as we can. And make it look like an accident or murder or something.'

'I could take him back to Primrose Hill. That's where he's been today.'

'How do you know?'

'Parsons saw him going there.'

'Did he seem odd?'

'No more than usual.'

'We'll need to find a pond or a ditch or something. Can't just leave him in the middle of a field.'

'I'll go over and take a look at the place. You can trust me, sir. I won't let the family down.'

'And in the meantime?'

'Look busy,' says Moor. 'Ask around. Do what you'd do if you hadn't found him.'

'Thank you, Moor. We're very grateful. For your loyalty, and so on.'

'I'll need your coach. And a man to drive it.'

'Of course. Of course. Anything. Just ask.'

'I ought to report it. Legally, I mean. Criminal offence not to.'

'Don't worry. We'll see you don't lose by it.'

'Two hundred guineas.'

'Two *hundred*? That's ridiculous.'

'It's nothing compared with what you'll save. And you'll need to pay the coachman to keep quiet. I don't want him turning King's evidence.'

'Yes, of course. Maybe twenty guineas for him? Or would five be enough, do you think?'

'I'll have to leave that to you. Just bear in mind he could inform on all of us.'

'You'll need to make it look like a robbery or something,' says Benjamin.

Moor looks up at his master's body and the sword still in its sheath.

'I think I can do that,' he says.

Chapter Eight

In which we meet Constable Brown

'You can't be certain it happened exactly like that,' I say.

'Of course not. As a writer, I'm permitted to embellish here and there. But there's nothing I've described that contradicts the evidence we have.'

'But definitely suicide?'

'Based on what we know at present, suicide because of his debts or suicide because of Coleman are both perfectly possible,' says Aminta.

'Possible but not certain,' I say. 'We've agreed that only a fool would have believed Godfrey died by stabbing. The brothers aren't fools.'

'That's why I'm convinced they delegated the disposal of the body to Moor. And Moor's certainly hiding something.'

'There is a further objection, though – the brothers left Godfrey with a considerable amount of money in his pockets, when to have taken it would have made for a more convincing robbery. They could have emptied his pockets at their leisure and in complete safety wherever they found him.'

'They made great play of the fact that the money in his pockets proved he was killed by the Jesuits.'

'It's an expensive way to prove something that everyone was quite ready to believe anyway. But I agree that may be the reason. If he was going to pay creditors as Moor thought, though, why did he still have the money?'

'Maybe Moor was very wrong that he was going there to pay creditors. There are other things that go on in low taverns. What if he was going there to gamble?'

'To recover the money lost by Godfrey Harrison?' I ask.

'Maybe his money problems really stemmed from his losses at cards anyway. It's why Lady Castlemaine never has enough, according to my aunt. And it would certainly explain why he didn't want to take Moor with him – more so than for a meeting with creditors actually.'

'He wouldn't be the first to ruin himself at the card table,' I say.

'And to say nothing to his family about it.'

'So, is that it? I go to Williamson now, say it's *felo de se* and we return to Essex?'

'Not quite,' says Aminta. 'I have to admit there's another problem with my version of the story. The broken neck. As we've agreed, that's unusual with a suicide.'

'Benjamin said the men who recovered the body might have slipped and dropped him,' I say.

'Would that be enough?'

'Quite possibly,' I say. 'I think that we should go to Primrose Hill ourselves. It may make it easier to work out what happened.'

'I'll wear my oldest dress. It could be quite muddy there.'

I think of Godfrey deciding not to wear his new camlet coat.

'Quite right,' I say. 'Old clothes will serve the day well enough for us both.'

Primrose Hill is a pretty enough place, even on a damp autumn afternoon, with the clouds low and rain once more in the air. True, there are no primroses here, nor will there be until the spring. But the trees are gold and the ragged green fields have attracted a number of Londoners wishing to escape the smoke of the City for an hour or two and visit a charming scene recently connected with violent death.

The White House tavern, the location of Godfrey's inquest, seems as good a place as any to start. It is, as Moor has told us, the lowest sort of establishment, soot-streaked, dirtily thatched and with wooden shutters to do the work of glass. We leave the muddy lane and step over the threshold into the parlour.

'You're lucky to have found me here,' says the constable. 'My duties rarely allow me the leisure to sit and drink ale at this time of day. Almost never, in fact. Most times you'd have had to search all over, me being busy with legal matters come rain or shine, neglecting my own interests out of loyalty to His Gracious Majesty. But today, the autumn weather making me unusually thirsty, I dropped in for a quick pint of ale. Just the one. Another five minutes and I'd have been gone. Might not have found me in here for another sennight.'

'Then we are fortunate indeed, Mister Brown,' says Aminta. 'You were there when Sir Edmund's body was found?'

'I was there when it was found *officially*,' he says. 'Others found it unofficially first.'

'Who?' I ask.

'Two men called William Bromwell and John Walters were on their way here when they saw a sword scabbard, belt, stick and gloves lying by a hedge. They thought they must belong to somebody who would be coming back for them sooner or later and, not wishing to be accused of stealing, they very properly left the gear alone and continued along the lane. They mentioned them in passing, however, to John Rawson, the landlord here. Rawson offered the men a shilling to fetch them, thinking perhaps that getting caught was less likely than Bromwell and Walters supposed – and anyway it would be Bromwell and Walters who'd be hanged for theft, not him.' Brown looks over to where the landlord is talking jovially to a group of customers and sneers briefly at him. 'Not that he'd admit that, of course. Says he just wanted to keep the valuables safe for their rightful owner. Anyway, it was cold and raining, and Bromwell and Walters reckoned they'd rather keep their necks unbroken and do without the shilling, thank you very much. So, Rawson stood them a drink or two and then, when the sky had cleared and the men's minds were cloudier, they all went back to investigate what might be done without alerting the authorities to anything illegal. Of course, they found that the rightful owner had been there all along, only he was head down in the ditch and very dead, which they could tell from the sword sticking out of him. That was when they called for me, as an expert in unexpected death.'

'Why don't you show us where it was?' I say.

Brown looks me up and down to work out how grateful I might be if he complies.

'Come this way, my good sir, and lady. It will be my pleasure to assist you.'

*

The place in question is no great distance from the tavern, a quick descent of a muddy path, fringed with the lank, broken grasses of autumn. The ditch itself is half obscured by brambles, though the vegetation around it has been trampled and flattened by the many people who have come here to view the site of Godfrey's blessed triple martyrdom. The channel is now full of the autumn rains, but Brown assures us that the water level was lower then.

'Dark, of course,' he adds, 'by the time they fetched me, the year already being so far advanced and the light summer evenings sadly just a memory for us all. But I could make things out by the glow of my lantern. The body was laid lengthways in the ditch, see? It looked odd to me – unnatural. The left hand was under his head on the bottom of the ditch – like this – and the right hand was a little stretched out, and touching the bank on the right-hand side – like that.' Brown pauses in his portrayal of a corpse to check that we have understood. I'm not sure I have entirely, but I nod encouragingly. 'The knees,' he continues, 'were resting on the bottom of the ditch, but his feet weren't touching the ground – not at all. The whole body was lying so strangely and crookedly that just bits of him got wet. His clothes were bone dry, mainly, but when you touched his flesh he felt as cold as damp mud and as stiff as baked clay. His periwig and hat were lying in the bottom of the ditch, a little in front of the body. And, like I say, there was a sword sticking right through him. I'd brought men to help carry the body and one of them commented that the deceased was a tall man. "Then I pray God it be not Sir Edmund Godfrey", I said to them. But sadly it was.' Brown removes his hat as a mark of respect, then quickly puts it on again. I think it may rain again very soon.

'You took the body back to the tavern to examine it?' I ask.

'The light was better there, though our main task, we knew, would be to prepare the body for the coroner. We had to remove the sword, of course, in order to get him on to the poles and carry him up the hill in a seemly manner. And we didn't want to stab ourselves by accident. One death was plenty. We were slithering about the whole time, in the dark and the mire, and anything might have happened.'

'You didn't drop the body, I hope?' I ask.

Brown swallows hard. 'Of course not, sir. Wouldn't be so careless and disrespectful. Glad to reach the tavern and get him on to a table, though, I can tell you. Once we were there, in good candlelight, it was obvious to anyone he hadn't been stabbed to death. No blood, you see, or none to speak of. Just a dribble of yellow when the sword came out. Almost nothing on the clothes.'

'You apparently had difficulty in getting the shirt off?'

Brown furrows his forehead, as if trying to recall an event an impossibly long time ago. 'Yes, we just managed to get the coat and waistcoat off but the shirt was too difficult. Eventually we had to cut it away.'

Unlike my suggestion that the body might have been dropped, this question has not troubled him at all. His conscience is clear.

'Did you keep the shirt?' I ask.

'Showed it to the coroner but he said he didn't need it. Somebody took it, I think, for cleaning rags. No point in wasting good linen, just because it's been on a corpse and it was too cut up to wear.'

Again, I wonder why Michael Godfrey was reluctant for me to have this information. As Brown has told us, the coroner knew and wasn't at all concerned. Perhaps if the shirt had been preserved it might have told us something, but it wasn't.

'He had money in his pockets?' I ask.

'Yes, I didn't count it – just gave it to the coroner, as was right and proper. But there must have been several pounds-worth, I'd have said by the weight in my hand, some of it wrapped in paper, two small gold coins loose at the bottom of one pocket.'

'Anything else on the body?'

'No, nothing. His brother – Mister Michael – did come round here asking if we'd discovered a pocket book. Quite large, apparently. We couldn't miss it. Very keen to have it, he was. Said there'd be a reward if anyone brought it to him.'

'But there wasn't one?'

'Sadly not. Not when we found him.'

'It couldn't have been in the ditch? Under the water perhaps?'

'We looked there the following day in case anything of value had been thrown in and missed in the dark. Somebody noticed he wasn't wearing his cravat and we wondered if that was in the ditch. We did a fairly thorough search, looking for that and maybe any missing money. We'd have seen a pocket book if it was there – especially a large one. Like I said, there wasn't that much water then. Nothing like enough to cover a man – hence the dry shoes. Actually his shoes were completely clean, as if he'd stepped out of his house only moments before. Which is odd, bearing in mind the state of the road. Ours were muddy enough when we got to the inn. He didn't walk here – I can tell you that for certain.' He looks at me significantly as if about to deliver information of certain monetary value. 'There were the marks of coach wheels in the road just beyond that field.' He points to the line of a hedgerow about a hundred yards away. It's not an impossible distance to carry a dead man.

'That's unusual?' I ask.

'Very. In my experience. Fine coaches don't come out this way much. Saint James's Park, yes, of course. Pall Mall, can't move for them. But not that lane. At the inquest they didn't take much notice of it, but it seems to me that Sir Edmund may have had powerful enemies – well, enemies who can afford to run a coach, anyway.'

Though there are probably carriage owners who murder nobody for weeks on end, it's a good point. It's likely whoever brought the body here owned a coach, which reduces the number of possible suspects quite a lot. A member of the nobility, perhaps. And the Godfrey brothers, of course. But, as evidence goes, a couple of ruts in the road don't take us much beyond where we already were.

'A coach could have passed by at any time during the last few days and have nothing to do with the murder,' I say.

'Ramsey, Lord Danby's man at the inquest, said it was prob-ably a cart anyway,' says Brown. He clearly resents Danby's intervention. Where was the King's chief minister when a body needed to be pulled out of the ditch? Where was he when they were struggling with the shirt? Nowhere, that's where.

'Had you seen Sir Edmund on Primrose Hill before?' I ask.

Brown pauses and looks at me sideways. 'Sometimes.'

'What did he come here for?' I ask.

I reach into my pocket and take out half a crown. I let Brown see it then close my fist on the coin.

Brown licks his lips and swallows. 'There's a club,' he says. He looks at my closed fist, but it is staying closed for the moment. I'll need a bit more than that. 'It meets at the tavern.'

'And Sir Edmund was a member?'

'Not exactly. It wasn't that formal. Just tradesmen from the City. Not gentry or anything. Sir Edmund sometimes joined them. I'd have said it was a bit beneath him, him being a knight of the realm and a magistrate, but there it is.'

Yes, didn't Elizabeth Curtis comment on Godfrey's liking for relatively lowly company?

'What did they do?' I ask.

'They talked. They played cards.'

'For high stakes?'

He laughs. 'I doubt it. This isn't Whitehall Palace. They wouldn't have had the money.'

Well, you can ruin yourself with low stakes, if you play often enough. Still, there's an omission that strikes me as odd.

'Rawson didn't mention any of this at the inquest,' I say.

'He didn't want to end up in Newgate,' says Brown with a crooked smile. 'It was a Catholic club. Rawson's breaking the law by allowing treason to take place in his establishment.'

'You didn't feel, in that case, that you should stop it, or report it? Wouldn't that have been your duty as constable?'

Brown looks a little less smug. I wonder if Rawson pays him for his silence. 'Never caught them at it, did I? Anyway, I can't swear anything treasonous was done there. Not for certain. Just that they met there.'

'Can you name any of the other members?'

I wait to see if he will name Coleman or even one of the great Catholic lords, but he shakes his head. Then he says: 'They come in from the City. They don't live here. There's one called Miles Prance. I think he's a member, or was. I haven't seen him much lately.'

The name means nothing to me. Nor is Brown saying Prance is any danger to the King. He's just trying to get me to release the coin in my hand. Still, it's a name, and that's always a useful starting point.

'Who is Miles Prance?' I ask.

'He's a silversmith. Does a lot of work for the Queen and the Duchess of York at Somerset House. Idolatrous silverware. Crucifixes. Candlesticks. Saints. Incense burners, I shouldn't wonder.'

I drop the coin into his hand.

'Thank you, Mister Brown,' I say. 'If you think of anything else, please send me a message.'

'Of the two things the club did,' I say, 'I think its being Catholic may have been more relevant to Godfrey's downfall than its card playing.'

'And that's probably why he came here that Saturday morning. In the end, nothing to do with paying off his creditors, though just for a moment I thought we finally had evidence that he had been losing money gambling. It looks as though, following his ill-advised disclosure of information to Coleman, Godfrey came out here to speak to his other Catholic contacts.'

'With money in his pockets,' I say.

'And a notebook, which somebody subsequently took,' says Aminta.

'So, who took it? Another mystery to add to the ones we already have. The introduction of Mister Prance's name is also an intriguing development,' I say. 'He doesn't sound terribly dangerous in himself, nor does his silverware threaten the Church of England. The connections are significant, though. Godfrey knows Coleman, who works at Somerset House, where Mister Prance goes to get custom for his silver, from Mister Coleman's employer's wife. I think we need to investigate Godfrey's growing circle of Catholic friends more closely,' I say. 'We should attempt to speak to Coleman, if we can get past his guards at Newgate. I'll get a letter from Williamson to introduce us.'

'We shouldn't speak to Miles Prance?'

'Prance,' I say, 'seems to have been introduced into the conversation mainly to speed up payment of a bribe. Brown said he hadn't even been to the club lately. It may be that we'll get to speak to Prance later, but there are other more important witnesses first.'

'Coleman next then,' says Aminta.

Chapter Nine

In which we meet Mister Edward Coleman

'I was told to let nobody see the prisoner,' says the jailer. 'Even gentry like your good selves.'

'But, as you see,' says Aminta, 'we have a letter signed by the Secretary of State. He has agreed that no harm can come of a brief visit by old friends.'

'It's very irregular and I can't possibly allow it ... still, thank you, sir, that's very generous of you. I'll unlock the door for you both immediately. Please take as long as you wish. Poor Mister Coleman gets few visitors. I wish more of his rich friends like you came here.'

I put my purse back in my pocket. Aminta sweeps into the small cell ahead of me. Edward Coleman looks up from the filthy straw pallet that is the only item of furniture with which he has been supplied. He's lucky to get that.

'Who are you?' he asks, blinking two bleary, deep-set eyes. His face is long and cadaverous. The hand that he holds up, quivering, half pointing at us, is bony, the hand of a man twice his age – a hand of which a saint or martyr would be proud. Yet there remains a worldly silkiness in his manner, even after many days of incarceration.

'We're friends,' says Aminta.

Coleman's mouth twists in a hopeful half-smile.

'Sent by Williamson,' I say.

The smile fades.

'I am Sir John Grey, a magistrate,' I add. 'This is my wife, Lady Grey. We need to ask you about Sir Edmund Berry Godfrey.'

Coleman views the pair of us from his low and malodorous bed. He would have preferred us to find him in a more appropriate setting, all things considered. 'Why does that require two of you?'

'Sir Joseph thought it would attract less notice if we seemed to be friends visiting, rather than my being sent in any official capacity,' I say.

'Williamson wishes things to be obscure?'

'Always,' I say. 'It is part of his job, as I'm sure you will already be aware.'

Coleman finally struggles to his feet. He is weak and exhausted but he clearly finds himself at some disadvantage with us towering over him. He must also feel it's occasionally worth getting away from the ever-present stench of his pallet. It will have been used many times before, by men who have long since passed away from one cause or another, but not before pissing themselves with fear.

Even standing, however, Coleman presents a sorrowful sight. His fine velvet coat is creased. I suspect he has been sleeping in it, having no blanket. His periwig has not been combed for some time. His linen is grubby. For obvious practical reasons, his sword and sash have been temporarily taken away from him. So, it would seem, has his razor. This is a shadow of the man who entertained politicians, peers and bishops by the light of fine wax candles.

'If I help you,' he says, 'I want you to help me. Those are my terms. They are not negotiable. You may take them or leave them.'

'Williamson has authorised me to offer you nothing. He has simply suggested that I threaten you with worse conditions than these if you do not cooperate.'

'There are worse conditions than these?'

'You have a straw pallet.'

'I have fallen thus far. Do you think I care if I fall a little further?'

'You may when you get there,' says Aminta. 'Look, Mister Coleman, we can, as my husband says, promise you nothing. But it is most unlikely that anyone more helpful than us will visit you for some time. Our gratitude may be worth more than you think. We're not much, but we're all you have at the moment.'

Coleman considers this carefully, as well he might.

'Lady Grey? You're the playwright, aren't you?' he asks.

'I'm certainly a playwright,' she says.

'I know you now. You write scandalous comedies. Plays of a most impious nature. Full of deceit and trickery and praise of women's guile.'

'You clearly visit the theatre a great deal. Thank you for your valued custom. Sadly we are also your last hope, unless Williamson has very much misrepresented your case. And I would not disparage women's guile too much, Mister Coleman. You may yet have need of it.'

Coleman allows himself a brief, unsaintly sneer. 'The Duke of York will not let me be executed,' he says.

'How do you know that?' she says.

'I just do.'

'You are aware that Oates wishes to bring the Duke of York down?' I ask. 'Your patron may be in no position to help anyone.'

'Oates has a ridiculous face and a mind like a sewer. He won't succeed.'

'He's doing quite well so far. That's why you are here and he has rooms at Whitehall Palace.'

Coleman considers this too.

'What do you want to know, Sir John?' he asks, as if we were keeping him from the many things he has to do this morning.

'You were a good friend of the late Sir Edmund Godfrey?' I say.

He pauses. 'It depends what you mean.'

'When did you first meet him?'

'I don't recall.'

'How did you meet him?'

'I'm not sure.'

'You saw a great deal of him, anyway.'

He shrugs. Does he want to distance himself from the murder as much as he can?

'I've been here since the first of October,' he says. 'I was under lock and key when Sir Edmund died. Williamson knows that perfectly well. His death was nothing to do with me.'

'But Godfrey saw you immediately after Oates's deposition to him?'

'Yes.'

'What exactly did he tell you?'

'He showed me the deposition that Oates had made.'

'Did he seem aware that might be treason?'

'He was a little nervous, I suppose.'

'So, why would he come to you?'

'He wanted to consult me. He wanted to know if there was any possibility that the story was correct.'

'What did you do after your discussion with Sir Edmund?'

'I made enquiries. I was able to tell Sir Edmund there was no truth in it at all.'

'Did he say he would inform the Privy Council?'

'That was his affair.'

'You didn't think to inform the Privy Council yourself? You must know all the Counsellors personally.'

'It was not for me to do so. My loyalties are to the Duke – not to them.'

'You are very frank.'

'Sir John, Oates's statement was a pack of lies. Only the most inconsequential details are true. There is no plot. There is no treason. Sir Edmund could have shown the document to the Pope or to the King of France without the slightest risk of harm to anyone. Why should it matter if I saw it? Why should it matter if either of us did not immediately tell the Privy Council? Why should I seek to conceal that I saw something that is now public knowledge anyway?'

'You could have warned some of your Catholic friends to flee the country.'

'That was very unlikely, my friends not being cowards and there being no danger.'

'Many have been arrested.'

He makes a noise that Aminta would probably render in her plays as 'pshaw'.

'They will soon be released,' he says.

'The Duke will see to it, no doubt,' I say. 'Who gave you the advice that there was nothing in the accusations?'

'All you need to know is that my friends, Catholics as you say, cooperated fully, to the great benefit of the King and the State. Being a Catholic does not mean being disloyal.'

'Might your friends have had anything to say, in confidence, about who killed Sir Edmund Berry Godfrey?' I ask.

'How would they know about that?'

'There is a rumour that he was murdered by the Jesuits.'

'You shouldn't believe everything you hear. Especially what people in this city tell you about the Catholic church. Their ignorance and spite never cease to astonish me.'

'I don't believe everything I hear. But I do believe you might have heard something that I haven't.'

'If I knew anything of any importance, and had been told in confidence, I would scarcely tell you.'

He looks at me as a priest might if I had asked him to reveal the secrets of the confessional. Mildly shocked yet infinitely forgiving. Perhaps he should have become a priest – a stern confessor, prone to imposing, for his parishioners' good, the sort of harsh penances he himself might rather enjoy.

'Is nothing Oates says true?'

'Oates lies all the time. He can't help himself, poor man. It is how God made him. We should pity him and pray for his putrid soul. But occasionally he speaks the truth. He was certainly at Valladolid and Saint Omers. He was expelled from both. He was forced to leave Valladolid because he lacked the capacity to study there. He proved equally ignorant of Latin, Spanish and theology. He was forced to leave Saint Omers for other reasons. It is a school for boys, not grown men. I cannot think why Father Strange, the former Jesuit Provincial, sent him there. He caused trouble. He left reluctantly but it was made clear to Oates by the new Provincial, Father Whitebread, that he had no choice but to go.'

'He claims to have been a spy there.'

'I cannot say what was in his mind, but nobody would have told him anything worth knowing. The boys wouldn't even sit with him at mealtimes. If it helps at all, I can confirm he was received into the Catholic church in March last year, and into the Jesuit order shortly after that. That is how he was able to study in Spain and why, when that understandably failed, he was found a place elsewhere, however unsuited he was to it. He was something of a pet of Father Strange, who is a good and charitable man and who helped him in many ways – something which Oates has repaid by denouncing him to the Privy Council.'

'Was Godfrey such a bad friend that you don't want to find his killer?'

Coleman says nothing.

'Do you know anything of a Catholic club that meets at the White House on Primrose Hill?'

Coleman says nothing.

'Do you know a Mister Miles Prance?'

'Prance? What has Prance got to do with anything? He couldn't have killed Godfrey. I know his name. Of course I do. I've met him once – maybe twice. He's a silversmith. He made some candlesticks for the Duchess. Good work at a fair price.'

We wait to see if he will add to that. He doesn't. Prance is not his concern. Still, he seems to have ruled him out as a murderer very confidently.

'You are said to be a diligent correspondent,' I say. 'The Privy Council has your letters, or at least the older ones. Williamson thinks you destroyed the more recent ones. You seem to have been a very good friend of Père La Chaise, the French King's confessor.'

Coleman makes no attempt to deny that he sometimes writes in a suspicious foreign tongue. 'There is nothing of consequence in those letters. Our discussions were on philosophy and history for the main part.'

'And religion?'

'There can be no serious discussion on anything that excludes God.'

'You said to Père La Chaise that England was happier in the days of Queen Mary.'

'How do you know?'

'Williamson told me about some of them,' I say.

'Well, it was. Much holier and much happier. People are coming to realise that now.'

'You mean happier in the days when Protestants were burnt at the stake?'

'No more than was necessary. A few hundred to save millions from the everlasting flames of hell. True cruelty, Sir John, lies in leaving people to be damned for all eternity – not in inflicting pain that will last scarcely ten minutes. I'd put a match to the fires myself if I had to. We need a monarch who can lead his people upwards and towards the light. Towards salvation, not towards Newmarket or the Theatre Royal in Drury Lane. Every year we have a professed Protestant on the throne, more souls are lost for all time, simply through wilful neglect. The King has much on his conscience, sir, and he knows it. He is delaying his conversion too long.'

'You wrote that to Père La Chaise?'

'Who could possibly object to somebody giving their honest opinion on the history of this country?'

'You said England would soon have a Catholic monarch again. Did you mean that the King will convert?'

'That remains very uncertain. I obviously meant the Duke. The King's health has not always been good. He has no legitimate son or daughter. Only a fool would believe that the Duke will not one day be king. It is those, like the Earl of Shaftesbury, who promote the cause of the bastard Duke of Monmouth, who are the true traitors, not those who support the rules of succession, as handed down by generation after generation of loyal Englishmen. Why don't they arrest Shaftesbury? Or Peyton – there's a traitor if ever I saw one. He wants Richard Cromwell back.'

'You also speculate in your letters on how much it will cost to win over Parliament to the Catholic cause.'

'In jest. Purely in jest. I was not suggesting that the members of the House of Commons were truly bribable *en masse*. Surely that is obvious from the words I use?'

'It was not obvious to the Privy Council that the Commons could not be bribed. It wasn't obvious to Williamson either. They all clearly thought it was just a question of price.'

'In that case, I hope the King at least has a sense of humour.'

He does and it may amuse him to see Coleman on the scaffold. He's always found Coleman an interfering nuisance, whose boundless lack of caution threatens the Duke, his brother.

'Did you yourself have funds to bribe some Members of Parliament at least?' I ask.

'No more than was strictly necessary.'

Coleman rubs his eyes. I am now tiring him with irrelevant questions.

'Well,' says Aminta. 'We both hope that you will shortly be released from your bondage, Mister Coleman.'

'They have no evidence against me, or none worth mentioning. And the Duke ...'

'. . . will save you. Yes, you said.' Aminta smiles at him encouragingly, but only one of us in the room believes that is true.

'Thank you, Mister Coleman,' I say. 'I shall report back to Sir Joseph.'

'You will ask him to release me? It must be clear to you that I present no threat to the King?'

Strangely the answer to that is 'yes', he is completely harmless. And I shall say that to Williamson. But I doubt that it will help in any way. The prisoner seems determined to condemn himself. Truth will be the death of Coleman, just as lies pave Oates's path to greatness.

'I'll do what I can,' I say.

'He was very frank,' says Aminta, as the prison gate closes behind us. The yellow, sulphurous London air feels fresh and welcoming.

'Except over his relationship with Godfrey,' I say. 'Where he met him and why they became friends.'

'It's difficult to see what a Catholic fanatic had in common with a lapsed supporter of Sir Robert Peyton,' says Aminta.

'Perhaps all fanatics have something in common,' I say. 'Perhaps they are all more like each other than they are like us.'

'Not like me, certainly, but I don't exclude you. Let's not forget you were once a Puritan.'

'No, I wasn't,' I say.

'Yes, you were,' says Aminta. 'You still would be if Cromwell had survived.'

'I'm not sure how he ruled Prance out as a murderer,' I say. 'I think, even in prison, he's heard something he's not telling us about. And, as you say, he was frank enough on other matters. Just what he told us today, willingly to two total strangers, was enough to hang him.'

'He doesn't care,' says Aminta. 'Edward Coleman is a born martyr.'

'He is certainly in love with the idea of martyrdom. I doubt he will enjoy the practical side of it, but he is ready to embrace it in theory. It's how he wishes to die, with winged angels carrying him off to heaven.'

'My father has always said that he wishes to die in bed with a glass of Canary in one hand and a tart's tit in the other.'

'A much wiser choice.'

'I've assured him that, if I think he's dying, I'll send at once for a tart.'

'Ever the dutiful daughter,' I say.

'I've warned him not to pretend to die, though,' she says. 'I'm only doing it once. The second time it will be the vicar and a glass of water.'

Chapter Ten

In which we meet Mistress Gibbon

'You may as well sit down, since you're here,' says Mistress Mary Gibbon. She is the elder Mistress Mary Gibbon, as she has already informed us twice. She wants us to know we are getting the genuine article.

'We simply wish,' I say, 'to convey our most sincere condolences over the loss of your good friend, Sir Edmund.'

'No you don't,' she says. 'Who do you work for? Williamson? They've all been poking their noses into my private business. That's what you want to do too, I shouldn't wonder.'

'There's no pulling the wool over your eyes, is there, Mistress Gibbon?' says Aminta.

'Don't try flattery on me, young woman. I'm old enough to be your mother. Almost. Well, ask me whatever it is you have to ask me.'

'I'm sure you have nothing to hide,' I say.

'What gives you that idea?'

I'll start with an easy question then.

'You and your family are, I think, amongst Sir Edmund's closest friends?'

'Closest? I've no idea,' she says, helpfully. 'But we knew him well enough. I and my husband, Captain Gibbon, and our daughter Mary. My husband is somewhat related to Sir Edmund. Don't ask me exactly how. He has explained more than once but I always drift off halfway through. His family's less interesting than he believes.'

'Sir Edmund was also a good friend of Edward Coleman's?' I ask.

'So I understand. We also knew Coleman a little. Our daughter Mary once worked for him. Oh yes, we're Catholics. Always have been. Not proud of it. Not ashamed of it. It's just what we are. People seem to think that Catholicism is some strange foreign religion, but we're not the ones who have changed – it's the rest of you, with your dreary new German heresy of Protestantism. I don't think Edmund attended many of the gatherings at Coleman's house, though. He didn't like grand dinners. He'd dine with his fellow wood-mongers on their feast days, or with a few close friends. Some said Edmund demeaned himself by the company he kept – happier playing bowls with tradesmen and labourers than dining with the gentry, they said. Well, the Godfreys are scarcely nobility, for all that Michael and Benjamin give themselves airs and drive around in their carriages. But even so ... There was gossip about it. Mixing with the lower orders just because he liked them. Oh yes, there was gossip.'

'Did he ever mention a club at Primrose Hill – a meeting place for Catholic tradesmen from the City?'

She shakes her head. 'He never talked of going there at all.'

'But he was a sociable enough man?'

'Sometimes. Other times ... Black moods came upon him, you see. And lately, more and more often. On the Tuesday before he vanished he came to me and do you know what he said? He asked if I had heard the news in town that he was to be hanged? Not really, I said. Would he like some tea? Then he mumbled about a Catholic plot – I didn't catch it all. Which Catholic plot is that then? I asked, because he was making little sense and I was stirring the teapot again. The water the maid had used when making it hadn't been hot enough – not nearly. He said something about Oates having outsworn himself and so it would come to nothing. That's good, I said. I may as well pour it now. It's as strong as it's ever going to be. Edmund shook his head, rather ungratefully I thought, and told me that he had taken Oates's deposition and had never spoken of it to any man, even though he had dined with the Lord Chancellor and the Attorney General. He was the master of a secret, he said, that would be fatal to him. But his security in the business was Oates's deposition. Well, there you are, I said. You've got security. So, you've nothing to worry about. Worse happens at sea, I said. Then our silly maid came in and Edmund wouldn't utter another word. Not that she'd have reported him or anything – it just goes in one ear and out of the other with her. The water, I said to her, has to be boiling – boiling, do you hear? I don't buy good China tea just so that you can spoil it with half-cold water. On the Thursday before Edmund was killed, though, he sent for me and I went over to him, once I had seen to my sick mother. He was in some disorder, I can assure you. He said to me something about his father's sharp melancholy and not being able to shake it off. He said it was hereditary but he was the only child of his father that took after him, which was true. I've never seen Michael or Benjamin feeling sorry for themselves. Or for anyone else come to that. But Edmund was another matter. In Kent, where the family comes from, they were famous for being peculiar. God's truth, they had to tie his father to his bed. I think it always played on Edmund's mind – that he'd end up the same way, roped up hand and foot, raving, attacking his family with a stick, which his father did more than once, for all the family now denies it. He said he'd been let blood. I said: more fool you, paying a surgeon for something that's never worked for anyone I've ever known. He said if that was all I had to say he was best alone. I said, seemingly you are, Edmund. Seemingly you *are*. He didn't like that. Too much truth for him.'

'Did he show other signs of instability?' I ask.

'A few weeks ago, I came round and found him eating just whey and brown bread. So, I made him some calves-foot jelly – to build up his strength a bit. When I visited him next he was eating whey again. I wanted to know why had he asked me to make him jelly then? He said it was his father's fault. There was no getting any sense out of him half the time. It made me cross. He was getting as thin as Mister Coleman.'

'You thought he'd kill himself?' I ask.

'And he did, didn't he? I'm not often wrong there. Not with family, anyway.'

'Michael and Benjamin say he didn't do it.'

'And you know why as well as I do. They got the coroner's jury to say it was murder, after a little persuasion, which was convenient for everybody, I suppose. I just hope some poor man doesn't hang on the gallows as a result because, mark my words, they'll want to hang somebody. Nasty lot, that Privy Council. I've always said so.'

'And after the murder? What happened then?' I say.

'It's all as I told the inquest. First, Mistress Pamphlin was sent to look for him, but all I could say was that he wasn't with us. Later Michael and Benjamin came by, as if I maybe hadn't noticed their brother in our sitting room and they needed to check. I said, he's not yet been gone a day, you boobies. It's too soon to worry. First, you waste Mistress Pamphlin's time, now you're wasting mine. Don't you think we women have work to do? There must be a thousand reasons why Edmund hasn't come home yet. Name three, they said. You know Edmund. Name three reasons why he'd stay out all night. I said, that was very true and when I last saw him I thought he might kill himself. So, they were probably right after all and his money was as good as in the King's purse. Happy now? I asked. At that Michael Godfrey lifted up his hands and eyes and said: "Lord, we are undone! What shall we do?" Just like that. "Lord, we are undone!" It made you want to laugh, it really did. I asked if they'd like to stay for some tea, but they said no.'

'And you told this to the inquest?'

'Yes, but I was the last to give evidence and I think they'd lost interest by then. The clerk couldn't be bothered to write half of it down. Well, if that's all, I'll get the maid to put the kettle on, shall I? Don't worry – I'll stand over the silly little mauther while she does it.'

A thick fog has descended on the city while we were at Mistress Gibbon's house – one of those ochre miasmas that are becoming increasingly common as coal rather than wood is burnt by its inhabitants. Anything more than ten yards away is lost completely, but we can still see the shadowy outline of the buildings on either side of us.

Aminta coughs and then puts her scarf in front of her mouth.

'I wonder that Londoners are not all dead from these fumes,' I say.

'The thick air is at least good for losing any pursuers.'

'You think somebody is following us?' I ask.

'Why should nobody be following us?' she says.

I stop and look behind. I can just make out a black shape that ducks into a doorway a moment or two later than it should have done. I don't think it's one of Williamson's men, unless they have become as sloppy as Mistress Gibbon's maid. Maybe Oates is interested in what I'm doing. Maybe it's the Jesuits. But I don't think I was imagining it. We'll find out soon enough.

'Mistress Gibbon made a good case for suicide,' I say.

'That's clearly what she believes. There does seem to be a complete consensus amongst those who really knew him. What Mistress Gibbon has added to the mix is a hereditary disposition to madness. She's also confirmed he had a very real fear that he might be hanged, drawn and quartered for treason. That would be enough for most people.'

'Vastly more likely than a Catholic plot, for which we've found no evidence at all. Godfrey never said that it was the Catholics whom he feared. He had no shortage of Catholic friends – to whom we must now add the Gibbons.'

'What are we to make of what Godfrey told Mistress Gibbon?' I say. 'What was the dangerous secret? How was Oates's deposition his security? Actually, the business of Oates's deposition was what threatened to condemn him, not to save him.'

'Mistress Gibbon implied his ramblings were all part of a general derangement, along with the perverse refusal to eat the jelly she had made him. She's right, of course, that some innocent person will probably hang.'

'Unless we can show Godfrey did commit suicide. I should have liked to have examined the body when it was found,' I say, 'rather than as it is now.'

'Too late to be thinking of that now. You made the mistake of being in Essex.'

'I can do the next best thing,' I say. 'Williamson has given me the name of the surgeon who examined it at the inquest. Zachariah Skillarne. He lives a few streets away. It's getting difficult to know exactly where we are, but hopefully we can get to our next destination while we can still see our hands in front of our faces.'

Chapter Eleven

In which we meet Surgeon Skillarne and discuss anatomy

Zachariah Skillarne consents to see us. He was just going out to visit a patient but has a few minutes to spare. The patient is unlikely to die until he starts to operate on him. He ushers us into a little sitting room, the ceiling of which he almost brushes with the top of his periwig. Even in here, the air is not completely clear. In addition to the smoke from Skillarne's own fire, the smoke of other Londoners' chimneys is creeping in from the street, underneath and around the poorly fitting sash windows.

On the table at his side is a range of instruments that he was about to pack up into his bag. I know the use of most, since that was my father's trade too. I recognise the trepan, the double-bladed bistoury, the forceps and the heavy surgical saw. Skillarne is a tall man and strong, as surgeons need to be. He bids us sit and takes a seat himself. He smiles at us, dextrously twisting a delicate scalpel between his thick fingers. I think it would not be advisable to pick a fight with him.

'You've read the report of the inquest?' he asks.

'Yes,' I say.

'I doubt I've much to add to what you know then,' he says. He holds the scalpel up to the light to admire the sharpness of the steel. 'I first heard that the body had been found on the Friday, when Michael and Benjamin Godfrey came to see me. They wanted me to go with them straight away to view the corpse at the inquest. It had been stripped ready for examination. The breeches, coat and so on were folded neatly beside it. All in order, other than that the constable had removed the sword from Godfrey's chest, but it was obvious where it had been, so no harm done, eh? You saw the body yourself?'

'Yes,' I say, 'but some days later at Hartshorne Lane.'

'Well, I don't need to describe the wounds in any great detail then. The marks round the neck were interesting. Cloth rather than rope, I'd have said. Maybe his own missing cravat. Slanting, but that doesn't necessarily mean it was a hanging – it could have been a taller man at one end of the cloth and a shorter one at the other. It would have looked much the same. The neck was completely broken. Snapped in two.'

'And what did you make of that?' I ask.

'Well, it's normal with judicial hangings, where the body drops a good way under its own weight before being brought up short by the rope. Or if it is a murder and the killers apply a great deal of force to the neck. But not an ordinary suicide, where death is by slow strangulation rather than breaking the neck.'

'That's what I thought too' I say. 'But could it have been broken when Sir Edmund was dragged out of the ditch or perhaps if the body was dropped on the way to the inn.'

'Was he dropped?'

'The constable said not.'

Skillarne considers this for a moment, then he smiles. 'The path from the ditch to the inn was certainly treacherous when I went there. The men summoned to retrieve the body had, by all accounts, been drinking at the inn beforehand. It was dark. It wouldn't surprise me in the slightest if they'd dropped him on his head half a dozen times. Mud from the path would have looked much like mud from the ditch. And, while a broken neck from suicide is very unusual, it's not entirely impossible. If all the other evidence points to *felo de se*, then I wouldn't let the broken neck alone make you decide otherwise. Not at all.'

'What was the body like more generally?' I ask.

'There was still little putrefaction. No obvious stench until we opened him up, then not much. The limbs were loose.'

'So the rigidity after death had worn off?'

'What do you mean?'

'It begins between one and six hours after death and ends twelve to thirty-six hours after,' I say.

'You have made a study of corpses, Sir John?'

'Yes, when I was a child. In those days there were many battlefields where one could study anatomy entirely free of charge. My mother was good enough to take me to several. She was searching for my father's body, but since he had left the army and gone to the Spanish Netherlands with his mistress, she never found it. I would amuse myself as best I could, studying some of the many ways of dying. Since then, as a magistrate, I have frequently put those lessons to use.'

'Most of my work is with the living,' he says. 'So, I'll have to take your word for it. I've seen corpses stiff and I've seen them limber but I've never troubled myself to catalogue them. Some of my colleagues say, however, that all those who die of strangulation are limber and all those who die naturally are stiff.'

'A little practical anatomy would tell them they were wrong.'

'Our fees depend on cures rather than being able to say why and when our patients died. In any case, all it shows is that Godfrey's death was more than twelve hours before I examined it and, since it had been found the previous evening, I knew that anyway. As I say, we saw some putrefaction when we ripped him open, but maybe not a lot. From that and from the last sighting of Sir Edmund alive, and because the weather was cold and putrefaction slower to set in than during the heat of the summer, I placed the time of death as being four or five days before – probably the evening of the day he disappeared. What you say about rigidity would seem to support this, or at least not contradict it, in that I saw none. The marks round the neck and the lack of blood from the sword wounds made it clear that it was strangulation. So did the prominence of his eyes. Mister Cambridge, the other surgeon present, was good enough to agree with me. The jury concluded that it was murder, because they were told to do so. The coroner could see there was no definite proof of suicide and it's always better, if there's any doubt at all, that a verdict of *felo de se* is avoided. For the family, I mean. But you imply you've other evidence?'

'Mistress Gibbon told us that Sir Edmund had been melancholy for some time and that his father had suffered from the same thing. It is also clear that he was worried about the consequences of not reporting Oates's testimony to the authorities. She seemed to have little doubt it was suicide.'

Skillarne nods. 'I think that juries often give too little weight to the testimony of ladies. If she had been questioned properly at the inquest and due notice taken of her replies, then perhaps we might have reached a very different conclusion. Anyway, the state of his mind was outside my remit, then and now. I gave evidence only on the state of his body. I'm still not unhappy with the verdict of murder or the time of death as Saturday.'

'But nothing you saw absolutely rules out suicide?'

'Not at all. There is the bruising – which suggested to me ill-treatment before his death. But it may be a settling of the blood after death, not a bruise at all. There's a lot we don't know about what happened to the body between Sir Edmund's death and his being found in the ditch. Did you see in one of the witness statements, by the way, that somebody was told, the day before the body was found, that Godfrey was lying dead with his own sword through him in Leicester Fields? Near the Earl of Pembroke's house, apparently. Could it mean that's where he died?'

'The witness accounts often contradict each other,' I say. 'And some seem like pure imagination.'

'Odd though that, the day before he was found, somebody heard he'd been stabbed with his own sword. That would have been a good guess, as these things go. Pembroke's mad, of course, and a convicted murderer.'

'But with no grudge against Godfrey that we know of.'

'True enough. But there's another strange thing of which I'm certain without witness testimony. The brothers didn't want a post mortem, so we did a less thorough job in that respect than I'd have liked. But when we cut open the stomach it was empty – Sir Edmund had, in my view, eaten nothing for at least two days. He must have been fasting most conscientiously just before he died.'

'He was certainly eating very little,' says Aminta. 'According to Mistress Gibbon anyway.'

'Well, perhaps his appetite had gone,' says Skillarne. 'Which adds to the evidence for melancholy and suicide.'

'One last thing,' I say. 'Sir Edmund's shirt was cut away and disposed of.'

Skillarne nods. 'Yes, that's right. They showed it to me. I told them at the time that it was of no importance. There was no blood on it – just a little staining from fluid after the sword was withdrawn. It told us nothing that we did not already know.'

'But why cut it away?'

'Well, a shirt is more difficult to remove than a waistcoat, I suppose. I doubt it was more than that. The fellows who assist the courts are an idle lot and take the easiest way. Sometimes, Sir John, we can look for problems that simply are not there.'

I nod. We have plenty of problems that definitely exist. We really don't need the other sort as well.

The fog is, if anything, worse on the way back to our lodgings. The buildings now are less than grey smudges. The people are like wraiths, floating past us, silent expect for the muffled sound of their coughing. Twice we take a wrong turn in a neighbourhood that we would know well on a clear day. We are relieved when our own front door finally closes behind us and we breathe in the scent of the clean rushes on the floor and hear the pleasant sound of supper being prepared in the kitchen.

'There's a person to see you, Sir John,' says our maid, before we even have the chance to take off our cloaks.

'Who?' I ask.

'He wouldn't give his name,' she says. 'But he's wearing the royal livery. Thinks he's quite something, lounging in one of your chairs.'

'I'd better see him then,' I say.

The man is indeed lounging. And his clothes are certainly intended to get him noticed. His scarlet, gold-laced coat and breeches make our parlour dull by comparison. If he wants to look dignified, however, he'd do better not scratching himself like that.

'Can I help you?' I ask.

'You Grey?' he enquires economically.

'I am indeed. Who are you?'

'Sent by His Majesty. You're to come with me. Now.'

'Where to?'

'Whitehall.'

'For what purpose?'

'Can't tell you.'

'Who am I to meet there?'

'Couldn't say.'

'Are you sure you can guide me there in this fog?'

'Do it with my eyes closed. Right, you coming or what?'

He gets to his feet and, with two grubby palms, brushes a little of the dust of the street from his breeches onto our floor.

We pass Aminta in the hallway. She has only just handed her cloak to the maid to hang up.

'I'm commanded to go to Whitehall,' I say to her. 'To see somebody who won't tell me his name.'

'For how long?' she asks.

'As long as it has to be,' says my chaperone. 'Hours. Days. Weeks. Months. Years. I'm not a fortune teller. Some I take there never come back.'

'If I've not returned by midnight, tell Williamson,' I say.

My guide proves to be as good as his word. This London fog is no more hindrance to him than the darkness of night is to an owl. Occasionally he pauses and squints at a half-hidden shop sign above our heads, but most of the time he presses on at a brisk pace. Occasionally too the shadow-people we pass glance at me and my escort, as if wondering what fate holds in store for me. Then they shudder silently and vanish into the gloom, thankful it isn't them this time.

When we finally reach our destination, I can see only the bottom half of the great entrance gate. The rest has disappeared into the universal murkiness of the late afternoon. We enter via a small wicket, stepping over the threshold on to the glistening cobbles. A sentry salutes my guide rather than me, but there is no time to acknowledge the gesture. Time seems to be of the essence.

Whitehall Palace is a strange collection of buildings, erected at various times for various purposes, some remembered, some forgotten by any still living. They are all linked by winding paths, stone courtyards, gravelled roads and patches of garden. Wandering through it, you're never sure who or what you will encounter next. Other than the new Banqueting House, there is little worth seeing. If the French King ever came to visit London, our own monarch would be embarrassed to have to welcome the owner of Versailles to such a hotchpotch of stone and brick and timber. Its sole advantage is that it is large. It resembles, in fact, a small town haphazardly clinging to the banks of the river. It is spacious enough that mistresses and wives can live there without ever needing to catch sight of each other. It has sufficient apartments and suites of rooms that a new royal favourite can always be found a bed at short notice.

I know we are now in the privy garden, mainly because of the gravel path beneath our feet and the clipped box hedges that brush damply against our breeches. Then, without warning, we plunge through a low archway into the irregular mass of buildings that flanks the Thames and the air is reasonably clear again. Even so, in this rabbit warren of a palace, only one of us has any idea where we are going. Eventually, in one of the grander corridors, we come to a sudden halt. My companion knocks on the oak door.

'Enter!' says a rich and booming voice on the other side.

The door is flung open for me. Suddenly the gloom of the day is gone. There is a blaze of light from many fine wax candles, rippling across the yards of polished floor that separate me from a man sitting at a desk. The desk is large and piled high with papers. The man is Titus Oates.

Chapter Twelve

In which we meet Doctor Oates again and I do after all discover new problems

'Welcome to Whitehall, Sir John,' says Oates from the middle of his face. 'I've been expecting you.'

He seems happy, as well he might be. He is dressed in the black silk gown of a doctor of divinity, with a fine white lawn collar. He has acquired, and possibly even paid for, a new periwig since I saw him last. He certainly no longer looks like a renegade Catholic priest on the run. But of course, though he did his best to run, he only ever pretended to be a Catholic. He lied cunningly to become a Jesuit, but he is now telling the truth as an Anglican. That's what the Privy Council believes and, according to Williamson and Aminta's aunt, I'd be wise to believe it too. I'll certainly do my best. I'd rather sleep in my own bed tonight than join Coleman in his.

'Good afternoon, Doctor Oates,' I say. 'I am pleased to find you in happier circumstances than last time we met.'

His welcoming smile fades. Our previous encounter is clearly not something of which he wishes to be reminded.

'Should I take a seat?' I say, indicating a chair on my side of the desk.

'But of course,' he says. 'Only the most ill-mannered host would force a guest to stand.'

I pull back the chair a little and sit down. 'Good,' I say. 'You wished to see me, Doctor Oates? The person you sent to fetch me implied that it was an urgent matter.'

'I hope he did not inconvenience you in any way? Palace officials can, in my own experience, sometimes be rather peremptory. Until they know what sort of man they are dealing with.'

'I am entirely at His Majesty's disposal and, so it would seem, at your own.'

His smile has returned. I'm exactly where he wants me, then.

'I hoped that you might be able to help me with something, Sir John.'

'Of course, Doctor Oates. If I can. It would be as much an honour as it is a pleasure.'

'That is very kind of you, Sir John. As you know, the King has instructed me to carry out an investigation into a Popish Plot against the Crown. We are proceeding well. We are uncovering traitors where we never expected to find them. Traitors the Privy Council never suspected existed. I think it is fair to say that the King is both shocked and disgusted by what we have told him. But dozens, perhaps hundreds, of the plotters remain at large. And the papists have struck back, sir! They have callously murdered the upright and industrious magistrate, Sir Edmund Berry Godfrey. It is essential that the perpetrators are hunted down so that they may feel the full force of the law. I am sure that you agree with me on this?'

'A magistrate struck down while doing his duty is certainly a bad precedent,' I say.

Oates looks at me, uncertain of my precise meaning.

'You make a jest, sir, of the death of such a man?'

'On the contrary. I hope that we are agreed that the ill-treatment by anyone of any magistrate engaged in the King's work is reprehensible.'

'All those involved in the King's work deserve protection,' says Oates with great firmness. 'And, should that ever fail – should they suffer violence from the King's enemies – they would be entitled to expect that the authorities will exact a terrible revenge. That is why the matter of Sir Edmund's murder is being looked into by the Privy Council and myself with the utmost zeal. We have hardened our hearts and intend to be entirely merciless. We fortunately have considerable resources at our disposal. And, praise God! we are making excellent progress. Which is my point, Sir John. Any additional investigations, particularly those of an unofficial nature, are not needed – indeed, they would be unhelpful. Do I make myself clear?'

'You make yourself perfectly clear, Doctor Oates. I am sure that the Privy Council will act swiftly and efficiently, as it always does.'

Oates looks as if he may be about to reprimand me again for levity, but he just shakes his head sadly. 'I understand, Sir John, that Sir Joseph Williamson has nonetheless asked you to undertake certain enquiries on his behalf?'

I smile and say nothing.

'Sir Joseph has, inadvertently I'm sure, failed to inform myself or the Privy Council of the nature of those enquiries.'

I smile and say nothing.

'To save having to disturb Sir Joseph at a time when he is very busy, it occurred to me that the best course of action was to ask you to visit me and give me a summary of what you have done so far.'

Oates dips his quill pen into an ink pot, ready to take notes.

'I am sure that Sir Joseph would be more than happy to meet you whenever you wished,' I say.

'Are you claiming that he has given you no such instructions?'

'Whatever his plans are, he will be able to explain them to you much better than I can. Williamson, almost as much as Arlington in the old days, rarely tells me more than he needs to.'

'You do not deny, then, that you have seen Williamson?'

'Is there any reason why I should deny it?'

Oates leans back in his chair and narrows his eyes, like a man who has given somebody a fair chance and been sorely disappointed.

'We know that you and your wife have been to Primrose Hill,' he says.

'So have a lot of Londoners.'

'We also know that you have visited Mistress Gibbon.'

'To convey our very deepest condolences at the loss of her kinsman.'

'We know you have been to visit the traitor Coleman – in spite of the Privy Council's express prohibition on his receiving anyone.'

I smile and say nothing.

'You were followed there,' he says. 'You and your wife. I can tell you the precise hour you arrived and when you left and how much you gave that rascally jailer. What did you discuss with the traitor? I advise you, for your own sake, to tell me everything. It will go hard with you if it is later found that you have left anything out.' Oates, pen still poised, raises an eyebrow.

'We talked about history and philosophy,' I say. 'Oh, and he told me when you were received into the Catholic church and when you became a Jesuit. Why you left Valladolid. Why you left Saint Omers. Things like that.'

Oates carefully returns his quill to the ink pot. 'I merely pretended to become a papist,' he hisses. 'You know that perfectly well. The dates are unimportant. And I left Saint Omers because my work there was complete.'

'You were very convincing,' I say. 'The Jesuits thought you were sincere. And Father Strange apparently offered you every kindness. I congratulate you. You must be a consummate actor.'

Oates raps a fingernail on the desk several times, as if to bring an unruly meeting to order.

'Your remarks, if you will permit me to say so, Sir John, border on the impertinent.'

'I apologise, Doctor Oates. Your very good friend, Lord Arlington, frequently told me the same thing. It is a habit that I am probably too old now to grow out of.'

'Arlington is a fool. I had hoped he would assist me in my endeavours to root out popery from this court but he proved woefully inadequate for the task. Well, the Earl of Danby was more perceptive in seeing what needed doing. Arlington's loss is Danby's gain. My Lord Danby has risen greatly in the King's esteem as a result of his support for me. I have no need for Arlington now. Let him strut around Whitehall with that ridiculous nose patch and his white staff of office. He could have sat side by side with me, planning and controlling this great work, but he seems content to be a figure of fun and nothing more.'

For once I have to agree with Oates. Arlington was clearly presented with a chance to regain some of his lost power and elected to turn it down, merely because Oates was a rogue and a liar. Danby saw what Oates might be made into and, after a brief hesitation, grasped the opportunity with both hands. That difference in approach is why Danby is now the King's chief minister and Arlington isn't. Of course, I'm not the King's chief minister either.

'Both my former master and I must have been a great disappointment to you,' I say. 'We simply delayed your inevitable progress.'

Oates's face is split across its circumference with a broad smile.

'Enough, Sir John! I accept your apology. The conduct of your constable was reprehensible, and may yet cost him his position and his liberty, but I accept you felt you had no choice but to investigate the matter as he mendaciously presented it to you. You must now accept in turn that I had always intended to pay and, indeed, I did pay without any protest at all. That is all there is to be said. I think neither of us needs to mention the incident again, in any context.'

Nothing he has accused me of so far remotely amounts to treason and he'll have a fight on his hands if he wants me to sack Ben as constable. He'd have liked to make me stand in front of him now, just in case I've forgotten how he was treated in my dining room. Giving me a seat means there's a limit to how much he thinks he can insult me. There's still something he wants.

'Sir John,' he begins, 'you are spoken of very highly at court.'

'I am rarely here,' I say. 'My work now is almost entirely in Essex.'

'Unless Williamson asks you to undertake some task in London, as we've agreed he has now.'

So, we're back to that? I smile and say nothing. I can do it all day if I have to. I've become quite good at it over the years.

'It would help me greatly if you were willing to work with me,' says Oates, 'and to report to me rather than Williamson.'

'I'm sure you could find other people in his office to spy on him, if that's what you need done.'

'You would of course be paid.'

'Promptly and in full?'

'Yes.'

'That would be a very pleasant change, but the answer is still no.'

'Do not make the same mistake as your former master made. You are spoken of as a man of some talent. You cannot really want to spend the rest of your life amongst fools and country bumpkins. You belong here at court, every bit as much as I do.'

'I have no wish, Doctor Oates, to ingratiate myself with the King or anyone else. And I really do have no ambition to be anything more than a country magistrate. I am happy that Danby takes full credit for all you do. I assume you're aware that's his plan?'

'You are confused as to who is the puppet master and who is the puppet. Danby will remain Treasurer as long as it suits me and no longer. You would do well to think about my offer, which is a generous one under the circumstances.'

'I've thought for as long as I need to.'

Oates narrows his eyes. 'You were not a supporter of the King during the late wars, I think?'

'I was much too young. My father was a surgeon in the King's army. My mother remained loyal to the King throughout his exile, though that did not stop her marrying a roundhead colonel who owned a house that she particularly wanted to possess. As you doubtless know, I worked for Cromwell and the Republic, once I was old enough to work for anyone.'

'As a spy.'

'That's right. I was recruited by John Thurloe when he was the Lord Protector's spymaster. His Highness the Lord Protector, as we called him then. Of course, we don't do that now. *Tempora mutantur, nos et mutamur in illis.*'

Oates looks at me suspiciously, as if I were testing his knowledge of Latin, which is not good, according to both Coleman and Aminta's aunt.

'You have made some poor decisions, Sir John.'

'If it helps, Doctor Oates, I have had this conversation many times with Lord Arlington in the days when I worked for him. He would wish me to do something dangerous or disreputable or illegal or all three. To help me make up my mind, he would remind me that I had previously been an enemy of the Stuarts, who had nonetheless graciously forgiven me. The thing he wanted me to do would show exactly the right amount of gratitude for that forgiveness. In reply, I would remind him that the scar you see on my cheek and others that are thankfully hidden beneath my clothing were acquired working for the present regime. I owed it less than he thought.'

'But you accepted Arlington's assignments?'

'Sometimes. My law practice brought in as much money as I needed and Arlington often forgot to pay me anyway.'

'Are you saying you don't need money?'

'Everyone needs money, Doctor Oates. I have never met a man who claimed to have more than he was comfortable with. But the estate that my mother acquired by marriage to the enemy is now mine. My wife earns less than she deserves from her writing, but it is a not inconsiderable sum. I am perfectly happy.'

'You are very fortunate. I assume, however, you would be less happy if separated from your wife and family, as Coleman sadly is?'

'I'm more careful with my correspondence than he was with his, Doctor Oates. If you wish to send somebody to Essex to seize it, tell my steward he may hand it over with an easy conscience.'

'Your constable stated quite clearly before me that you failed to take action against Catholic conspirators in your parish. If so, that would be treason.'

'I think you will find that he did not say anything of the sort. He said that I did not always fine my neighbours for failing to attend church on Sunday, as required by law. That is true, but it is not treason. Unless somebody chooses to denounce a neighbour or two, it would be unreasonable to expect me to note every absence. My pew is after all at the front of the church and my eyes are always very properly on the altar or the pulpit. One or the other, depending on where we are in the service. The Book of Common Prayer never commands us to turn round and check which of our fellow parishioners is missing.'

'Is that so? You would still be well advised to mark what I said. One day, Sir John, you will discover that you are not as clever as you think you are.'

'I did that long ago,' I say. 'At about the same time I acquired the scar on my cheek.'

'Tell Williamson that he is to desist from his operation at once. I do not permit it. And don't think Williamson will be able to protect you if I do discover that you have been assisting a Catholic plot. Don't think the Duke of York will be able to protect Coleman either. He will be tried as a matter of form, but he's as good as dead already. Note his fate carefully – the hanging, the drawing and the quartering. You have clearly made your decision. I hope you do not live to regret it.'

'We can agree on that at least,' I say.

Chapter Thirteen

In which we discuss a suicide

'Are you sure,' says Aminta, 'that on meeting a powerful but untrustworthy and vindictive man, the best thing to do was to annoy and insult him?'

I run a familiar finger down the raised line on my cheek. 'Not entirely,' I say. 'And he was quite right that I can't count on Williamson digging me out of any trouble I get myself into.'

'He may not have the power. Oates has imprisoned Coleman, in spite of Coleman being protected by the Duke of York.'

'So Oates reminded me. He said Coleman was going to die painfully and he could arrange the same for me.'

'There you are then.'

'Our cases are somewhat different. Let's not forget Coleman has written extensively and quite openly to the French on the advantages of England becoming a Catholic country and how the French King might help in that respect. He then left the letters in a box, waiting for them to be found.'

'The letters weren't in code?'

'Of course, but the code was in the box too, according to Williamson. Edward Coleman is the worst spy I have ever come across. He also confessed to bribing some of Parliament, even if he didn't have enough money to bribe all of it.'

'Mister Coleman's tongue is the enemy of his neck. He cannot resist admitting to treason. He would have been well advised to fast less and spend more time covering his tracks,' says Aminta.

'I conversely have never plotted against the King—'

'Or not since 1659.'

'It was quite legal to plot against him until then. He was merely the treasonous Pretender Charles Stuart in those days.'

'I'm sure that, if you remind the King that's what you and Cromwell called him, it will help your case greatly.'

'I shall also point out that my wife and my mother never wavered in their loyalty to the Stuarts and that my father-in-law bankrupted himself supporting both the present King and his late lamented majesty, King Charles the First.'

'I agree that I am your most valuable asset,' says Aminta, 'but there is a limit even to what I can do.'

'If I tell Williamson that Oates knows what he is doing, I suspect I shall be stood down anyway. The whole point of using me was that I could investigate without Oates or the Privy Council suspecting anything. Now they do.'

'Is Williamson wise to run an operation independently of Oates and the Privy Council?'

'I've wondered whether he is running it independently of the King too. In which case, he's not wise to do it and I'm surprised he has chosen to. Anyway, Godfrey committed suicide. That's what we've decided. There's nothing more to investigate and no murderers to pursue. The King just needs to claim Godfrey's estate for himself, give the money to one of his mistresses to gamble away on the single turn of a card and then that's that.'

'How secure is Williamson in his post, if he has offended Oates?' asks Aminta.

'Williamson has for almost twenty years been an indispensable part of the government of this country. We couldn't run an intelligence network without him. He knows things that nobody else knows. He knows things nobody else would want to know. The King simply can't dismiss him. Danby conversely could be sacked without the slightest risk to anything of any importance. He is clinging to power by his fingertips. Williamson will outlast Danby as he outlasted Arlington. And he'll certainly outlast Oates.'

'What will you do now?' she asks.

'I'll go and see Williamson in the morning. I'll pass on Oates's message. I'll tell him it was suicide. Then I suppose we'll go back to Essex. Ben probably has a few more petty thieves for me to deal with. Our constable is never happier than when he's got somebody in the stocks.'

'It's what you'd expect of Oates,' says Williamson.

'Which part?' I ask.

'All of it,' he says.

'Well, that's as far as I can get, anyway,' I say. 'It looks very much like suicide but Oates will most certainly try to stop me investigating further.'

Williamson stares out of the window at the street below, as if expecting Oates to be spying on us from behind some tree. I think it may be raining too hard for that. Williamson has listened patiently to all of the reasons why Godfrey killed himself. He hasn't yet told me I'm wrong. Maybe he will very shortly. At the moment he is fully occupied in his deep and lasting resentment of Oates.

'Just out of interest, does Oates really have the power to have me convicted of treason?' I ask.

'This is England, not France. We have a Parliament that is ever watchful against tyranny. We have independent courts that will, in the last resort, stand up to the King.'

'It won't save Coleman,' I say. 'Oates is right about that.'

'Coleman is guilty. Oates won't need to lift a finger there. Everything is already in Coleman's letters, some of which he wrote before Oates even became vicar of Bobbing.'

'I'm sorry for Coleman,' I say. 'I promised him I'd tell you he's harmless, which he of course is. He enjoys gossip and he enjoys being indiscreet. I think he had little idea that others might object to him gossiping indiscreetly with Père La Chaise. He may have bribed a few Members of Parliament but I've seen no evidence they've delivered anything in return. You could free him without the slightest danger to the State.'

Williamson shakes his head. 'Nothing can be done to save Coleman now, unless he receives a royal pardon, which the King may grant if his brother requests it. I have no plans to petition the King on his behalf, if that's what you want. I'm already under enough pressure to find Godfrey's killer.'

'Well, that's easy enough because, as I explained, he did it himself. There's the madness of Sir Edmund's father. There are Godfrey's financial problems, albeit that they now seem less than before. But most of all, Godfrey, instead of taking Oates's deposition to the Privy Council, had shown it to Coleman. He feared that he would be hanged for treason.'

'I'm sure you are right that the last of those might have worried him.'

'And there was an immediate danger that Coleman might reveal that fact to Oates during interrogation.'

'It was always possible, I suppose.'

'But Godfrey apparently said that his security in the business was Oates's deposition. Do you know what he meant by that?'

'Not really. You say that Coleman told you Godfrey simply wanted to check some facts with him?'

'Yes.'

'Does that seem an unreasonable thing for a magistrate to do? I mean, if he doubted Oates?'

'No,' I say. 'He clearly held up the deposition reaching the Privy Council and he was openly proclaiming that he mistrusted Oates, but it was not unreasonable. Quite the reverse.'

'Had Godfrey come to me on the Saturday morning,' says Williamson, 'rather than running round London like a headless chicken, I could have reassured him that his having interrogated Coleman was perfectly in order.'

'Was it?'

'Of course. In any case, there was never any suggestion of a lack of loyalty on Godfrey's part.'

'Do you know anything about a Catholic club that meets at Primrose Hill? It seems that Godfrey may have been a member.'

'Who told you that?'

'Brown, the constable who found Godfrey's body.'

'Did he say why he hadn't reported it?'

'Lack of proof that it was in any way dangerous.'

'Did he name any other members?'

'Miles Prance, silversmith who has worked for the Duchess of York, amongst other people.'

Williamson nods. No scrap of information is too insignificant not to be squirrelled away. He still hasn't said if he knew that Godfrey was a member.

'Nor was any mention made at the inquest of the Peyton Gang,' I say. 'A proscribed organisation. Godfrey was also a member of that, in the past. That can't be brushed away.'

Williamson nods again. 'One of a group of twelve hand-picked men plotting to have Richard Cromwell restored as Lord Protector.'

'Sir Edmund had clearly changed his mind since then.'

'Clearly. It happens. You were a republican once yourself, as Lord Arlington frequently reminded you. I don't hold it against you in any way. Nor did I hold it against Godfrey, once he'd dropped Peyton.'

'Very well,' I say. 'What we are left with is this. Even if you would have condoned his consultation of Coleman, Godfrey clearly did not know that, because he'd failed to ask. He was terrified Coleman would tell Oates under questioning and that Oates would have him charged with treason. A family tenancy to melancholy would have heightened his fears to an irrational extent. Perhaps he could have saved himself if his investigations had borne fruit, but he thought he needed more than Coleman had provided and Coleman was now in Newgate. I believe one of the two messengers who visited him was from Coleman, who advised him to talk to his contacts at Primrose Hill. The money he had with him suggests he was willing to pay for information if he needed to. But he had no success. Those who saw him in the afternoon confirm how dejected he was. He took the only option he believed he had. He went home and quietly hanged himself in one of the sheds in the yard. The brothers delegated the disposal of the body to Moor. We thought the stabbing was the key to it all but we assumed that it was done for a reason. We had not considered that it could be explained as easily by the incompetence of somebody unacquainted with dead bodies, instructed by two men who were inclined to panic.'

'You make a very persuasive case,' says Williamson, thoughtfully. 'It would be unfortunate if we suggested that Godfrey – publicly hailed as a hero – was actually a traitor, especially since we agree he may well have acted in good faith. But we can certainly tell the Privy Council of his melancholy and of the family history of insanity, both of which were wrongly kept from the inquest. We can give Mistress Pamphlin and Mistress Gibbon free rein there. Skillarne has said that suicide cannot be ruled out. We can get the inquest verdict overturned. Oates will look foolish and it will please the King, because the Catholics are no longer to blame in any way at all. The brothers won't like it, of course, but they are nothing to me.'

'So my investigations are complete?'

'You've done well,' says Williamson, 'exactly as I expected you would. I assume your expenses were in the end relatively modest? If so, it would be unfair to put you to the trouble and the effort of submitting an account.'

'I'd be happy to prepare you a list if you wished. I have had to spend a few guineas seeking information, not to mention the cost of the journey to London.'

'A few guineas? No more than that? Then I wouldn't wish to inconvenience you, Sir John. Let me just wish you and your wife a safe journey back to Essex.'

Chapter Fourteen

In which an old witness returns with new information

'I am pleased,' says Aminta, 'that Williamson is happy with our conclusion that Godfrey died by his own hand. His plan to reveal Godfrey's suicide but not his treason is nicely judged.'

'Williamson seemed unconcerned that Godfrey had spoken to Coleman before he went to the Privy Council. Perhaps Godfrey badly misread things.'

'It would be ironic if he died simply because he failed to check with Williamson before putting the rope round his neck. There's certainly every evidence that he was not thinking clearly just before he disappeared. But Williamson knew about the club at Primrose Hill?'

'He seemed to,' I say. 'It wouldn't surprise me if one of the members was already reporting to him.'

'Well, whatever Williamson is doing, I think you are well out of it. Did he pay you your expenses or did he suggest you declined any financial reward out of humble gratitude to His Majesty?'

'He felt our outgoings were too modest to worry about,' I say.

'Even though we've bribed half London for him?'

'Perhaps I should have accepted Oates's proposal after all. He claimed to offer better terms in all respects. Like Arlington, I have missed my chance. We can start packing as soon as you wish.'

'Not before you speak to your visitor.'

'My visitor?'

'Our visitor, I suppose. But she insisted on seeing you as well as me. She imagines that you have deeper pockets. Writers are notoriously badly paid.'

'Mistress Pamphlin?'

'Mistress Curtis, but the terms are likely to be much the same.'

'Where is she?'

'In the parlour.'

'We'll hold off packing for ten minutes or so, then. I fear she has had a wasted journey, though.'

'Anyway,' says Mistress Curtis, 'I was racking my brains in case I had missed anything that you might want to know. Because I do so want to help you. Out of loyalty to the master and without thought of personal gain, unless you really wished to give me a little something for my trouble. Not that I'm asking for it. Only if you wanted to, because you thought I deserved it.'

'But of course,' I say. 'I must warn you that we believe we now know as much as we need to about Sir Edmund's unfortunate death. But, since you have taken the trouble to come here, please do tell us what it is that you have now remembered.'

'What it is,' she says, 'is this. When they brought the body home and I was washing it and dressing it, Mister Michael came by and asked me to tell him if I found any pocket book in the clothing – hidden, most likely, he said. Maybe in the lining of the coat? Well, there was nothing, of course, but he was very anxious to find it. I thought you should hear about it straight away. From me. So, I put my mantle on and came, in spite of the foul weather.'

She looks at me and is disappointed that I don't immediately reach for my purse and shower her with gold.

'Yes,' I say. 'We know that he was looking for a notebook – indeed that he was very anxious to have it. The constable told us. Mister Michael had asked him too.'

'Well, there it is. I thought you should know,' she says.

'Thank you for coming to tell us,' I say.

Elizabeth Curtis furrows her brows. She tries again. 'There was wax on his coat,' she says. 'I did find that. Wax from candles.'

'Is that so unusual?' I ask.

'We don't have wax candles at home. Just cheap tallow. But the Catholics burn wax candles. In their churches.'

'Most of the richer people in London burn wax candles in their homes,' I say. 'And it was an old coat. It doesn't show that wax was dropped on to it recently.'

'I brushed it often enough,' she says indignantly. 'The wax wasn't that old, I can assure you.'

'It doesn't need to be that old,' I say. 'Just older than the Saturday he disappeared. When did you brush it last?'

She shrugs. 'I thought you might be interested. Seemingly not.'

'I'm grateful to you anyway,' I say. 'Thank you for coming, Mistress Curtis.'

Reluctantly she rises from her seat. She looks at us both and makes one final attempt. 'He was sore melancholy for so long,' she says.

'Well, if that's all,' I say, rising from my own seat.

'How long?' asks Aminta. 'When did it start?'

Mistress Curtis is already pulling her mantle back round her shoulders, but pauses for a moment while she thinks. 'Oh, months ago, my Lady. When the master came back from France, really. Yes, it was then that we all noticed it.'

'France?' I say.

'That's right. France. He was away a long time.'

'How long?'

'Well, he came back in July, I do know that.'

'Having left when?'

'That's more difficult. No, wait, I do remember – it was just after the trial. I should have thought of that.' She smiles at us, pleased at our interest, even if the information has no monetary value. 'Thank you for seeing me, Sir John. Thank you, Lady Grey. I had best start back before they miss me in Hartshorne Lane. I'm sorry that—'

'What trial?' I say.

'The master was on – oh, what's the name for it? A grand jury. That's it.'

'To decide whether to commit somebody for a full trial?' I ask.

'Yes. I was forgetting you knew all about the law, sir. Just like the master. That's it exactly. He was foreman and had to deliver the verdict to the court. They found it was a true bill, as the saying is. So, it went to trial before the House of Lords.'

'The House of Lords?' I ask. 'Why?'

'Oh, because it was a nobleman who did it. He'd kicked a man to death – Cony he was called, the man who was killed. They were in an argument in a tavern and the lord knocked Cony over and stamped on his chest. Not for any reason. He just did it. The poor man died a week later.'

'And the lord was convicted and sentenced?'

'Manslaughter. But he pleaded privilege of peerage and was released with a warning not to do it again. He said he wouldn't.'

'And who was the nobleman?' I ask, though I think I already know the answer. News of this strange case reached us even in Essex.

'It was Philip Herbert,' says Mistress Curtis. 'The one they call the Mad Earl of Pembroke. Why, do you know him at all?'

Mistress Curtis has departed, pleased with another half guinea that I shall probably never get back from Williamson.

'So,' says Aminta, 'it's not only you who gratuitously provokes dangerous men?'

'It takes little to enrage Philip Herbert,' I say. 'And becoming Earl of Pembroke has not taken the edge off his temper in any way. Godfrey was brave when he agreed to be foreman of the grand jury and to deliver the verdict. Pembroke is not one to forget an insult of any sort. Especially from a commoner. He'd have remembered who sent him for trial.'

'Then, in April, the House of Lords found Pembroke guilty but released him to do whatever he wanted to do.'

'And, almost immediately, Godfrey decided to leave the country for four months,' I say.

'I suppose people do buy less wood and coal during the summer, but even so . . .'

'Godfrey had no partner to take care of his business in London,' I say. 'And he was seemingly short of money anyway.'

'He returned in July,' says Aminta. 'Thinking he was safe.'

'And by October he's dead,' I say. 'Of course, Pembroke may not have heard he was back straight away.'

'Godfrey had severe bruising to his chest,' says Aminta.

'Just like Cony. I think we'd all overlooked that aspect of Godfrey's death. The marks on his chest seemed to be a relatively unimportant issue – perhaps not even bruising but just a settling of the blood after death. It was the marks on the neck and the sword wounds that were interesting. That's what Skillarne thought. That's what I thought, on balance.'

'And you still think that?'

'Maybe not,' I say.

'The other thing Skillarne said,' says Aminta, 'was that there was a rumour that Godfrey's body was seen in Leicester Fields, near Pembroke's house.'

'So he did,' I say.

'I think you need to talk to Williamson again,' says Aminta. 'Because I think Godfrey's journey that Saturday may have taken a slightly different route.'

Godfrey's Journey

He can hardly see from one side of his woodyard to the other. They blamed the sea coal for the foul air, but would they prefer to freeze? He doubts it very much. People do say odd things.

He checks his pockets. It's all there. The broad gold pieces wrapped in paper. The silver. The three small gold coins. He's about to open the gate onto the lane, then he pauses. What if he's made the wrong decision?

The first messenger had worried him, but not too much. Just a letter from somebody he knew in Whitehall to say that the Earl of Pembroke had been drunkenly muttering about revenge. He'd replied that he didn't know what to make of it. Then this morning a second messenger had arrived. The Earl sends his compliments and requests the pleasure of Sir Edmund Berry Godfrey's company at his house hard by Leicester Fields at four in the afternoon. Wine will be served. So, Pembroke was no longer angry, then? But the messenger had seemed nervous, when there was no cause to be. Moor had overheard what the messenger said and looked worried.

Maybe the Earl didn't mean what he was saying? If so, there were clearly two possibilities. He could run again. Or he could stay and explain things to Pembroke logically. He hadn't liked running before and didn't now. Cowards ran, everyone knew that. Surely a man like Pembroke, once things had been properly explained to him, would share his view that he'd had no choice – he'd simply done his duty in bringing in the verdict he had? So, he had called for his best coat. Pembroke would at least see he was dealing with a gentleman. But even as Moor was buttoning it up, he wondered if what he planned to do was as wise as he'd thought. He often found it difficult to read faces, even Moor's, but everything in his clerk's expression this morning told him he'd made the wrong choice.

Maybe he should just empty the cash box and go, then. To the country this time. Kent would be far enough. Stay with his cousin. For a month, say. Enough time for Pembroke to forget again or, better, drink himself to death. He told Moor he'd wear his old coat after all. Better not to be too noticeable on the road.

His clerk had watched him stuffing the money into his pockets. He wasn't sure the old man approved of that either. But he couldn't stay where he was, in his bedchamber, beside the still-unmade bed. Leicester Fields or Kent. He was definitely going somewhere.

So, he's got as far as the gateway leading into Hartshorne Lane anyway. That's progress. The ever-present Moor is now watching him like a dog from the doorway. Time to think. That's what he needs. He'll take a walk. Somewhere. Anywhere. Clear his head. Run through his well-reasoned justification for his actions.

What's the worst Pembroke can do? Well, kill him obviously. He can work that out without help from Moor or his brothers.

He slips like a wraith into the lane and closes the gate behind him. By the time he reaches the Strand, he's almost worked out what he'll say. But somebody else is talking to him. He turns and sees Parsons, the churchwarden. The man is asking him a question. Why does he want to know that?

'What do you mean, where am I going?' he says in reply. Suddenly the thought occurs to him: could Parsons be in the pay of Pembroke? Stranger things have happened. He looks into Parson's face and sees nothing that will help him.

Parsons is smiling amiably. 'You look as if you're anxious to get there, wherever it is.'

'Primrose Hill,' he tells Parsons, mainly because it's in the opposite direction to Kent.

Parsons asks if he plans to buy the place. It's some sort of joke apparently. He never makes jokes himself. Why say something that clearly isn't true just to make somebody laugh?

'I have business there,' he says, perhaps a little too sharply. He immediately regrets it. Parsons appears to mean no harm, after all.

'You'd best take the left fork ahead, then,' says Parsons. 'If you try the other way, you'll get lost in this fog.'

He takes the left fork. Why not? Primrose Hill is as good as anywhere else to walk and think. By midday, he's decided. He's going back and he's going to have it out with Pembroke. Man to man.

Probably.

Another turn round Primrose Hill, perhaps.

The bells of Saint Martin's are chiming four as he knocks on the enormous oak door. He's regretting not returning to Hartshorne

Lane to change into the new coat. But the old one will have to serve. He adjusts his cravat. The door opens on well-oiled hinges.

'Sir Edmund Berry Godfrey,' he announces. 'I'm the Court Justice. I'm expected by his lordship.'

But when he is shown into the drawing room the Earl just blinks at him. For a moment he sits there, glass in hand, almost empty bottle on the table, clearly puzzled why his afternoon drinking has been interrupted.

'Who ... who you?' he asks.

Godfrey explains Pembroke asked him to come.

'Why?'

Godfrey says he doesn't know.

'Well, I don't know if you don't. Sit down. We'll get drunk. Four o'clock and I'm still that other thing. Not drunk. What's it called?'

Godfrey says that, under the circumstances, if he's not needed after all, he'll just go home.

'You refusing drink with me?' says the Earl. 'My wine not good enough for you?'

'Well, perhaps just one glass,' says his visitor.

He drinks almost nothing. He lets Pembroke talk and occasionally sleep. Twice he risks getting to his feet, but each time Pembroke is instantly awake and glaring at him.

At nine o'clock Godfrey recalls that he still hasn't eaten that day, but his host doesn't seem to need food.

At midnight, Pembroke notices that, for some unaccountable reason, he's been drinking with the foreman of a grand jury.

'I'm not paid to get rid of bodies,' says the younger of the two footmen. 'I had to take the letter, don't forget. Why is it always me?'

'You'll do what the Earl tells you to do,' says the steward. 'Just help get it into his lordship's carriage. Pretend he's drunk, like half the people who leave here.'

'He's got a sword sticking through him.'

'Nobody will notice if you're quick with it.'

'Where's the body going, anyway?'

'The Earl says Primrose Hill. Unless you've got a better idea.'

'Why there?'

'The fewer questions you ask the better, don't you think?'

'Maybe. It is always me, though.'

Chapter Fifteen

In which we meet Mister Chiffinch

'When I got up this morning,' says Williamson, 'I was certain that the Catholics had murdered Godfrey. By dinner time I had been convinced that he had, after all, committed suicide. Now, before supper is even on the table, you are telling me he was kicked to death by the Earl of Pembroke?'

'Then strangled. And at some point stabbed. I still think it's the strangulation that killed him, but it's the bruising that is important. It's exactly what Pembroke did to Cony. Repeated kicks to the chest when he was lying on the floor. It explains why Godfrey was so worried in the days before his death. He'd stayed out of Pembroke's way for four months, but he had to come home sooner or later. He crept around London hoping that Pembroke had forgotten . . .'

'So it was madness or drunkenness, rather than ignorance, that led to the pointless stabbing?' asks Williamson.

'We must assume so. The report that Godfrey's body had been found in Leicester Fields, close to Pembroke's house, was largely dismissed, but did somebody actually see the body being carried, the sword still in it, by a nervous footman, from the house to the coach?'

'And the evidence that Godfrey had been seen near Somerset House?' asks Williamson.

'At least half the reports we've had must be untrue – he can't have been in all of those places. Anyway, Leicester Fields isn't that far from Somerset House. The two things aren't mutually exclusive.'

Williamson seems to find my explanation convincing, or at least convenient.

'Very well, not a suicide but it's still not the Catholics,' he says. 'Not unless Pembroke has changed his religion.'

'He doesn't have time,' I say. 'Drinking keeps him busy.'

'That solution should still please the King, which is all that's important, when you think about it. What plans if any do you have for bringing Pembroke to justice then?' Williamson is genuinely curious, as well he might be.

'You mean, if Pembroke killed Godfrey simply for being on a jury, what might he do to somebody who provided incontrovertible proof that he was a murderer a second time round – when he would not be able to plead privilege of anything?'

'Yes. That.'

'If he's hanged, he will be no danger to anyone.'

'Unless the Lords simply refuse to convict him, not wishing to see an earl with a rope round his neck, or he obtains a pardon from the King.'

'I can see that witnesses may be few and far between,' I say. 'Amongst his servants more than anywhere.'

'If they've any sense. And we'll need at least two.'

'There may not be much other evidence.'

'I certainly wouldn't count on Pembroke confessing,' says Williamson.

'I'm not,' I say. 'But you can't transport the body halfway across London and nobody know about it. Even if the accessories don't want to come forward as witnesses, they'll end up telling somebody.'

'Who in turn will tell others. Yes, that's how rumours spread. Especially at Whitehall, where rumours are legal tender for most sorts of transactions.'

'So,' I say, 'I need somebody who knows all the gossip at court.'

'Nobody knows all of it.'

'Chiffinch does,' I say.

'He's a busy man too,' says Williamson. 'It would be better to try a less important figure. I definitely wouldn't involve Chiffinch in this.'

'You're right,' I say. 'Like Pembroke, he has much to do. I am grateful for your advice.'

Mister William Chiffinch sniffs and looks at me down his nose. Well, he's an important figure. He's entitled to do it.

'Why should you think I know anything about that?' he asks.

'Because you know most things,' I say.

'And Williamson sent you?'

'I've just come from his office,' I say.

Chiffinch is Page of the Bedchamber. You might think of a page as an angelic youth, rosy-cheeked, polite and cheerful. Chiffinch is seventy-five, if he's a day, and sixty of those seventy-five years have been spent living hard and drinking hard. You don't get a face like his on small beer and going to bed every night at nine o'clock. Of all the men who serve him, Chiffinch is the one that the King trusts most. If His Majesty is wrong about that, it's already too late to do much about it. There's no bribe received from the King of France, no married lady secretly conveyed via the backstairs to the King's bedchamber, no quietly attended Catholic mass, no blasphemy uttered by the King in his cups that Chiffinch doesn't know about. You'd do well to drink with Chiffinch if he asks you to drink with him. Much better to have him as a friend than as an enemy. But don't drink too much. He is said to keep a stock of powders that he slips into wine to get people to say more than they had planned to say when the evening began. In some ways, I am warier of Chiffinch than I am of the Earl of Pembroke. You can, after all, see an honest sword thrust or a kick in the guts coming.

Strangely, the mention of Williamson's name has not endeared me to the wrinkled cherub in front of me. Perhaps he sees Williamson, another eager information gatherer, as a rival.

'You are investigating the death of Sir Edmund Godfrey for Williamson?' he asks.

'Yes.'

'And he told you to talk to me?'

'He obviously warned me you were a busy man. But everyone knows that little escapes your attention. I shall not take up more of your time than I have to.'

'Say what you have to say.'

'We believe that the Earl of Pembroke may have beaten Godfrey and then strangled him.'

'Why?'

'Godfrey was on the jury that indicted him.'

Chiffinch nods thoughtfully. 'Yes, he was. He was a fool to do it. Brave, of course, but a fool for all that.'

'I think it will be difficult finding witnesses, either to the deed itself or to Pembroke boasting of it later.'

'So do I.'

'You, on the other hand, may hear things that neither Williamson nor I would.'

'That doesn't mean that I'm going to tell you what I hear.'

I smile and say nothing.

'I can arrange for you to meet Pembroke,' says Chiffinch. 'Entirely at your own risk. I've no way of arranging for him to be sober. Drunk, his temper will be worse, but he'll be slower on his feet. He may confess or he may not. That's the best I can do. Take it or leave it.'

'That will do nicely,' I say.

'I distinctly told you not to trouble William Chiffinch,' says Williamson.

'I delayed him no more than a couple of minutes,' I say.

'Did you tell him I sent you?'

'Is there any reason why I should not have done?'

Williamson scowls at me. 'Why should there be?'

But of course. Williamson's concern has nothing to do with how busy Chiffinch is. He knows Chiffinch will mention my visit to the King. It rather confirms Williamson doesn't want the King to know he is carrying out his own investigation, independently of Oates and the Privy Council, any more than he wanted Oates to find out. Because it's not only Oates but it's also the King who might now order him to stop. Well, if that's the case, Williamson should have warned me and not relied on my guessing it. He wouldn't have made a mistake like that in the old days. He used to be good at detail.

'You have no objection, I assume, if I go and see Pembroke? Since Chiffinch is willing to oblige?'

Williamson rubs his eyes. He's not looking too well at the moment. I'd say he was a little melancholy. Yes, that's the word. Melancholy.

Chapter Sixteen

In which we meet Lord Arlington

'So, that's the final proof – Williamson is definitely running an operation without the King's knowledge?'

'Not necessarily against the King,' I say.

'But he might be?' asks Aminta.

'If it was merely against Oates and the Privy Council the King would have every reason to approve.'

'It sounds dangerous, then.'

'I would have advised against it,' I say.

'So, why is he doing it? It verges on treason. He can't really care much about Godfrey, can he?'

'Only as an important but ultimately replaceable cog in the great machine of the state.'

'Then there's more to it than we can see. What is the thing that he has not yet told you? Why does he in fact care very much? Enough to get you up from Essex, albeit cheaply, and potentially put your life and freedom in danger?'

'We mustn't assume that he is behaving as Arlington used to.'

'Why mustn't we?'

It's a good point. If anything, he seems to be concealing more even than Arlington would have done.

'So, if he's imitating the methods of his former master,' Aminta continues, 'who might best enlighten us as to his motives?'

I consider this point carefully.

'It's worth a try,' I say. 'Tomorrow morning seems as good a time for a social visit as any. I'll ask that the carriage is ready for us at nine o'clock.'

Arlington House has risen like a phoenix from the ashes of the old Goring House. The latter building was not a victim of the fire of 1666 but of one of those accidents that happen all the time in London. A clumsy maid carrying a candle. An overenthusiastic cook. An unswept chimney. Fire has many friends. But every disaster is an opportunity. Lord Arlington may have lost his old house and his old job, but he now has a magnificent new residence and much free time in which to plot his return to power. The new house is gloriously lit in the evenings, just as the last one was, though the guests are perhaps no longer quite as distinguished as in former times. Today I, with Aminta on my arm, am one of them.

'So, what's Williamson up to?' asks Arlington before we have even had a chance to sit down. 'I'd heard you'd been visiting him.'

'He has many things on his mind,' I say.

'I'm sure he has. But he would not have summoned you to London without a reason. Which of those things did he want to consult you on? Godfrey?'

'Yes.'

'Isn't the Privy Council dealing with that?'

'Sir Joseph nevertheless hoped I could offer some additional insights,' I say.

'Doesn't trust them, you mean. Quite right. They're a parcel of knaves. Danby more than any of them. He made a speech in Parliament saying Oates was a liar then quickly changed his mind when it suited him to believe something else.'

The last few years have not been kind to Arlington. Being out of office – real office, not the meretricious one he now fills – does not suit him. It is true that the black patch across his nose is as glossy as ever. It still conceals a long-healed wound that he sustained at a minor battle, fighting for the royalist cause during the civil war. But being in the shadows has taken its toll on every other part of Arlington. His face is almost as lined as Chiffinch's and the stubble on his cheeks is greyer than it used to be. His shoulders are more hunched. His arrogance is now scarcely greater than that of any other courtier. This is not the Arlington I knew and suffered under for so long. He is a mighty oak, not felled by gales but stripped of many of its branches and left lopsided and vulnerable. The sort of tree that Godfrey would have regarded as being just so much firewood in waiting.

'You know the King refused to make me Lord Treasurer?' he adds. 'When Clifford resigned?'

'Yes,' I say.

'There are envious men who speak against me at court, John, and His Majesty is being poorly advised, as a result.'

'But, as Lord Chamberlain, you see the King almost daily, do you not?' asks Aminta.

'I'm not at the meetings where the real decisions are made,' says Arlington. 'Danby sees to that. That man spends so much time plotting, I'm surprised he has the leisure to shit.'

'Williamson has little enough leisure these days,' I say.

'He was always good at the intelligence side of our work,' says Arlington, rubbing his chin. Has he been shaved this morning?

I suppose he reasoned that, if we were to be his only visitors today, it wasn't worth summoning his valet to fetch the razor. Valets are busy men. 'But Williamson knows nothing about the rest of it. He stands there in Parliament, looking round him as if the chamber was full of London fog and he can scarcely see from one side to the other. And when he speaks, he might as well be reading from one of the less exciting chapters of Leviticus. They take no notice of him, John. And, if they had a mind to it, they'd have him removed tomorrow.'

'He's in real danger of removal?'

'Daily. And the King won't save him. You know that as well as I do. His gratitude is spread widely but very thinly.'

'I thought Williamson was indispensable,' I say.

'That's what they said about Walsingham in Queen Elizabeth's time. And about Thurloe in Cromwell's.'

And, though he hasn't mentioned it, about Arlington until four years ago. Everyone has to go eventually.

'Williamson has always seemed a good and decent man, anyway,' says Aminta.

'Parliament is no place for good and decent men, my Lady,' says Arlington. 'Parliament eats good and decent men and spits out their bones.'

'So, if Williamson could discover why Godfrey died – find out before Oates and the Privy Council do – that might save his career?' I say. 'But the methods he is having to use are such that he knows the King would never condone them?'

'It depends what he finds,' says Arlington. 'The King will wink at anything that proves it wasn't the Catholics, though he might choose not to say that in so many words. He'll like any result that doesn't touch his brother or affect his right to succeed to the throne. Succession to the throne is not something to be debated or conceded. It just is what it is.'

'But if it was suicide?'

'Perfectly acceptable in dynastic terms. And it will make Oates look stupid. Which will make Danby look stupid. Which will make the Privy Council look stupid. Can you find that it was suicide?'

'Yes, but there is another possibility. Have you heard the Earl of Pembroke's name mentioned in that context?'

'Young Philip Herbert? No. Should it have been?'

'Godfrey was foreman of the jury that indicted him.'

'Yes, I remember that now. But that was in February? March?'

'March, I think. The trial was in April.'

'Herbert is a man of violent moods. He'd have kicked Godfrey to death if he could have got hold of him the day the House of Lords let him go. But he has a shorter attention span than most people think. I'm not saying that he wouldn't have killed Godfrey if he came across him by chance and he was drunk and happened to recognise him. But he wouldn't have sought him out, just as he wouldn't get up to swat a fly that had already stopped buzzing in his ear. Pembroke is unforgiving, but lazy.'

'What if Godfrey went to him, unwisely seeking a reconciliation?'

'Why would Godfrey do that?'

'Because he has a tidy mind. He likes to have things settled one way or the other. He received two messages shortly before he died. One could have been from Pembroke.'

'I don't think Herbert would have written demanding to see him, if that's what you mean.'

'Could somebody else have done it?' asks Aminta.

'Out of malice? To trap him? Yes, that's possible, my Lady. They might have sent a letter purporting to come from Pembroke, with the aim of luring him there and relying on Pembroke's temper to do the rest.'

'Did Godfrey have enemies who would have been prepared to do that?' I ask.

Arlington thinks for a moment. 'Peyton,' he says.

'Because Godfrey switched his loyalties to the Catholics?'

'I'd say he wisely chose a middle way,' says Arlington. 'But Peyton thought of him as a turncoat. Peyton also resented the fact that when other supporters of his were dismissed as magistrates, Godfrey kept his position. Still, if there's any evidence of it being suicide, I don't think you should look any further than that.'

'Because that's what you believe happened?'

'I don't need to believe anything. It could have been Pembroke alone, or Pembroke and Peyton together, but suicide is more likely to please the King. That's all that matters.'

'You'd be happy to see Pembroke go unpunished?' asks Aminta.

'He went unpunished before. He'll go unpunished again most likely. That's how things are. The King wouldn't want to see an earl, of ancient lineage, go to the scaffold just for killing somebody. For treason, yes of course, but not for the simple murder of a commoner. Anyway, I'd rather see Oates hanged. Or at least discredited. He's the greater danger to the state.'

'He called on us earlier this year in Clavershall West,' says Aminta.

'Oates did?'

'He stayed at our local inn and forgot to pay his bill,' I say. 'My constable wanted to put him in the stocks.'

'Ben Bowman would have been wise to do that,' says Arlington. Remembering names is one of the essential skills of those who wish to influence others. Arlington can still do it. He hasn't given up quite yet.

'He came to see you first, I think.'

'It was clear at once he was a charlatan,' says Arlington. 'And, unlike Danby, I don't change my mind.'

But there is a look in his eyes that suggests he might not send Oates away if he had a second chance. Oates could have been his creature rather than Danby's. He could have been the puppet master pulling Oates's strings, making that great mouth open and close, spewing venom on his own enemies, not wasting it on Danby's.

Tea arrives, served with greater formality than we manage to do at home. We discuss our respective families. Arlington's only daughter, Isabella, is now ten and is married to the Duke of Grafton, the King's bastard son, though for practical reasons she remains for the moment at Arlington House. I think that Arlington still hopes for a son of his own and a long line of Earls of Arlington, who will look back on him as the founder of a great noble house. Perhaps there will instead be a long line of Dukes of Grafton, who will look back to him with equal warmth and gratitude, but more likely they will choose to remember that the King was one of their ancestors. That's why a son to inherit his title would be so much better. But he still doesn't have one and probably never will. Life for Arlington is, in so many ways, not quite what he had hoped.

Just as Aminta and I are leaving, he says: 'One last thing, John. Don't imagine, not even for a moment, that you are the only person that Williamson has asked to look into the murder.'

I nod. The same thought had occurred to me some time ago.

*Our coach rattles over the gravel roads of Saint James's Park. Arlington House is on the very edge of London, where the air is cleaner. It still has fine views of open fields from many of the windows and of the park from others. But the area is more built up each year. Soon only merchants will choose to live within the old city walls with smoke belching from thousands of chimneys. Fashionable London is moving westwards, almost as we watch.

'That was a neat theory of yours,' I say to Aminta, as she reclines against the leather seat.

'That Peyton or somebody lured Godfrey to the Earl of Pembroke's house with a forged letter and just waited for him to do their dirty work for them? Yes, it just suddenly came to me. The perfect murder, when you think about it. Not a trace of blood on the hands of the correspondent. And even Pembroke would have no idea how Godfrey had been delivered into his hands.'

'They couldn't be certain that the Earl would be drunk enough, of course.'

'They could be reasonably certain,' says Aminta.

'Well, however Godfrey fell into the trap, Pembroke had the motive,' I say. 'He had the violent temper to see it through. He had a reputation for inflicting beatings. He had servants who would be terrified to betray him to the Privy Council. He had the carriage to convey the body. He even had the wax candles.'

'So, you'll go and see Pembroke?'

'If Chiffinch has been able to arrange it. And yes, I'll be careful.'

'Do you think Williamson really has got two of you investigating the same thing?'

'It's what Arlington would have done himself,' I say. 'I think my Lord is simply assuming Williamson works in the same way. One of us working on one side of the problem, the other working on a different one, with Williamson the only person to see and understand the whole story. Just so long as Williamson doesn't send us both to interview Philip Herbert. I think that the second one might get very short shrift indeed.'

Chapter Seventeen

In which we meet the Mad Earl of Pembroke

'You got my message then,' says Chiffinch.

'Not until I returned home,' I say.

'He's upstairs,' says Chiffinch. 'In the Matted Gallery. Nothing I can do about the state of him. You should have come sooner. He's been drinking with Sir Charles Sedley all morning. Sedley's pleaded a dinner engagement, real or imaginary, and gone. I'm not sure Pembroke has yet noticed his absence.'

'Maybe I should come back later,' I say.

'By one o'clock he'll be unconscious,' says Chiffinch. 'The goods come as seen. You don't have to take them if you don't want to. Just don't try to return them to me.'

'I'll have to make the best of it,' I say.

'So you will. This way, if you please, Sir John. I've already asked for another jug of wine to be sent up. Just in case you need it.'

As with Arlington, the last few years have not been kind to the Right Honourable Philip Herbert, Earl of Pembroke. But you'd expect that: Herbert is trying to live his life twice as fast as anyone else and it shows under his eyes. He is twenty-five years old but looks forty. He sits slumped in a chair. The dregs from his glass have spilled, red and unheeded, on to the new rush matting. The glass itself dangles precariously from his fingers. He is dimly aware that he may still need the glass for something and that it would be better not to let it fall.

He looks up and sees me standing in front of him. Chiffinch has already vanished silently. It's a useful trick he has acquired.

'Good afternoon, my Lord,' I say.

He looks at me through a red-wine haze that is almost as thick as the fog outside.

'Do I know you?'

'I'm Sir John Grey.'

'Grey? Grey? Grey? Wait! Your wife. Your wife. Actress? Yes?'

'My wife is a playwright,' I say.

'What I said. Playwright. Bloody good playwright. Wrote *The Summer Birdcage*. Very funny. She here?'

'No,' I say.

'That wine over there?'

I turn to the side table. With the same dexterity that Chiffinch made his exit, somebody has entered, placed a fresh jug of wine and two clean glasses on it and left. Pembroke decides that he can finally release his own glass. It shatters on the floor. The sound seems to please him.

'Better pour that,' he says. 'Need new glass though. Some bloody fool just broke mine.'

I fill two glasses and hand one to him.

'Toast!' he says.

'To truth and virtue,' I say, raising my glass.

'Really?' He shrugs, raises his own with the greatest polite-
ness, then swallows the contents down in one gulp. He belches.
'Truth and virtue,' he says. 'Bloody good things, in moderation.
Another one. Quick.'

I replenish the glasses, though I have no more than sipped
from mine. Fortunately he is interested only in his own
glass, which he now raises. 'Red wine and willing maids,' he
announces. 'The more the better. Eh? Eh? Can't get too much
of either, me.'

I raise my glass almost to my lips. Another belch from my
friend confirms that the toast is complete.

He frowns. 'Your wife. Actress, yes?' he says.

'She's a playwright,' I say. 'Comedies mainly.'

'Wrote that play I mentioned . . .'

'*The Summer Birdcage.*'

'Bloody funny,' he says. 'I prefer actresses, though. Might see
if I can find one later. Or two. Can't have too many.' He belches
again. I hope the wine stays down until I've asked my questions.

'Did you know the late Sir Edmund Godfrey?' I ask.

'Don't think so. Late? He dead or something?'

'He was murdered,' I say.

Pembroke frowns again. 'Bad luck. Should have been more
careful. London, dangerous place.'

'Killed by the Catholics, so they say.'

'Ah well. Explains it. Peyton told me – not a sin for them to
kill Protestants. Godfrey Protestant?'

'As far as I know.'

'Me too. You?'

'Yes.'

'We'd better be careful, then. Lots of Catholics here. Duke
of York. Duchess of York. Queen. Duchess of Portsmouth.'

He shakes his head in disappointment. 'Petre. Bellasis. Not Shaftesbury, of course. Bloody good man, Shaftesbury.'

'He was a magistrate,' I say.

'Who? Shaftesbury?'

'Godfrey.'

'What's he like?'

'Tall, thin. A wood-monger.'

He thinks for a long time, or at least he doesn't speak. 'Yes. I remember now. Godfrey. Bloody good man. Brave. Did things during the Plague. But he's dead, I think. Somebody told me.'

'Yes, I did. Just now.'

'No, weeks ago. Somebody said to me that this man . . .'

'Godfrey?'

'That's it. Told me Godfrey had been killed. And I said when? And they said this afternoon. And I said, where they found his body, then? And they said, they haven't yet. So they found it now?'

'Yes.'

'About time. What was his name, again?'

'Godfrey,' I say.

'That's it,' says Pembroke. 'Godfrey. Did something during the Plague. Forget what it was. Bloody good man.'

'But one against whom you had a grudge?' I ask.

'Godfrey?'

'He was foreman on a jury, earlier this year. A murder charge. Do you recall that?'

There is another long silence, as if Pembroke is considering all sides of my last question. Then I hear him snoring. I walk back across the rush matting, as quietly as I reasonably can. I think he needs the sleep and this is as good a place as any.

*

'So, Pembroke claimed he didn't know Godfrey?'

'More or less. He also said you were an actress, though.'

'He likes actresses.'

'Probably,' I say. 'He's never killed one, anyway.'

'As far as we know.'

'I'm sure he'd have told somebody if he had.'

'So he doesn't kill the sort of people he thinks I am?'

'Exactly.'

'I'll take it as a compliment, then.'

'No reason not to. He also said he liked *The Summer Birdcage*.'

'He has excellent taste. Did he kill Godfrey, though?'

'I'm not sure he knows the answer to that question himself.'

'Perhaps you should try to see him when he's sober.'

'I don't think I'll live that long. I've already reported back to Williamson as best I can.'

'What did he have to say about it?'

'We agreed that, since neither Pembroke nor anyone else can recall him murdering Godfrey, it was going to be difficult. But the more important thing is this: seeing him again reminded me what Pembroke is like. It's as Arlington told us: when Pembroke murders somebody, he does so on a whim and then gets caught. Even if he had help, from Peyton or his servants, it's all too neat.'

'Could Peyton have done it without Pembroke's assistance?'

'I did mention Peyton to Williamson as a possible killer in his own right, but he simply dismissed the idea. I think he still has agents watching Peyton's every move. He will report to the King, in due course, that it was suicide. He has no objection to our returning to Essex. In fact, I think he'd rather like me to do that. I am released.'

'Perhaps his other investigator is doing better and he no longer needs you.'

'Perhaps. Oh, and Williamson asked me, in passing as I was about to leave, if I'd heard of three men called Green, Berry and Hill.'

'And had you?'

'No.'

'Further proof he's got somebody else working for him on this,' says Aminta. 'Did he offer payment this time?'

'He said he never asked me to investigate Pembroke,' I say. 'I wonder who Green, Berry and Hill are?'

'People we'll never hear of again,' says Aminta. 'At least, I hope not, for their sakes. This is a good time not to be noticed.'

Chapter Eighteen

In which we meet Doctor Lloyd, who poses a question

A few days later, Sir Edmund Berry Godfrey is finally laid to rest. His body has already been moved to the more convenient location of Bridewell for a formal lying in state. Now, on the very last day of October, the coffin has been draped in black velvet embroidered with an approximation of the Godfrey coat of arms and is being carried along Fleet Street by six strong, black-clad men. Godfrey is returning to his old church of Saint Martin-in-the-Fields, where he was once a vestryman. The coffin is followed by a vast cloud of white-surpliced clergymen and by thousands of lesser mourners, many of whom actually knew Godfrey in life.

With a nice touch of irony the skies have cleared for the interment of the wood and coal seller. Above the streets is a canopy of pure, uninterrupted blue. Only the slight smell of sulphur, noticeable even above the stink of rotting cabbage and discarded offal, reminds us all that this is still the London we love.

Williamson has arranged for Aminta and me to be near the front of the slow-moving crowd. This is not, I think, out of respect for my distinguished service to the state, but rather that he wants one last gratuitous favour before I leave London. He'd like me to be his eyes and ears in case any papists attempt to disrupt the proceedings. It would, of course, be a brave Catholic who ventured out into a crowd so desperate to tear somebody – almost anybody – to pieces. I try to look as Protestant as I possibly can. Not too difficult. After all, according to my wife at least, I was once a Puritan.

'I do hope they've put the Duke of York somewhere out of harm's way,' says Aminta.

'And the Duchess,' I say.

'And the Queen and most of the King's mistresses,' says Aminta. 'Oh dear. The palace will be almost empty if this mob gets its way.'

'Have you seen Oates?'

'He'll be somewhere in that collection of preening divines. Finally, an event worthy of the new clothes he has ordered for himself. It's a shame that the King did not agree to a state funeral at Westminster Abbey.'

'You think Godfrey merited it?' I ask.

'No. But then we could have gone in our carriage and I could have worn my new black silk.'

'Black wool must serve,' I say.

'I do hope Oates isn't preaching the funeral oration?'

'Doctor William Lloyd,' I say. 'Dean of Bangor and a most zealous man against popery.'

Our conversation is interrupted by a woman at the side of the road who chooses this moment to exclaim: 'Oh, Sir Edmund! Our poor, brave Sir Edmund!'

Not wishing to be outdone, the man next to her yells: 'Revenge! Death to the Jesuits!'

This cry for justice is taken up by others in the crowd but it is a ragged one. I think they have been yelling threats all morning and are beginning to realise that nobody is going to be hanged today. But still, if they say nothing they'll look like papists themselves. That wouldn't be a good idea. 'May God rot the Duke of York!' calls somebody at the back of the crowd. There is much nodding. That's something they can all agree on.

'Would this be an appropriate time to explain to these good people that Godfrey was actually a traitor who withheld information of a Catholic plot?' asks Aminta. 'And then committed suicide.'

'Unless he was killed by a Protestant nobleman with the help of Sir Robert Peyton,' I say.

'My aunt says that the court is now convinced it was suicide,' says Aminta. 'And the King has stated publicly that Godfrey was a dangerous fanatic. Still, a state funeral would have been nice. We really should have them more often.'

Doctor Lloyd is not alone in the pulpit. Two stout clergyman are there with him, both armed with staves, just in case the Catholics should push their way, *en masse*, through the packed church and make an attempt on his life.

'My text is from the second Book of Samuel, chapter three, verse thirty-three.' Lloyd pauses and surveys the packed congregation. *Second* Samuel, his face seems to say. You're all in for a treat. Then he spits at us: '*Died Abner as a fool dieth?*'

The startled congregation look at each other. It's a good question. Did he or didn't he? Nobody seems quite sure.

'And David said to Joab, and to all the people that were with him, rend your clothes, and gird you with sackcloth, and mourn before Abner. And King David himself followed the bier. And they buried Abner in Hebron. And the king lifted up his voice, and wept at the grave of Abner, and all the people wept. And the king lamented over Abner, and said, "Died Abner as a fool dieth?"'

'No!' calls somebody from the back of the church. Lloyd looks up disapprovingly, but whether because it's the wrong answer or because he doesn't want the right answer revealed yet isn't clear. There's a time and place in every story to explain how somebody was killed, and this isn't it. Not yet.

'Thy hands were not bound,' Doctor Lloyd continues, 'nor thy feet put into fetters: as a man falleth before wicked men, so fellest thou. And all the people wept again over him. And the king said unto his servants, *Know ye not that there is a prince and a great man fallen this day in Israel?* And I am this day weak, though anointed king; and these men the sons of Zeruiah be too hard for me: the Lord shall reward the doer of evil according to his wickedness.'

Well, that's clear enough. Godfrey is Abner, a prince and a great man, and our own King is David, who has been weakened by his death. And God is personally tasked with ensuring that the evil ones aren't going to get away with it. Not this time, anyway. But did Abner die as a fool? That's still not entirely clear.

Doctor Lloyd has, however, moved on. 'This Innocent Blood speaks and cries in the ears of God,' he hisses. 'It speaks and cries aloud to him for vengeance: *How long, O Lord, holy and true, dost thou not judge and avenge?*'

'Revenge!' calls somebody. 'May the Jesuits all burn in hell!' And this time, Doctor Lloyd simply beams in benediction.

*

The fire crackles in the grate. Outside night has fallen and the stars shine. Godfrey has been laid to rest. Lloyd's sermon is being discussed and freely misquoted in every tavern in the City. Wise Jesuits are drinking at home tonight behind closed and barred shutters.

'I thought that Lloyd stretched the Abner–Godfrey comparison as far as it would go,' says Aminta. 'His Majesty was in no way complicit in Godfrey's death, if that's what we were supposed to conclude.'

'Godfrey would have been pleased to hear himself described as the best Justice in England,' I say. 'And no mention of anyone's misprision of treason.'

'Being a martyr rules out being a traitor,' says Aminta. 'The two things are incompatible.'

'Lloyd was right to point out Godfrey's conduct during the Plague,' I say. 'He did well. And Lloyd's summary of the evidence was remarkably accurate – the problem, for example, of where Godfrey's body was kept after he died.'

'And Lloyd had heard about the wax on his clothes,' says Aminta. 'And the empty stomach. And his clean shoes.'

'Lloyd ruled out suicide,' I say. 'But then he also specifically said that Godfrey's wounds bled copiously, which he must have known they didn't.'

'It's what martyrs' wounds do,' says Aminta. 'Everyone knows that. Just as Jesuits think it no crime to kill Protestants.'

'A timely reminder to the congregation.'

'Lloyd compared the King very favourably to David, didn't he?'

'In the end. That was wise of him, with so many informers in the church. And we must now apparently follow the King as Israel followed David.'

'I didn't understand all of his parallels between Abner and Godfrey, though. Abner was about to change sides from Saul to David. Godfrey's allegiance to the King had not changed in any way.'

'If we ignore his previous support for Peyton and the restoration of Richard Cromwell,' I say.

'Well, anyway, Abner's death had little to do with his change of sides. He was killed by Joab and Abishai in revenge for something else entirely. They invited him into a room on some pretext and stabbed him to death. David might have prevented it with a little foresight, but it wasn't his fault.'

'Is Doctor Lloyd trying to tell us something?' I ask.

'That Godfrey was in the process of changing sides again, but died largely by accident?'

'Yes.'

'It would be an odd way to make that known.'

'I suppose it would,' I say.

'You don't think that Lloyd might be Williamson's other investigator?'

'It's possible,' I say.

We sit in silence for a while and watch the flames consume the coals. Coals that Godfrey will never sell again.

'So, did Abner die as a fool dieth?' asks Aminta.

'Ask Doctor Lloyd,' I say.

There is one further task that I have to undertake before we return to Clavershall West, just for completeness.

The skies are again heavy with snow clouds as I take the short walk to the Palace of Westminster. I am pleased to escape from the first of the flurries as I dodge into cavernous Westminster Hall. I ask one of the porters if he can tell me where to find Sir Robert Peyton.

'Are you a papist?'

'I try not to be,' I say.

'It's just that I've felt the rough side of his tongue enough this week. If I were to send him any class of papist this morning, there's no knowing what he'd do.'

'I'm as good a member of the Church of England as you'll find in Westminster,' I say.

'In that case, he's the gentleman over there with the large black moustache and the sneer from one side of his mouth to the other.'

'Williamson?' asks Peyton. 'So, he's taking an interest in me again, is he?'

'Not in you personally. He has asked me to investigate the murder of Sir Edmund Berry Godfrey.'

'Every other fool in Westminster is doing that. The Privy Council thinks they're investigating. So does the Commons. So do the Lords. Oh, and Doctor Oates, no doubt. Well, I know nothing worth telling you. It's months since I last spoke to him. I heard rumours he'd been killed on the Sunday after he vanished. I didn't bother to attend his funeral.'

'But Sir Edmund was formerly one of your associates?'

'Once. He seemed a sound enough man in those days. Then his courage failed him.'

'What do you mean?'

'I'm surprised you don't know if you're working for Williamson. Two or three years ago your master kindly prepared a report for the King on what he was pleased to call "fanatics". A number of friends of mine lost their places as a result. Godfrey managed to remain a magistrate. I'll leave you to wonder why that might be.'

'You think Godfrey betrayed you to Williamson?'

'No, that's not what I mean at all. Nobody needed to betray us. We were open enough in our views, even if we didn't let people know all of our plans. And if somebody was stirring things up, I don't think it was Godfrey. He was as surprised as anyone when the arrests began. Afterwards, when he was allowed to retain his place as a magistrate, I wondered if he had reached some accommodation with Williamson – a deal not available to the rest of us. Godfrey, as the Court Justice, had a lot of well-positioned friends. They might have told Williamson to leave him alone. After the arrests, we saw very little of him anyway. Too scared to associate with us, once the dangers were clear to him.'

'I never thought Godfrey was a coward.'

'Nor did I. Until then. But we knew he was lost to us when we discovered he was now consorting with Edward Coleman. The man is simply a turncoat, waiting to feather his nest when the Duke of York becomes king. We were well rid of him.'

'His death, ostensibly at the hands of the Catholics, must have seemed fitting punishment,' I say.

Peyton frowns. 'Punishment? Are you suggesting I was in some way responsible for Godfrey's murder? You are a long way from the truth there, Sir John. He may have escaped by the skin of his teeth when stouter citizens were dismissed, but we'd long decided we were better off without him. If a man doesn't know, from one day to the next, whether he's a papist or a true Englishman, then he's no use to anyone.'

Chapter Nineteen

In which we hear of Captain Bedloe

November arrives with the first heavy snowfall. We have returned to Essex just in time. The roads are impassable to carriages. Maybe soon to horses and riders too. Aminta busies herself in a new play. It includes a character named Doctor Blowfish of the famed University of Santiago de Compostela. He attempts to speak Spanish and Latin but does so very badly. I fear this may be a parody of Oates, though I doubt if the butt of the joke will recognise himself. I spend much time tramping round the estate with my steward, sometimes with the snow almost up to the top of my boots, checking that all that needed to be done has indeed been done. Winter has come early this year.

But London has not forgotten us. Within a few days of our return a very cold messenger arrives with a letter from Williamson.

'I thought he no longer needed you,' says Aminta. 'I suppose he hasn't just remembered that he should have paid you after all?'

'He says he's had further intelligence.'

'I thought that, in the absence of evidence against the Earl, he was content for it to be suicide?'

'As far as I can tell, he still is, but he reports that a man named Captain Bedloe, a known rogue and informant, has written from Bristol, claiming that he had been asked by two priests, Father Le Fevre and Father Walsh, to kill an unnamed enemy of the Catholic church, who had information that was a danger to them.'

'So, was Bedloe admitting to murder?' asks Aminta.

'He was very properly horrified and refused to do it, but a few days later he met Le Fevre again, who accused him of cowardice in not coming to their assistance. This time Bedloe, stung by the accusation, agreed to help, but when he arrived at Somerset House, he was told that he was too late and the murder had already been carried out by better men than himself – somebody called Pritchard and an unnamed servant of Lord Bellasis, apparently. Bedloe was taken to a small room and shown a body.'

'The body of Sir Edmund Berry Godfrey?'

'You sound sceptical.'

'No, I just saw it coming a mile off. Anyway, this is beginning to look like the hero's threefold refusal to embark on the adventure – a well-used literary trope. Bedloe's not the most original storyteller. What happens next?'

'Bedloe promised to assist in moving Godfrey's body but, on reflection, changed his mind.'

'And that makes three – what did I tell you? Then Le Fevre finds him and rebukes him again?'

'Indeed. This time Bedloe was given the entire history of the murder – how Godfrey had been lured into Somerset House and threatened with death if he did not hand over Oates's deposition. When Godfrey refused, he was smothered then strangled.

The following Monday, his body was taken by sedan chair from Somerset House to Primrose Hill, where it was run through with a sword to make it look like suicide. Bedloe, realising he now had very dangerous knowledge indeed, fled to Bristol in fear of his life, but then decided to inform the authorities, who he hoped would reward him for his assistance.'

'Ah, the reward – now we get to the point,' says Aminta. 'Well, the preamble to his request for cash is nicely judged in that he really confesses to nothing except constantly arriving too late – not in itself a criminal offence – but at the same time, he knows enough to inform on the killers. He sounds as if he might have done this sort of thing before.'

'A veritable knight of the post,' I say.

'I wonder how much he is expecting to get paid? Do you think any of it is true?'

'Bedloe says Godfrey was killed because he would not hand over Oates's deposition. But we know he'd already given it to Coleman. So his killers were, at the best, not very well informed.'

'That answers that question then. And does Williamson believe any of this?'

'He says neither he nor the King believe a single word of it,' I say. 'Oates does, though. These days, that seems to make anything true, however improbable that thing is.'

'So, why is Williamson writing to you about it?' asks Aminta.

'He wants to know what I think.'

'From a literary point of view, I can assure you it's rubbish.'

'I think he means whether it could be true.'

'I suppose he's already asked his other investigator and they've said they don't know.'

'Possibly.'

'And what do you think?'

'As I say, I think Bedloe is simply a knight of the post – a common liar hoping to become a paid common liar. I'll write to Williamson and point out the obvious flaw in the story – though he must have spotted it too. No charge.'

'One way or another, Williamson will put a stop to Bedloe,' says Aminta.

'Let's hope so,' I say, 'or every rogue in the country will soon appear on the doorstep of the Privy Council, swearing that some poor innocent told them that he had killed Godfrey and demanding five hundred pounds for the information.'

'Five hundred pounds will buy you a lot of suspects,' says Aminta. 'The courts will be busy.'

'A letter from my aunt,' says Aminta. 'Somebody has been provided with new accommodation.'

'Don't tell me Bedloe has been given rooms next to Oates at the palace?'

'No. But Williamson has been sent to the Tower,' says Aminta.

'For opposing Oates?'

'Not exactly. I think you were right that Williamson was struggling to manage Parliament as Arlington did. The Duke of Monmouth had approved some commissions for officers in Ireland. The officers all turned out to be Catholics. Parliament was outraged.'

'What's that got do with Williamson?'

'He countersigned the list without checking it properly.'

I nod. Williamson was hopelessly overworked before Godfrey was killed. The papers piled on his desk showed that clearly enough. Something like this was bound to happen. Parliament has found a way to remove a minister they never liked.

'So, is he still in the Tower?' I ask.

'No, the King ordered his release.'

'That will not have endeared Williamson to Parliament,' I say.

'Or to the King.'

'No, he won't have liked having to dig his Secretary of State out of a completely unnecessary hole he'd fallen into. It will have weakened Williamson in every possible way.'

'The one relatively sane individual at the centre of government will soon have no influence with anyone,' says Aminta.

'And Oates will have even greater freedom to strike at anyone who offends him whenever he chooses. Speak the slightest word against the good doctor or the Privy Council and it could spell your ruin.'

'I think I shall make one or two small changes to the play I'm working on,' says Aminta. 'It may be wise to remove Doctor Blowfish.'

'We're all going to need to tread carefully from now on,' I say. 'There are times in history when it is simply not safe to write comedy.'

'Another letter?' asks Aminta.

'From London again.'

'Williamson?'

'No, from Arlington. They've executed Coleman.'

'I'm sorry to hear it. But it would have taken something quite remarkable to save him.'

'He certainly shouldn't have sneered at your offer of women's guile. His trial was quite short, apparently. He asked for, and was refused, legal representation. He admitted to writing the letters but claimed that they did not make him a traitor. He told the court that he feared that the mere fact he was a Catholic would be enough for him to be found guilty, a notion that the

Lord Chief Justice airily dismissed. Bedloe and Oates were then called to give evidence against him, to which Coleman could only say that he'd never met either of them, and was out of town at the time Oates claimed he was plotting in London. But the letters alone, which were quoted at great length, were enough to condemn him without Oates's blatant falsehoods. The jury was told, as an inducement to be quick, that they could make up their minds there and then or be locked in for the night. They were also told that to find Coleman innocent was to find Bedloe and Oates guilty of perjury. Tempting though that must have been, Coleman was condemned. Arlington says he met his death bravely. Apparently he continued to hope for a pardon from the King up to the very last moment. Somebody had certainly promised him one. His final words were "there is no faith in man".'

'At least he died a martyr,' says Aminta.

'That is a question of canon law that would need to be confirmed by Rome. But he's certainly halfway there in that he's dead.'

'I wonder how many more will die before this is all over.'

'They're apparently still hunting for the Jesuits who killed Godfrey,' I say.

'You mean the men accused by Bedloe?' says Aminta.

'Le Fevre and Walsh? Yes, I assume that's who Arlington means.'

'Do they really exist?'

'I doubt it. Why should they? Nothing else in Bedloe's statement is true.'

'Williamson hasn't been able to convince the Privy Council that it was suicide, I suppose?'

'Apparently not,' I say. 'But nobody's listening to Williamson any more.'

*

The snow continues until the end of the month, then turns to rain, then to something that is neither one thing nor the other.

On Boxing Day I arrive back at the house after a ride round the estate and find a very cold and wet rider talking to Aminta in our hallway. I immediately deduce that he has come some distance and has been where he is long enough to excite pity from our own servants. He clutches a glass of steaming mulled wine in one hand and a letter for me in the other.

I break the seal and read the missive carefully.

'Arlington thinks I should return to London,' I say.

'Now?' asks Aminta.

'He wrote the letter late on Christmas Eve and urges me to be with him by this evening. He seemed to think it would reach me instantly.'

'I did my best,' says the rider. 'Only I don't have wings. The journey can't be done on horseback in under two days. Not with the roads being flooded and what's not under water being thick mud. I passed three coaches that will be stuck where they are until they can be dug out in the spring. Only a fool would travel, begging your pardon, Sir John. Shall I tell them that you can't get to London?'

'If you can ride here in two days, then I can get to London,' I say. 'I doubt if Arlington would summon me in the depths of winter without good cause.'

'But what could you possibly do?' says Aminta. 'You've presented Williamson with the case for its being suicide. It's not your fault if nobody believes it. Leave Bedloe to accuse non-existent priests if he wishes to do so. He can't hurt them.'

'The letter says that a great injustice is about to be committed,' I say.

'What injustice?'

'He says he will tell me when he sees me.'

'Was he afraid that Oates would try to intercept his letter?' asks Aminta.

'Oates doesn't have that ability.'

'Who knows what new powers he's acquired?' says Aminta.

'I'd better return now, sir,' says the rider. 'What message shall I take to my Lord?'

'Tell him I'll leave tomorrow at first light,' I say. 'That will have to be good enough. You've had a difficult journey. Do you wish to stay the night here? We can ride to London together in the morning.'

He shakes his head. 'Lord Arlington will be happier once he knows you're coming,' he says. 'I'll finish this wine and be on my way.'

Aminta persuades him to take some food first, but half an hour later we watch him canter off down the drive, towards the London road.

'I'm sorry,' I say. 'But I don't see that I can do otherwise.'

'Just try not to upset Oates,' says Aminta. 'I don't want the next letter from my aunt to be about you.'

Chapter Twenty

In which Green, Berry and Hill tell us their story

The sleet lashes down so that I can scarcely see the road ahead, but I am glad that I followed the advice not to bring the coach and four. My mare nimbly circumnavigates the seas of mud that seem to have replaced much of the highway. They would have swamped our carriage up to its axles. Every hour or two I stop at an inn to dry myself out a little in front of the fire and give my travelling companion some respite in a warm, hay-filled stable. Then we head south again into the teeth of a freezing gale. It takes me almost two days to reach the capital, riding from dawn until the sun is nearly down. I obtain lodgings near Whitehall, change out of my wet clothes and set off at once on foot, my boots crunching on the new snow, guided by a link boy with a blazing torch, for Arlington House.

'You took your time,' says Arlington. 'I'd hoped I'd made it clear that this was an urgent matter.'

'I apologise for my tardiness, my Lord,' I say. 'But it is Christmas.'

'Essex is the same distance from London in December as in June.'

'Well, I'm here now, as you can see. My family hope that I shall be back in Essex as soon as possible. So do I.'

'Well, I need you in London.'

I detect a renewed confidence in Arlington. Things may be bad but he senses an opportunity. Rumours have been growing all month that Danby is in trouble and may be impeached. Perhaps that is what has put a smile on to Arlington's face again.

'What is the injustice that you think my presence will forestall?' I ask. 'I assume now I'm here you can actually tell me.'

Arlington smiles. Of course, he could have told me at any time, but then I'd have had a chance to consider whether it was worth coming.

'Have you heard of Captain Bedloe?' he asks.

'Yes, of course,' I say. 'I've never met him, but both you and Williamson have told me about him. He's a paid informer. He fled briefly to Bristol, then gave evidence against the late Mister Edward Coleman, along with Oates. I know nothing more than that.'

'You don't need to. In fact, you will soon be able to forget Bedloe completely. He's a smirking villain, who hopefully one day will die with a rope round his neck. He thinks a devil-may-care insolence will get him out of any hole. Do you know what he told the House of Commons? He said: "Mr Speaker, I have been a great rogue, but had I not been so I could not have known the things that I am about to tell you." The fools would have applauded him if the Speaker had allowed it.'

'It would seem he and Oates are now great men anyway.'

'Not for much longer. Coleman was convicted in spite of Bedloe's evidence rather than because of it. His testimony was laughable. Even the judge, who was determined to convict, gave him a pretty hard time. As for Oates, he's made the mistake of trying to include the Queen in his ridiculous plot. Said he'd heard her utter treasonous views at Somerset House. The King was furious. Got Oates taken back to Somerset House to identify the place where it occurred. Of course, he couldn't because it hadn't happened. The King had Oates confined to his quarters at the palace.'

'Is that the end of them both?'

'No, Danby and the Privy Council still need them – Danby in particular. The House of Commons wants to impeach him for, amongst other things, his relative lack of zeal in hunting down Catholic plotters. For all that Danby knows Oates is a fraud, he won't let him go under unless he has to. And Bedloe has obligingly found a new traitor.'

'Who?' I ask.

'Miles Prance,' says Arlington.

'I've actually heard of him,' I say. 'But I don't think he's a traitor. He's the Duchess of York's silversmith and a member of a club that meets at Primrose Hill. What is he supposed to have done?'

'He made the mistake of saying that some of the Catholics denounced by Oates were in fact honest men. He was overheard by one of his tenants, who, as it happened, owed Prance money. Thinking to get Prance off his back for a few weeks, the tenant denounced him as a Catholic – which he possibly is – adding that Prance had been suspiciously absent from home at the time of Godfrey's murder. Prance was taken to the House of Commons for questioning, where Bedloe spotted him and was happy to confirm Prance was definitely a popish plotter. Prance was sent to Newgate prison. It was made clear to him that he should either admit to killing Godfrey himself or, if he preferred, tell the Privy Council who had done it. To assist his memory he was kept chained to the floor in a small and very cold cell known as Little Ease.'

'I saw Coleman's cell at Newgate,' I say.

'Well, Little Ease is much worse. No chair. No bed. No bedding. He lasted two days, then decided he'd better name somebody.'

'So,' I say, 'who did he name?'

'Green, Berry and Hill,' says Arlington.

Once again, I am hearing names that are already familiar to me.

'Williamson mentioned them some time ago,' I say. 'In November, it must have been. He asked if I knew who they were.'

'And did you?'

'Not then,' I say. 'And I still don't. I'm not sure Williamson knew who they were himself. But you clearly do?'

'Yes, but the answer is probably much less interesting than you are expecting. They are all minor officials at Somerset House. Henry Berry is a porter, Robert Green is the cushion layer in the Duchess's chapel, Lawrence Hill is the servant of Dr Thomas Godden, a Catholic priest who is almoner to the Queen. They were all arrested on Christmas Eve and have joined Prance in Newgate.'

Arlington's right. That isn't very interesting. Except for the three men accused, of course.

'It probably spoilt their Christmas as much as you've spoilt mine,' I say.

'It is disappointing,' says Arlington, 'that you would consider your own personal comfort at a time like this.'

'But surely they are innocent?' I say. 'There's no danger for them. Or are you saying there's a chance Prance is telling the truth?'

'I am surprised that you even ask that question, John. But since you have been in the country you can be forgiven for not knowing how things work these days. The men are of course innocent but they will nevertheless be hanged unless something is done.'

'So, Prance is simply repeating names he has been given by Oates?' I ask.

'Again, I'm surprised you have to ask. Had Prance truly known that they were the murderers when he entered Newgate, then I think he might have remembered that fact slightly faster than he did. He would not have enjoyed the delights of Little Ease for two days first. But sadly he could not denounce them until he was told who to denounce.'

'If Williamson knew their names in November, doesn't that suggest they really could be involved in some way?'

'There are always false rumours circulating. You know that, John. Williamson heard of them in November, probably investigated and found nothing. Oates or Bedloe have since heard the same thing, whatever it is, and, showing greater imagination, decided to use it to incriminate the three men.'

'But why?'

'Well, Bedloe knows he performed badly at Coleman's trial. Like an actor, he's aware people remember only your last performance. Oates has been severely reprimanded and publicly shamed for suggesting that the Queen might be caught up in the plot. The two of them realise they need to restore their own crumbling credibility. And their targets are well chosen. One is the servant of the Queen's almoner. Another is a cushion layer in the chapel she uses. Nicely judged – not another stab at the Queen herself, but at people close enough to her that it makes the point anyway, rather as arresting Coleman made a similar point to the Duke of York. Before long they'll have the three so-called suspects up before Lord Chief Justice Scroggs, as Coleman was before them. And with exactly the same result. Three deaths to save Oates's skin. And maybe Danby's, God rot him.'

'Is anyone concerned about saving Bedloe's skin?'

'Oates has had enough of Beldoe's incompetence. He'll abandon him as soon as the trial is over, but he'll keep him afloat in the meantime.'

'Coleman was well educated, possessed a reasonable under-standing of the law, had friends at court and was used to dealing with men like Scroggs as equals,' I say.

'Whereas these three are a porter, some sort of chapel care-taker and a priest's manservant. And even Coleman struggled and ultimately failed to save himself. It's true he made telling points against Oates when cross-examining him and used his own witness to good effect. But if much of the case against you is kept secret until you are in court and the judge sees himself as the chief prosecutor, then it takes very special skills to mount a successful defence. Would an aged cushion layer have such skills, I wonder?'

'Is there any evidence against them, other than the accusation that Oates has extracted out of Prance?' I ask.

'Of course not.'

'You're right,' I say. 'If they go to trial, Scroggs will insult and patronise them by turns before suavely instructing the jury to find them guilty.'

'And if we don't act, nobody will. There's no point in hoping Williamson will do it.'

'But we should still seek his help. If Williamson already knew about Green, Berry and Hill, and chose to bring no charges against them, then surely it means he too thinks they are innocent? Indeed he may actually have proof of it. We at least have to try to get him to act – he has more influence with the King than either of us.'

Arlington flinches slightly at these last words, but then shakes his head. 'Williamson is a broken man,' he says. 'It took two whole nights in Newgate to reduce Prance to what he is now, but a day in the relative comfort of the Tower has done for Sir Joseph. Before his arrest he saw himself as the all-powerful spider at the centre of a web of his own ingenious design. His agents were everywhere. He was better informed than any man in England. He controlled the post. He controlled the ports. Then, suddenly, he saw he was nothing. A swarm of flies could bring him down after all and the King could save him only with difficulty. He should have been more obliging to Oates while he could.'

The rain lashes the window, making it shake in its frame. Arlington turns, as if hoping to view the garden beyond the glass, but the night is pitch black. All that can be seen from here is the water streaming down the pane, dancing in the silver light of the wax candles. Arlington is once again pondering his own failure to be as obliging to Oates as he might have been. It could have all been so different. Too late now, of course. London has become a dark and dangerous place. A shadowy, sulphurous pit, lit only by a cruel yellow light. But no night lasts for ever.

'Then my family may have to celebrate what remains of the twelve days of Christmas without me,' I say. 'What do you suggest we do?'

'You must go and interview Prance,' he says. 'In my view, you should have done that when you first heard of him. It must have been obvious to you that he was a significant witness.'

'I merely knew that he made candlesticks.'

'For Catholics, John. Candlesticks for Catholics.'

'*Mea culpa*,' I say.

'He's still imprisoned at Newgate, but they'll let you in. He's lying, of course. We know that. But we need to see in what way he's lying.'

'And the three accused men? They're imprisoned in the same place.'

'Don't expect to get much from them by way of facts. They won't have the first idea what's happened to them or why. But, yes, why not? It may give them some comfort to see you.'

'I'll go first thing tomorrow,' I say. After my long ride, my arms and legs are all aching. I am looking forward to a warm bed.

'No, go tonight,' says Arlington. 'In Newgate, night and day are much of a muchness.'

'In order to gain admittance, should I say you sent me?'

'Me? Certainly not. Tell them Williamson sent you. It can't hurt him. He's finished anyway.'

Captain Richardson, my genial host and governor of Newgate prison, greets me like a man whose supper will keep another few minutes but no more. Sir Joseph Williamson sent me? Then, yes, I can see Prance by all means. Everyone else seems to be talking to him. And the three Catholic conspirators? Of course, if I wish. They have little else to occupy them at present. It's obviously at my own risk – they are murderers – dangerous and unpredictable men. The warder will conduct me to whomsoever I wish to talk first. Tip him a couple of coppers at the end by all means, if I wish, but no more. The warders here are a pack of rogues. They'd actually let people in to see the traitor Coleman when he was resident here, if I can believe such a thing.

Prisons are never still or quiet. As we proceed down the long, damp passageways, we hear shouts and moans and sobs. Torment and despair seem both universal and unremitting. Hell must be like this, but hopefully a bit warmer. I resolve that, when I am next arrested myself, I shall make sure that it is during the summer.

Green, Berry and Hill are in a cramped cell together. It is below ground, damp and airless. A single tallow candle burns, just revealing a low, vaulted stone ceiling, from which water drips constantly. They are seated on an improvised bed of rushes but they instinctively jump to their feet as I enter. Having washed this morning at an inn near Harlow, I still smell strongly of authority.

'I'll be just outside, sir,' the warder says to me. 'Call if you need me. These are desperate killers and there's no knowing what they will do.'

'Thank you,' I say. 'I have my sword.'

The men look less like killers than anyone I have seen today. Green, when they introduce themselves to me and I can tell one from the other, appears to be about seventy years old and scarcely able to stand. I can see him, in happier times, shuffling around the chapel, contentedly rearranging the cushions, but I doubt he's capable of doing much else. Berry, the porter, looks strong enough, but has a vacant expression about him. Long periods of inactivity in his lodge wouldn't bother him, so long as he could tipple and joke with the soldiers on guard there. Lawrence Hill, Doctor Godden's servant, is tall, thin and very nervous. His long hair is plastered to his head by sweat or by the general dampness of his accommodation. He seems ready to burst into tears. Of the three, he understands best the trouble they are in.

'Is it day or night out there, sir?' asks Green.

'Night,' I say.

'And the month?'

'The same as when you were arrested,' I say.

Green nods at the other two, as if a long-discussed point has finally been resolved. 'And why are you here, sir, if you don't mind my asking?'

'I have been investigating the murder of Sir Edmund Berry Godfrey.'

'I swear to you it wasn't us, sir,' says Green. 'We told them that when we were arrested at Somerset House. And we've never even met Mister Prance, except for Berry, who thinks he sometimes let him in to see the Duchess.'

'So, where were you all on the night that Sir Edmund vanished?'

'I was at home, sir,' says Green, running his fingers through what remains of his short, grey hair. 'I was there all Saturday evening and my landlord and his wife will certainly vouch for me.'

'And you, Mister Hill?' I ask.

'I did not stir abroad that evening,' he says, 'as my master's niece and housekeeper will tell you. I could not have gone out without their noticing. Prance is making it up, sir.'

'And you couldn't get a body out of Somerset House without the guards noticing, sir,' says Berry. 'Can't be done. Not by sedan chair, which is what Prance says we did. And I should know, me being the porter and that being my business, man and boy.'

'What will become of us, sir?' asks Green. 'They say we'll hang.'

'They say we should confess, if we want to save our lives,' says Hill, 'but we don't know what to confess to. Could you find out for us, sir? We're not trying to be difficult. We'll say whatever they wish, within reason. We just want to go home.'

'Don't confess to anything,' I say. 'Whatever they offer you, don't trust them. Keep telling the truth. This may take some time, but you do at least have some friends. I can't make promises, but if we can stop this going to trial then we will. If we can't stop it, we'll at least make sure you are able to call your witnesses to show you were elsewhere. And now I have to go and speak to somebody that I should have questioned before.'

I bang on the door. The warder lets me out and we start to climb the stone stairs, up towards heaven and where Prance is now kept.

Chapter Twenty-One

In which Mister Prance tells his story

I would not choose Prance's quarters myself as a place to stay in London, but they are better than those in which I found Coleman and much better than those I have just left. Since his memory has improved, Prance has been promoted from Little Ease to a small, whitewashed room with a bed, a table and two chairs, a window that doesn't seem to be barred and, most important of all, a blazing fire of good sea coal. A dirty wooden plate on the table shows that he is being fed, which, I reflect, is more than I have been this evening.

Prance is a small, neat man. He's had a chance to tidy himself up a little in his new quarters. He certainly isn't worried by my arrival. He remains seated and looks me up and down. I'm not his most impressive visitor by a long way. Who else has been here, I wonder? The Earl of Danby? Lord Shaftesbury? Oates? A bishop or two? Like a prize hound chained in his kennel, Prance has become an important asset and he knows it.

He finishes picking a tooth with his forefinger, then says: 'So, when are you all going to release me?'

'That's not the purpose of my visit,' I say. 'I assume that you will be freed once the Privy Council's enquiry is complete. I just want to ask you some questions.'

'It's time their lordships made up their minds, then. I've told them what they wanted to know. If you'd like to remind me of anything else, I'll see what I can add to oblige them, but I can't stay here for ever just to keep the Privy Council happy. I've got a living to earn. I'm a silversmith. And a landlord. Who's taking orders for candlesticks while I'm here? Who's collecting my rents for me? You tell me that, Mister . . .' He pauses and looks at me. I'm not one of the usual gang and the warder's introductions were brief.

'Grey,' I say. 'John Grey.'

'You work for Oates?'

'No, for Sir Joseph Williamson,' I say.

He looks at me with suspicion. That's clearly the wrong answer to give.

'Williamson already knows all about this,' he says. 'He doesn't need somebody else to ask questions for him. What's going on?'

So, Arlington and I have underestimated the Secretary of State. He has clearly been busier than we thought. He has already interviewed Miles Prance, or sent one of his people to do it. He has also probably investigated whatever rumours had been circulating about the three men. But Green, Berry and Hill are still in danger, suggesting a job started but unfinished. Perhaps Williamson might have already resolved matters if he had not been rushed off to the Tower. A number of things may have slipped his mind since then. I must try to pick up wherever he left off. Arlington did well to send me here tonight. Still, I'll need to tread carefully.

'My questions are simply points of clarification,' I say. 'To add to what Sir Joseph already knows. But perhaps you would be kind enough to run through your evidence again from the beginning.'

I have done nothing to reduce his mistrust of me. 'It's all in my deposition,' he says. 'Williamson must have shown it to you. He has a copy.'

'I'd still like to hear what you have to say. Clerks often don't get down every word on paper.'

'Don't they? If you say so.'

His suspicion is growing by the minute. He's wondering if Williamson is trying to catch him out on something. Or whether I've been sent by Oates for some unknown purpose. This is probably as confusing for him as it is for me and the stakes may be equally high for both of us. He fixes me with his gaze, daring me to contradict anything that follows.

'The Sunday before Sir Edmund died,' he begins, 'I was approached by two men while I was drinking in the Plough Tavern, hard by Somerset House. I now know the men to be Father Gerald and Father . . . Father Kelly.'

'Not Walsh and Le Fevre?' I say.

'Never even heard of them. Different murder, probably. The two I met were Gerald and the other one I just mentioned . . . Kelly . . . that's it. They asked me if I was acquainted with Sir Edmund Berry Godfrey. I said that I was and that he had done me and my family much harm. They said that he was a persecutor of good Catholics and a particular enemy of the Queen's servants. They therefore proposed to do away with him and asked me if I would kindly help them.'

'And you said . . .'

He smiles, as if this question holds fewer dangers. 'I said that I could not do so, since murder was a mortal sin.'

'And they said?'

'They said it was in fact no sin, but actually a work of charity, to kill such a monster. Sir Edmund's intention was to ruin the Catholics and it was necessary to destroy him. Therefore I might do it with a clear conscience and be richly rewarded by some Catholic lords for my pains. And also by Almighty God, as and when He had the opportunity to do so.'

'Which lords?'

He closes his eyes. 'Lord B ... Bell ... Bellasis. That's it. Bellasis. And some others. It's all in my statement.'

'I'm sure it is, Mister Prance. The question is where it was before that. Were you to work alone?'

'They had already recruited three other men, all Catholics. They were Robert Green, Henry Berry and Lawrence Hill, the servant of Doctor Godden.'

'What happened then?'

'For the rest of that week, we dogged Sir Edmund as he walked about the streets. We also went to his home on some pretext—'

'What pretext?' I ask.

Prance looks startled. It would seem nobody has told him that.

'Business,' he says quickly.

'What business?'

'Wood,' he says.

'Were you offering to buy or sell?'

'That's my affair,' he says.

I leave him to ponder what sources of timber he possesses that might allow him to deal wholesale with a wood merchant.

'What happened next?' I ask.

'On the Saturday he was killed, Hill and Gerald dogged him all day, until he was back in the Strand.'

'*Dogged?*' I say. It's the second time he's used that word. I suspect it was impressed on him that that was what he had done.

'Yes ... dogged. Followed. Whatever you want to call it. In the meantime, Green and Berry laid a trap for him. When he approached Somerset House, Hill caught him up and told him that there was an affray in the courtyard there. Sir Edmund at first refused to go in but did so when he saw Green and Berry pretending to fight. Once in the courtyard, he was attacked by Green, Berry, Father Gerald and Father ...' He frowns. He knew the name a moment ago. 'Kelly,' he says suddenly. 'They kicked him and strangled him. Green wrung his head right round to break his neck. Finally they ran him through with his own sword.'

Prance breathes a sigh of relief. A lot of detail there, but it didn't go too badly.

'Why stab him?'

'They weren't sure he was dead.'

'But he was?'

'Well, he certainly is now.'

'So you were there when he was killed, Mister Prance?'

Prance takes a deep breath. He knows the answer to this question.

'No, I was not. I was eating at a tavern at the time—'

'Which one?'

'Don't recall. A nearby tavern. Anyway they found me and called me back to Somerset House. I arrived too late to save Godfrey, which I would have done, but he was dead. They told me how they'd killed him. Then they made me help carry the body. We hid it in the room of Doctor ... Doctor ... *Godden*, Hill's master. Doctor Godden. We kept it there until Wednesday night. Then we carried it in a sedan chair to the Grecian Church in Hog Lane, from where they took it on by horse to Primrose Hill and left it. Godfrey was propped up in the saddle to make it look as if he were still alive.'

'Did the guards not try to stop you leaving the palace?'

'We plied them with drink,' he fires back at me.

'What sort of drink?'

Again a look of panic comes into his eyes. 'Ale?' he suggests.

'Did you see the place at Primrose Hill where the body was left?'

'No. I helped carry the sedan chair only as far as the Grecian Church. Hill and Gerald went on with the horse and the body.'

'How did you get home afterwards?'

'I walked.'

'What happened to the sedan chair? Was it just left where it was?'

'I don't know.'

'It didn't go on the horse?'

'Of course not. Why on earth would you think that?'

'Because, judging by your narrative, the chair seems to have vanished into thin air. What are you saying happened to it?'

'Maybe we pushed it into a building.'

'Maybe?'

'We pushed it into a building. I remember now. Very clearly. That's what we did.'

'Large building? Small building?'

'Medium.'

'This medium-sized building was unlocked in the middle of the night?'

'Yes.'

'And the owners were absent?'

'Yes.'

'Well, I suppose it must still be there then,' I say. 'It would have been a strange surprise for the proprietors of the building when they found it there the following day. How odd they never reported it to anyone. You know Green, Berry and Hill have now been arrested?'

'Of course.'

'Where, then, are Gerald and Kelly?'

'They escaped. To France. With the help of the Jesuits.'

'Were they Jesuits themselves?'

'They didn't stay long enough for me to ask them.'

'Did anyone try to stop them fleeing?'

'No.'

'And Green, Berry and Hill decided to stay and take their chance?'

'Yes.'

'Is that because Green, Berry and Hill are real people and Kelly and Gerald are merely a convenient fiction? Imaginary go-betweens who are necessary if anyone is to believe the strange tale you've just told me? Because Green, Berry and Hill quite clearly could not have acted on their own?'

'Are you saying you don't believe me?'

'Yes, that is exactly what I am saying. Did Williamson believe you?'

'You claim to work for Williamson, Mister Grey. You tell me.'

I wonder exactly what Williamson said to Prance when they met, as they clearly must have done. It would be entirely like Williamson that he gave Prance no clue whatsoever what he thought. Or that he told Prance that he believed everything unreservedly, even if he didn't believe a single word.

'Let me inform you, Mister Prance, that I at least have no doubt at all in the matter. You and I both know you are lying. We also know what you have said will result in the deaths of at least three completely innocent men. Don't you think it would be better to tell the truth? I can talk to Williamson and ensure that you do not lose by it.'

He gives me a very odd stare indeed. 'Look, Mister Grey, if that's your real name – I don't know who sent you here, but I don't think it's Williamson and I'm pretty sure it's not Doctor Oates either. I've told you all I'm telling you, and you could have got it from my deposition if you'd bothered to read it. I've sworn an oath that it's all true, and that's what it is. All true. Green, Berry and Hill will hang. And there's nothing either you or I can do about it.'

'On the contrary,' I say. 'There is something I can do. You see, those who have persuaded you to tell this tale think you are innocent. So, they've promised you that, once you've given your evidence, they'll let you go. But we both know that isn't the case, don't we? You are much guiltier than you have told me or anyone else.'

'What do you mean?' he says. He licks his lips. They must have suddenly got rather dry.

'I have a witness who will say that you have been a member of a Catholic club at Primrose Hill. A club to which Sir Edmund Berry Godfrey also belonged. You knew Godfrey. And you have already confessed, on oath apparently, that you had a grudge against him because of what he had done to your family. It won't take long to pick apart your unlikely story about vanishing sedan chairs. It shouldn't be difficult to show that you never visited Godfrey's house in Hartshorne Lane, either to buy or sell wood. There won't be any need to bother the Lord Chief Justice with this tale of murder at Somerset House and the long journey through the night by horse to Primrose Hill. He can be presented with a much simpler explanation: that you met this man you say you hated at the Catholic club and you killed him exactly where his body was found, a place you already know well and where witnesses will swear they saw you often. What do you say now, Mister Prance? Bear in mind you're rumoured to be a Catholic and they want to hang a Catholic.'

'But it's not true. None of that's true. Or not much of it. I'm not saying Godfrey never came to club meetings, but I hardly even spoke to him there. It was just an informal gathering, once a week or so. Most of the members were Catholics but you didn't have to be. We played cards in the winter and bowls sometimes in the summer. We talked. No treason. Just what was going on. How long would Danby's ministry last? How long would the King's latest mistress last? Would there be another war with the Dutch? People came if they wanted to and stayed home if they didn't. What is this? I was told I would be safe if I confessed. And I have confessed – exactly as they asked me to.'

'I'm sure you were told that. I'm sure you also thought that, at the worst, your lies would show you were an accessory to murder, for which you would be pardoned in exchange for the information you had provided. Wasn't that the deal? But actually, from what you tell me, you are the most likely suspect for the murder itself. And the final proof is you've tried to blame three men who the court will see could never have carried out the murder. The rope, Mister Prance, is already round your neck.'

'I never hated Godfrey. I told you: I'd scarcely even met him.'

'But you have sworn otherwise. Are you claiming that was merely a little light perjury?'

'What I said – about Green, Berry and Hill – it was only . . .'

'What you were told to say? Yes, of course it was. Somebody needs a Catholic murderer and Green, Berry and Hill fit the bill nicely. Three times over, in fact. But you'd fit it equally well. I'm sure you see that, Mister Prance. And we wouldn't even need to manufacture the evidence. We'd just have to tell the truth.'

'You really think I did it?'

'Of course not. I don't believe in Oates's plot and I don't believe a Catholic killed Godfrey. Why would they? I have yet to discover a single thing that Godfrey did to harm the Catholics, jointly or severally. But I seem to have a difficult choice here – either three innocent Catholics die or one does. The one is you, in case you were wondering.'

'Or maybe nobody has to die,' he says quickly. 'What if I retract my confession? I could do that. What happens then?'

'Some people might give you a very uncomfortable time. You might stay here longer than you wished. But they couldn't hang you. Probably.'

'I don't understand what's going on and I still don't understand who you really work for. All I need to know is this: if I change my story, would Williamson look after me?'

'You've clearly met him and talked to him, so I must leave you to answer that question for yourself. But he's a man of his word and I'll also do what I can for you. Why don't you sleep on it, Mister Prance? You do now have a very comfortable bed, unlike Mister Green, Mister Berry and Mister Hill. I think that, in the clear light of day, you may well see what you ought to do.'

Chapter Twenty-Two

In which we are told of the existence of a grain of truth

Snow is falling on London again. Each flake is, courtesy of Godfrey and his fellow wood and coal merchants, more grey than white. My mare can rest in her stable today, but I must set out for Sir Joseph Williamson's house.

First, I scan the street as usual. Is anyone loitering improbably on the corner? Is anyone avoiding my gaze when a mildly curious glance in my direction might be more natural? I thought, last night on my way home from the prison, that I could hear the crunch of somebody's feet in the snow behind me. Perhaps it is reassuring that somebody thinks I am worth following. It may mean I am not wasting my time.

Williamson looks ill. I suppose I would if I had recently suffered the displeasure of the King and Parliament and had Doctor Oates constantly watching what I was doing. He sits, wrapped in a blanket, by his fire. There are dark circles under his eyes.

He coughs into a fine linen handkerchief, and then stuffs it firmly into a pocket.

'They won't get rid of me that easily,' he says. 'I know all of their secrets. I'm not finished yet. And Arlington had no business sending you to interview Prance. It's nothing to do with him. Not any more. I'm Secretary of State now. Arlington's just a man with a white wand and a nose patch.'

He reaches into his pocket, retrieves the handkerchief, coughs again and lapses into silence. He knows that soon he may be even less than Arlington.

'Are you sure you're well enough to deal with this?' I ask.

'Of course I am. I am suffering from a chill that has gone to my chest. Everyone in London is coughing and spluttering at the moment. It's the foul air. As for what I have to deal with, everything was under control until Arlington interfered. You shouldn't have threatened Prance. There's no knowing what a man like that will do if he feels he's in danger. He needs handling with the greatest care.'

'He's a liar who will cause three innocent men to be hanged.'

'The Privy Council will have somebody hanged. Who would you prefer it to be?'

'Nobody,' I say. 'The three men are innocent. Prance is contemptible but it's not his fault Bedloe falsely accused him. He doesn't deserve to die either. We'd agreed you would tell the King that Godfrey's death was suicide. There's no evidence against Green, Berry and Hill.'

'What we thought before may have been wrong.'

'You don't mean you believe Prance?'

'I won't insult you by suggesting Prance's tale of Godfrey being strangled somewhere as public as the courtyard at Somerset House could possibly be true. Or that Green could break Godfrey's neck.

Nor do I think Godfrey's body was carried around London in a sedan chair. But sometimes there's a grain of truth in the most unlikely of stories.'

'How large a grain?'

'Enough for me to be sure Godfrey was murdered.'

'When you asked me about Green, Berry and Hill in November, I assume you'd already heard rumours about them?'

'Their names had been mentioned to me. I've learned a lot more since then.'

'So you do have new evidence? Evidence that might clear them?'

'I promise you I have no information that would help Green, Berry and Hill in any way. If I gave you everything I have, it would change nothing. You are right that there's no evidence they killed Godfrey, but that is unimportant compared with the security of the state. If the alternative is renewed civil war, three deaths are acceptable. You know that.'

'You sound like Coleman, defending the burning of a few heretics to save millions from eternal damnation.'

'The two issues are very different. My calculations are based on logic and pragmatism, not blind faith. They do not depend on guesses about what God thinks of it all. Anti-Catholic mobs march through the streets of London every day. Half the population have bought knives with "Remember Godfrey" engraved on them in order to protect themselves from the Jesuits. Ladies are carrying pistols in broad daylight to shoot God knows who – each other if they're not careful. This is not going to end well. The only way to restore sanity is to convict somebody of Godfrey's murder and to do so very quickly. Don't look at me so disapprovingly, John. What I say is true. The best I can offer is that I might still be able to throw the Privy Council a bigger fish in their place. We'll have to see.'

'Thank you. In the meantime, I'll gather what information I can for their defence.'

'It will do you no good, but I won't stop you if you can't see the folly of it.'

'Arlington thinks that you have other people investigating Godfrey's death, by the way, not just me.'

'Arlington would think that,' he says. 'And you're no longer investigating anything for me. I'm grateful for what you've done, John, but my advice to you is to return to your duties in Essex as soon as the weather clears. Doctor Oates doesn't like you. Not at all. Staying in London simply places you and your friends and your family in danger. I don't want that. Just leave me to do what I need to do. Eventually you'll see why. You'll agree I was right to do what I'm doing.'

'Still, if I discover something new, would you like me to report back to you?'

Williamson coughs again. He really isn't at all well. 'No,' he says eventually. 'But if you see Arlington again, tell him to stick to his job as Lord Chamberlain.'

'I'll let him know,' I say.

As Williamson's street door closes behind me, I finally see the man who has been following me, this morning at least. He's not really dressed for it – the bright red coat and gold lace stand out on a grey winter's day. He touches his hat to me.

'Morning, Sir John. Always a pleasure to see you, sir.'

'Good morning,' I say.

'Whitehall Palace,' he says. 'You're needed.'

'The same gentleman as before?'

'Not for me to say. Find out soon enough. Follow me, if you don't mind, sir. Watch the snow. You can slip up nasty if you're not careful.'

Oates may be out of favour, but he still occupies his old quarters. He sits behind his desk in what is clearly episcopal dress – a silk gown, a cassock, a great hat with a satin hatband and long rose scarf.

'Am I to congratulate you, Doctor Oates, on your promotion to a bishopric?' I ask.

'It is purely honorary,' he says. 'The Archbishop of York thought it would be appropriate if I dressed in a manner that befitted my rank at court. I mix a great deal with the peerage. It is right that they see I am their equal, though I am not, of course, officially a member of the House of Lords.'

'Am I then to address you as a bishop?' I ask.

He smiles. 'Whatever you think appropriate. I place little store by such things.'

He waits for me to address him as 'your grace'.

'Why have you had me brought here, Doctor Oates?' I ask.

'I merely invited you to come, Sir John. I hope my messenger made that clear. You are not under arrest.'

'Good,' I say.

'You could be, but you're not. Not yet.'

'Good,' I say.

'I was hoping, however, you could very kindly clarify something.'

'You have only to ask, Doctor Oates.'

'Thank you. So, let me ask you: what in the name of God did you say to Miles Prance when you visited him last night?'

'We talked about the evidence that he has already given under oath – the evidence that you are already aware of.'

'Nothing else?'

'I don't think so. Does the warder say that I did?'

'Do you know what Prance has done this morning? No? Well, I'll tell you. He has gone to the King and fallen on his knees and begged forgiveness for lying about Green, Berry and Hill. That's what he has done. He has withdrawn his previous confession. He says he was never at Somerset House, other than to meet with the Duchess and take her orders for silverware.'

'I can assure you, Doctor Oates, that my conversation with Prance never touched upon the King in any way. The notion of falling on his knees before him is Prance's alone. I can only assume that his conscience has been troubling him, as well it might, and he has decided to tell the truth. I am sure that, whether as a bishop or a ship's chaplain or the vicar of Bobbing, you would stress that telling the truth and confessing one's sins are on the whole good things to do. And you could scarcely blame me for saying to Miles Prance that I agreed with you wholeheartedly.'

'Is that what you did?'

'I can't recall my precise words.'

'This is your doing, Grey. You have deliberately cost us our best witness, and you know it.'

'Are you saying Prance isn't now telling the truth?'

'I thought you were working for Williamson?'

I consider this. Well, Williamson warned me against discomposing Prance, for reasons he never fully explained. Oates is aware that is exactly what I've done. Yes, that must puzzle him. I am not behaving as I should. What puzzles me, on the other hand, is why Oates and Williamson seem to be so much in agreement. Has Williamson, in desperation, formed an alliance with Oates to save his job? Is part of the price for this new alliance that some Catholics will be convicted of Godfrey's murder? Green, Berry and Hill, unless a bigger fish can be found?

'Prance claims what he is saying now is the truth,' I say. 'I have no evidence to the contrary – quite the reverse, in fact. I don't quite know what you want me to do about it. You can't expect me, as a magistrate, to instruct somebody to lie. Even if I were a bishop I wouldn't dare do that.'

'Prance will soon regret trying to cross me,' says Oates. 'I would advise you not to do so either.'

'Has the King ordered the release of Green, Berry and Hill?' I ask.

'Of course not. The loss of our witness should prove only temporary. Prance, much to his dismay, is back in Little Ease. It took two days last time for him to see reason. We'll see how he feels tomorrow morning.'

'And if he remains steadfast?'

'Prance? Steadfast? I don't think so. But we can find other witnesses if he does.'

'Who?'

'Well, since you've cost me a witness, the least you can do is to replace him yourself.'

'I was in Essex at the time of the murder,' I say. 'I can be a witness to nothing.'

'The thing that you could be a witness to happened in your county.'

'What did I witness?'

'I think you know Lord Petre?'

I consider this carefully. Yes, Petre would be quite a big fish.

'I know he is one of the Catholic lords that you informed on and that the Privy Council has since arrested him and is holding him in prison,' I say.

A shadow passes over Oates's face. He doesn't like the words 'informed on'. It places him too close to men like Bedloe, men he despises, for all that he needs them.

'You also know him personally.'

'A little. He lives in the same county as I do – perhaps about thirty miles away.'

'I believe you have visited him?' says Oates.

'I did earlier this year, on county business. As a Catholic he holds no official office, of course, but I needed to consult him. He gave me good advice.'

'Earlier this year. Perfect. And when you were there, you will recall he told you that Sir Edmund Berry Godfrey was a great enemy of the Catholics in England and that there was a plan to get rid of him. He invited you to join the conspiracy. Naturally you were horrified. You refused. To help persuade you he named a number of other Catholic lords who were part of the plot.'

'Who?'

'Up to a point you could choose. I mean, one or two of your neighbours must have annoyed you?'

'I am happy to say I am on good terms with them all.'

'If you have no preference at all, then let me suggest Lord Bellasis. Perhaps together with a few of the lesser Catholic gentry in Essex. I would have to leave you to select them – you would already be well acquainted with them, because your own Catholic sympathies are notorious. Bowman mentioned how you overlooked treason in your village. I'm sure we could get him to sign a statement to that effect, if we had him here in London and a week or two to work on him.'

'He said nothing of the sort. He merely told you, and I have admitted this before, that I am not in a position to persecute my Catholic neighbours as much as you would like.'

'As much as the law demands, Sir John. My personal wishes do not come into it. Nor do yours.'

'Ben will simply tell the truth,' I say. 'In Essex or in London.'

'Let's see what truths he tells after a week or two in Little Ease, shall we? How long until Mister Bowman decides he'd just like to go home to his inn and his wife and his daughter? Nell and Beth, I think they are called? Maybe we could bring them to London too. To help Ben's memory. There's always room in Newgate for a couple more. How long would little Beth survive in Newgate, I wonder? Jail fever was very bad there last summer. How strong is her constitution?'

'Don't try to threaten me,' I say.

'I'm not threatening you, Sir John,' says Oates. 'I'm offering you a trade. One that should be very much to your liking. You get Green, Berry and Hill – and Prance, if you can think of a use for him. I get the bigger prize of Lord Petre. You don't care about Petre. You scarcely know him. It's nothing to you if he goes to the scaffold.'

'And, if I did that, you'd release the three men?'

'Yes, the moment you finish testifying before the Privy Council that Petre is a traitor and murderer. When Petre is formally charged, which we could do the same day, Green, Berry and Hill will be freed and their families will shower you with kisses. I give you my word, as a gentleman.'

'How would you achieve their release?'

'Bedloe or Prance would recall something new. Do we have a deal, Sir John?'

'I don't need to do any deals, Doctor Oates. Green, Berry and Hill are innocent.'

He smiles. So is Lord Petre, of course. He's a more important piece in the game than the cushion layer, but that's all he is. Another piece on the board. And, for the moment, Oates is treating me as a fellow player. An equal, almost.

'Take my offer, Sir John,' he says, silkily. 'It won't remain there in front of you for long. Save the men you want to save. Think how grateful they'll be. Think how grateful their families will be. Save them and leave me to do what I need to do. Nobody would dare criticise you. Not the Privy Council. Not the King. Not the other Catholic lords. Least of all your master, Williamson. Not a word of complaint from any of them. Because they'll all know you are my friend and protégé. My influence at court, I am pleased to say, grows daily. The King thought he could chastise me for telling him a few home truths about the Queen. But, as you see, I am still here.'

I shake my head.

'My offer is open until tomorrow evening, Sir John. Why don't you go away and sleep on it? As Prance did. Talk to Williamson if you feel you have to. Or just tell him that's what you're going to do. You don't need his permission to do anything. Not Williamson.'

'So, Prance has withdrawn his accusation, sir?' says Green hopefully. 'If that is your doing, we can't thank you enough. We, all of us, will be forever in your debt. Will we now be released? They can't keep us, can they?'

'They'll find reasons for holding you if they can. But they can't try you for treason. Oates thinks that Prance, back in Little Ease, will revert to his previous statement. But it will do Oates no good. Prance has perjured himself. He has sworn two contradictory things under oath. No judge will be able to accept his original evidence at a trial.'

'Not even Scroggs, sir?' says Berry.

'Scroggs is Lord Chief Justice. He has to have some respect for the law. Even he will have to abide by the rules.'

'You'll return to Essex for the New Year?' asks Arlington.

'Yes, if I ride hard tomorrow I should get there on time.'

The fire blazing away in front of us, crackling and spitting reassuringly, serves only to remind me of the rain and snow I've to face on the way. The red glow reflects back from the shiny leather bindings and the gold titles of the books on the shelves. Arlington still holds in his hand a letter that he had been reading when I came in. He wishes me to know that this interview will be short.

'Your actions have certainly spiked Oates's guns,' says Arlington. 'For the moment. Maybe for good. If he fails to get a conviction that will be another major defeat for him. And a defeat for that ridiculous popinjay, Danby. You have done well, John.'

Indeed. I have done exactly what Arlington hoped I would do. I have damaged – perhaps fatally – an important asset of Arlington's enemy, Lord Danby. I may have hastened the fall of Danby himself. My Lord has made no offer to assist in securing the early release of Green, Berry and Hill. They can enjoy the hospitality of Newgate for a little longer, all free of charge.

'And Oates had the temerity to suggest that you should trepan Lord Petre?' Arlington continues. 'Does he think none of us have any principles?'

It's an odd question on Arlington's lips. Up until now he's always assumed a lack of principles was normal – desirable, even. Perhaps, without informing me, he has developed a conscience.

'Seemingly not,' I say. 'He'll get Petre executed by one means or the other, though.'

'I don't think so. The whole edifice that Oates has constructed is about to fall on his head. Petre's as safe as he needs to be. Will you report back to Williamson?'

'No,' I say, taking a last look at the comforting fire. 'He doesn't want me to. Anyway, Williamson seems too concerned with his own problems. He wants to save his position as Secretary of State, above everything else. If he'd hoped to do that by placating Oates, I think he may have failed. Oates thinks Williamson counts for nothing any more.'

'For once, Oates is right,' says Arlington.

Chapter Twenty-Three

In which Sir Felix and my wife explain why I am wrong, and I agree with them

It's no longer snowing, but that just makes things worse. The road now is a sea of mud and slush and water and broken sheets of ice. At least a dozen times on the first day, it is only the good sense of my mare that saves her from stumbling and me from being thrown into the freezing morass. My face stings. My hands are so cold inside my gloves that I can scarcely grip the reins. I am sure my legs must be frozen to the saddle. But there is no need to urge my mount onwards. She wishes to get to Clavershall West every bit as much as I do.

'Is that a Godfrey knife?' asks the landlord of the inn we have stopped at for the night.

'Yes,' I say, as I cut into the sixpenny slice of beef before me.

'You got it in London?'

'I'm travelling back from there now.'

'Did you meet that Doctor Oates?' he asks.

'Yes,' I say.

'Then I envy your good fortune, sir. He is a hero and the saviour of us all. The Catholics, sir, they hate us. I was saying to my wife, it's only Doctor Oates who stands between us and having our throats cut in our own beds. It's happened before, sir, in the days of Bloody Mary. Everyone who was a Protestant – *everyone* – was burnt alive at the stake. Hundreds of them. Thousands. It's all in Foxe's Book of Martyrs, sir. If Doctor Oates was here, I'd give him the best room in the inn, and a fine supper and all the beer he could drink – no charge.'

'And what did your wife say to that?' I ask.

'Oh, she just said that the King had called him a rogue and that was good enough for her. But women don't understand these things, do they? Not the way we do. That man is a Protestant saint. And you've actually met him!'

'Yes,' I say. 'Several times.'

'Well, any friend of Doctor Oates is welcome here. There'll be no charge for your supper, sir.'

'I'm not his friend,' I say. 'Thanks for the offer but I'll pay the usual price.'

On the second day it rains. The fields on either side of me are flooded, almost as far as the eye can see. I wonder whether the three men from Somerset House have been sent home yet. The Privy Council seems quick to arrest but slow to release.

Everywhere I stop, there is a desire for the latest news from the capital, and there is fear.

'You've come from London?' asks the landlord of the inn I have stopped at for dinner.

'Yes,' I say, as I cut into the slice of ham before me.

'Did you meet that Doctor Oates?' he asks. 'The one who claims there's a plot against the King?'

'Yes,' I say.

'They say he's imprisoned Lord Petre.'

'He's certainly caused him to be imprisoned,' I say. 'For treason.'

'Just because he's a Catholic?'

'I know of no other evidence against him.'

'So how will they convict him with no evidence?'

'They'll find some paid informer to invent it.'

'If such a knight of the post stayed here, I'd cut his throat as he slept.'

'That would be a great service to everyone.'

'Lord Petre's well known in this county. People like him. He may not believe what the rest of us do, but he never did nobody any harm.'

'No,' I say.

'If they can imprison him, they could imprison anyone. These are evil days, sir, when a man can be thrown into jail just for what he thinks.'

'Yes,' I say.

'Maybe the less we all say the better then.'

'Yes,' I say.

I am finally sitting in front of my own fire, warming my hands. Aminta and her father have just finished listening to the account of my stay in London. I think I deserve the mulled wine on the table beside me.

'You did well,' says Sir Felix. 'You have struck a major blow against Oates. Even if Prance changes his mind again, the fact that he has perjured himself means that his evidence can't be considered.'

I nod. 'And without Prance's confession, the case against the three men will fail. Bedloe's testimony alone won't do – they need a pair of witnesses.'

'You say Prance was a member of a Catholic club. That could be used to discredit him further?'

'It was helpful to be able to threaten him with it,' I say, 'but in court I'd need the constable to swear that he was indeed a member and I'm not sure he would. Anyway, it seems to be a genuinely harmless gathering of Catholic tradesmen.'

'I agree,' says Sir Felix. 'The perjury is more solid. It does, however, still leave open the question of who did kill Sir Edmund Berry Godfrey.'

'You no longer think it was suicide either?' I say.

'We've had a chance to think about it while you were away and we were celebrating Christmas here,' says Aminta. 'Like Williamson, we now think he was murdered, but unlike Williamson, we're willing to share our reasons with you.'

'That's good of you,' I say, sipping my wine.

'First,' says Sir Felix, 'you'd assumed that Godfrey's crime was that he did not immediately report what he knew.'

'Yes,' I say, 'Godfrey had received Oates's deposition and did not believe it. So, instead of reporting it to higher authorities, he investigated further – by talking to his friend, Edward Coleman, and later consulting members of the Catholic club that Prance also belonged to. But that took time and meant that Godfrey feared he would be accused of treason simply because of the delay in reporting what he knew.'

'In fact,' says Sir Felix, 'Oates met the Privy Council the day after he made his deposition to Godfrey. So, everybody who needed to know, knew very quickly anyway.'

'Where did you learn that?' I ask.

'Christmas greetings from my aunt,' says Aminta.

'Oates has never blamed Godfrey in any way for delaying the revelation of the plot,' continues Sir Felix. 'Nor, clearly, did Williamson. Whatever Godfrey was worried about, it can't have just been the delay, which would have been no more than twelve hours or so.'

'But his fears that he would be hanged still related in some way to Oates's deposition,' I say.

'I would remind you he actually said the deposition was his security,' says Aminta.

'I agree it's more complicated than we thought,' I say. 'He also spoke of a secret that he held that would be fatal to him. The secret can't have been simply that he went and saw Coleman – or not according to Williamson anyway. It was something else that Godfrey was worried about.'

'Exactly,' says Aminta. 'And there is an important point that we missed concerning the brothers. One of the things that Mistress Curtis told us was that Michael and Benjamin asked her if she had found a pocket book on the body.'

'Yes,' I say.

'And they clearly wanted it very much. But if they'd kept the body for three or four days in one of the woodsheds, they could have recovered it for themselves easily enough. Alternatively, if somebody else had taken the book from the body before the brothers found Sir Edmund, they'd have already known it wasn't there. In neither case would they have had to beg a servant to check for them.'

'So, they never had the body?' I ask. 'In which case, it also explains another puzzle: why they didn't take the money.'

'Precisely. They spent the week frantically searching for the body not as a diversionary tactic but because they genuinely had no idea what had happened to Edmund, right up to the moment he was found in the ditch.'

'But the body had definitely been moved – it couldn't have been in the ditch the whole time. So, somebody else found it somewhere and took it to Primrose Hill?' I say.

'We then have to ask why would anyone except the brothers want to cover up a suicide,' says Aminta.

It's a good point. Why would anyone else, finding the hanged body of Sir Edmund Berry Godfrey, want to undertake the arduous journey, probably by night, to leave him in a remote ditch, some way even from the muddy road where the coach tracks were found? And then needlessly plunge a sword into his chest?

'So, if somebody wasn't covering up a suicide . . .' I say.

'They were covering up a murder,' says Sir Felix. 'We therefore considered the question of the broken neck again. Everyone's agreed that it's rare with self-hanging. So long as there was other good evidence for suicide then it was worth considering that rough handling of the corpse after it was found might have produced the same effect, but now . . .'

'The balance of probability undoubtedly shifts to murder,' I say. 'Which is what Williamson now thinks too. But he's not willing to tell me who it was, except that he's found no evidence that Green, Berry and Hill are murderers. If we rule out the Catholics and Pembroke and suicide, what's left?'

'The man who would have objected most to Godfrey's consultation with Coleman,' says Aminta. 'Oates.'

Godfrey's Journey

Somebody had been following him all day. Several times, he'd caught sight of the two rather clumsy shadows in the swirling yellow fog. At Marylebone, he thought he'd lost them, but they must have picked him up again on his way back, because they were certainly there now.

He had the money in his pockets to run if necessary, but first he'd wanted to check any rumours that they might have heard on Primrose Hill. In the end, the most worrying had been that Williamson and Oates had come to some sort of understanding. But of course, it might not be true. They'd laughed when they said it, as if they didn't quite believe it themselves. Or did they? As so often, he found it difficult to tell. Maybe they'd know more at Somerset House. He'd check there next, then head for Dover if London was now simply too dangerous. It would be too risky to go back to Hartshorne Lane anyway. They'd be watching for him there. He should have listened to his clerk.

*

Now he's back in the Strand, with two shadows still behind him. Are they the same as the ones this morning? If so, you can't fault their persistence. Coleman, perhaps under torture, must have already betrayed him to the Privy Council.

He quickens his pace. The Watergate of Somerset House is close by. Soon he'll be amongst friends.

They catch him only twenty yards from his sanctuary.

'Thank goodness we've found you, Sir Edmund,' says one of the men, placing a hand on his shoulder.

'Why?' he asks. His own right hand instantly seeks the handle of his sword. He'll have difficulty fighting them off, but he might take one of them with him.

'No need for that, sir, we've come from the Duke.'

'Which Duke?'

'Why, the Duke of York, to be sure, sir. He wants us to take you to somewhere you'll be safe. Safe from your enemies. We don't want to lose you as well as Mister Coleman. The Privy Council have men out looking for you.'

'Where are we going? To Somerset House?'

'No, not there, sir. That's the first place they'll search. They already have a warrant. Just come this way.'

'Down that alleyway?'

'That's it. There's a little house where we accommodate priests who shouldn't really be here. You really can take your hand off your sword now, sir. We'll look after you.'

'You don't need to grip my arm like that.'

'Just keeping you safe, Sir Edmund. Another few yards and we'll be where we want to be. It will be easier if you stop struggling, sir. Just in through that door. Then we'll have a little chat about things.'

Chapter Twenty-Four

In which Oates shows his hand

'Even if you're right, Aminta, that it was government agents who killed Godfrey, you still can't be sure it was Oates who ordered it,' says Sir Felix. 'Why not Danby and the Privy Council? Or Shaftesbury? Or Peyton? Or Williamson for that matter?'

'No, I agree with Aminta,' I say. 'Oates is my guess, too. It fits in better with what we already know. I think that Williamson worked out Godfrey's death must have been authorised by somebody close to the heart of government and that the Privy Council investigation would merely cover up the crime. So, he got me and some other person to find out what had happened. Williamson couldn't risk anyone in authority knowing what we were doing – but Oates was the one I was specifically told to beware of.'

'Well,' says Sir Felix, 'I'd put nothing past Oates, including murder. Too much of a coward to kill Godfrey himself, of course, but I can believe he'd get somebody else to do it for him.'

'I think that Williamson's other investigator eventually discovered the truth. Williamson confronted Oates. Oates denied it, of course, but made Williamson an offer that was too good to refuse. He'd support him in office. Together they'd bring down Danby.'

'Then Williamson stood you down before you could also discover what had happened,' says Sir Felix.

'Can your Williamson really have stooped so low?' says Aminta.

'I'm only guessing, and I still hope I'm wrong, but Williamson is clearly in trouble, especially after he signed the commissions. He is just one more mistake away from being sacked like Arlington. Oates blundered over accusing the Queen and can't trust Bedloe. They may despise each other but they are both desperate for allies.'

'So, who is Williamson's other investigator?' says Aminta.

'Could it be Prance?' says Sir Felix. 'He's unprincipled enough.'

'It would explain why Prance was so puzzled when I questioned him,' I say. 'But, if so, Williamson's protected him very badly.'

'I think, John,' says Sir Felix, 'that you would do well to trust Williamson even less than you trust Arlington. And, whatever he promises you, you should trust Oates least of all.'

There is a banging on the door. Before I can even say 'come in', it swings open and Ben's wife, Nell, appears. She has clearly run all the way from the inn. She is out of breath and the hem of her skirt is wet and muddy.

'Please come quickly, Sir John. And you, Sir Felix. And you, my Lady. There are some men from London. They came, stabled their horses and ate a good dinner. Now they are trying to take Ben away with them!'

That we are not too late is largely down to Ben's stable boy, who has thought to lock the stable door, behind which all of the available horses are now safely confined. He is standing defiantly, arms folded, the key in his pocket, while two men threaten him in a variety of imaginative ways. Since the taller of them is fully occupied holding on to Ben, the shorter one has limited options. The stable boy is nimbler than either of them and holds the only key they know of.

More ominously for the abductors, a trickle of customers is forsaking the inn and starting to gather in a circle round the little group. Their tankards are empty and they don't look happy that their landlord is now unable to refill them.

Both men look at us in dismay as we approach them, two drawn swords gleaming in the last rays of the winter sunshine. If they were not worried about being outnumbered before, they are now. They can see they've spent too much time lounging at the table, enjoying Ben's hospitality, before seizing him. Better to have been some way along the London road before sunset, but time has finally run out for them.

'What's going on?' I ask.

'We have a warrant for the arrest of Ben Bowyer,' says the shorter of the two, waving a rolled paper at me. He appears to be in charge of whatever they think they're doing.

'May I see it, please?' I ask.

He hands it to me with more hope than can possibly be justified.

'Unfortunately you have arrested Ben Bowman,' I say.

'Bowman. Bowyer. What of it? A minor error in a warrant does not make it invalid,' he says, puffing out his chest.

'It does if it's the name of the suspect. And it seems to be signed by Titus Oates. I realise that he now thinks he's a bishop, but when did he become a magistrate?'

'His signature is good enough for anyone.'

'Not here in Essex,' I say. 'You'll need another warrant from the authorities in London. With the right name on it. Until you get one, you'd better tell your friend to take his hands off Mister Bowman, unless you wish to be charged with assault.'

'Look, whoever you are,' says the taller minion, 'Doctor Oates is tasked with hunting down traitors and the murderer of Sir Edmund Berry Godfrey. We have evidence that Mister Bowman here was involved in a plot against the King. We're taking him to London for questioning.' He scans the growing crowd. 'On your way, all of you, or I'll summon the magistrate.'

He pauses, perhaps wondering who might be standing in front of him with a drawn sword, explaining the law in simple terms.

'That isn't going to be necessary,' I say. 'As you know well.'

'Are you Sir John Grey?' he says.

'Yes,' I say.

'You got here quickly. Doctor Oates said you couldn't arrive until tomorrow at the earliest.'

'I thought I'd make sure I was back for what remained of Christmas,' I say. 'Unless you want to be arrested yourself for abduction, I would suggest you release the prisoner now.'

'Arrest?' says the possessor of the warrant, perhaps somewhat inadvisedly. 'I'd like to see you try.'

But his taller more perceptive companion releases his grip on Ben. 'We'll return, Sir John. With a new set of papers. Maybe two, if Doctor Oates thinks you've obstructed the course of justice. Now, if you'll be so good as to order that boy to unlock the stable door, we'll be on our way. We've wasted enough time in this village.'

'Don't let them off that easy, Sir John,' calls one of the customers. 'They've tried to abduct Ben, like you say. We can sort it out, if you don't want to.'

Perhaps it's just that it's getting darker, but the crowd encircling Oates's minions seems closer to the men than it was before. 'Let's just string them up now,' says somebody. There is a murmur of approval for this modest and reasonable proposal.

'We demand the protection of the law,' says the shorter man, slightly too late. 'We look upon you, Sir John, to uphold it in every particular.'

'I shall most certainly do so,' I say. 'You have both attempted to kidnap my constable, an officer of the law, a man deserving of your respect. Arrest the two of them, Ben. We can try them straight away.'

'Try us?' they say more or less in unison.

'Just follow Ben into the parlour of the inn,' I say. 'Whatever verdict the jury brings, it won't be that you should freeze to death out here.'

It isn't too difficult to assemble a jury. The inn is full, as it usually is on a winter's evening, and I swear in twelve jurymen from amongst them. There is none of the usual reluctance to accept jury service. One day, they'll be able to tell their grandchildren about this one. Candles are lit, the sun now being down, and beer is served. Ben gives evidence of his attempted abduction, while the jury lean back on the settles, tankards in hands, and smoke their pipes. Nell and the stable boy are sworn and are pleased to confirm Ben's account. More beer is served. The two men decline to cross-examine the witnesses for the Crown. They add that they hadn't thought to bring any of their own. I direct the jury, which then takes less than a minute to bring in a guilty verdict and to relight their pipes. I sentence Oates's minions to a day in the stocks. Ben takes them away to one of his two guest chambers and locks them in for the night.

'That was edifying,' says Sir Felix as we walk back to the Big House and supper. 'Scroggs himself could not have dispatched a case in a more efficient manner. But, on reflection, was it wise?'

'It was the safest option for all concerned. Oates's men will at least get out of the county alive. And Oates will know that we bite if provoked. Hopefully he'll keep away from Clavershall West in future. Anyway, he has bigger fish to fry in this county than me. Or Ben.'

'I know. You said. Lord Petre's a good man. He fought for the King in Warwickshire during the war. Looks after his tenants well.'

'Oates nevertheless wishes to destroy him, like a child deliberately breaking something of value that he doesn't understand. He's attempted to get me to help him with that and he's failed, but he'll find somebody eventually to give false evidence against Petre. Being a knight of the post is now a respectable profession.'

'And Williamson's apparently ready to condone even that in order to remain in office,' says Aminta.

'Let's hope the Privy Council sees through Oates before that happens,' says Sir Felix.

'He's still too useful for them to drop him completely,' I say. 'So long as Shaftesbury and Danby have a few old scores to settle, Oates will keep his apartment in the palace and his rose-coloured scarf. And Williamson may have no choice but to work with him.'

The following day, I get the would-be kidnappers to sit in the stocks outside the inn for a bit. At nine o'clock it starts to snow again. I leave them until almost ten before releasing them several hours early. The stocks are not intended to be a means of execution. Anyway, it's hardly fair to expect the villagers to pelt them with rubbish in conditions like this. The men's horses are restored to them, and they ride away with less gratitude than they should have.

Three days later a letter arrives from Arlington.

'Prance has indeed changed his mind again,' I say to Aminta. 'Just as Oates predicted. He has decided that, on further consideration, he did see Green, Berry and Hill murder Sir Edmund Godfrey. Their trial has been listed for the fifth of February.'

'Well, you did your best,' says Sir Felix. 'At least, as a result of your work, Scroggs will have to set Prance's evidence aside. Without that, the prosecution will have no case at all.'

'Nothing can be depended on,' I say. 'Arlington predicts foul play. I'll need to go back and ensure that things are done according to the law in London, just as they are in Clavershall West.'

'You can't travel alone to London again through the ice and snow,' says Sir Felix. 'It's too dangerous. I won't allow it.'

'Exactly,' says Aminta. 'This time I'm coming too.'

I am again sitting at an inn, trying to warm myself, but this time with Aminta beside me. I can tell that the other customers think I am acting in an irresponsible manner, forcing my poor wife to travel on horseback in this weather, for all that she is wrapped in furs. But we have made good progress today.

'I still can't believe Williamson is working with Oates,' says Aminta.

'We don't yet know that he is. Not for certain. I think that, when he first asked me to come up to London, he genuinely wanted to discover who had killed Godfrey.'

'But not enough to tell you all he knew.'

'It would seem not. I'm not saying that he is behaving as my former master did. Arlington's loyalties are very simple – they are to Arlington and to the long line of Bennets that he still hopes will succeed him. He is loyal to the King because it is expedient and because he has been loyal to the King for so long that it might prove awkward now switching his allegiance elsewhere. Williamson is very different. His loyalty is to the state and good order. He would make compromises that Arlington couldn't consider. But even then I hope he would draw the line at working with Oates.'

'Perhaps he has some card up his sleeve of which we know nothing. Maybe he knows the men will never go to trial? Or maybe he wants them to go to trial and be found innocent, just to confound Oates and Danby?'

'You're on your way to London?' asks the landlord, placing two bowls of steaming mutton stew in front of us.

'Yes,' I say.

'If you see that Doctor Oates, you can tell him from me that he's the saviour of the nation,' he says.

'Thank you, but he already knows,' I say.

Chapter Twenty-Five

In which we begin to prepare a case for the defence

The cell in the bowels of Newgate is as cold as ever. The only heating is the warmth of the men's bodies. We've been given a lantern to take with us. It would be inhumane to expect us to interview them by the light of the single tallow candle that the three accused men usually have.

'So, we must stand trial after all, sir?' asks Green.

'Yes,' I say. 'It looks as if that's what will happen. But the case against you is as weak as it could be. You will be able to mount a good defence.'

'Can you speak for us in court?' he asks.

'No. There will of course be counsel for the prosecution, but the defendants are allowed no representation in a case like this, lest you escape justice by legal trickery.'

'Is there nobody there to help us, then?' asks Hill.

'The judge must offer you advice and explain things to you but you should not believe he will be on your side. Not for one moment.'

'It will definitely be Scroggs, sir? The man who condemned Mister Coleman?'

'So we're told,' says Aminta.

'He hates Catholics,' says Hill.

'But he must still abide by the law,' I say.

Hill shakes his head. 'What must we do, then?'

'You will need to listen carefully to the prosecution witnesses. If they get something wrong – if they claim you did something that you did not do, then you must challenge them. Ask them how they can possibly know that. If they contradict themselves, you must point that out to them. In particular, if Miles Prance is allowed to give evidence, you must ask why he swore to the King that his original testimony was a lie. You must say that the court should not accept his latest statement because it contradicts the earlier one.'

'That's perjury, sir?'

'Exactly, Mister Hill. That's perjury, plain and simple. Remember the word and use it well. Hopefully, if the judge accepts what you say, it will stop the trial in its tracks. But you must be prepared to cross-examine all of the witnesses if necessary, whoever they are.'

'Who will they call?' asks Hill.

'We won't know until the day of the trial. We won't even know exactly what you are charged with.'

'Is that fair?'

'No, but it's how it's done. They may accuse you of what Bedloe claimed happened or what Prance claimed happened or something else. If your objection to Prance's evidence fails, you will also need to be ready to call your own witnesses to swear that you were where you claim to have been on the night Godfrey was killed.'

'Will the judge believe them?'

'If they speak up and dress respectably, there's a good chance.'

'How do we make sure they'll be there?'

'Aminta and I can seek them out and explain things to them.'

'Talk to my wife,' says Hill. 'She'll help you. She knows where they are to be found.'

'So, who can speak for each of you?' asks Aminta.

'My landlord, James Warrier, and his wife will swear that I did not leave the house all evening,' says Green.

She makes a note of the name.

'Doctor Godden's niece, Mistress Tilden, can vouch for me that I never left his house after eight o'clock,' says Hill. 'So will his housekeeper, Mistress Broadstreet. They'll say I almost never go out after eight, and certainly didn't that night.'

'You must talk to the soldiers who were on guard that week,' says Berry. 'They'll confirm that no sedan chair left the palace on the Wednesday night. If we can show that's a lie, it will show everything Prance has said is a lie, won't it, sir?'

'It will certainly help,' I say. 'Every contradiction in their account will reduce the credibility of the charges. In the last resort, we shall need to chip away bit by bit at everything they claim is true. But our main hope is that Scroggs will dismiss Prance's evidence for the falsehood that it is.'

'Will the King need to swear that Prance retracted his oath before him?' asks Hill.

'That would be too much to hope for. But we'll need to make sure there is a witness to it. I'll find out how that might be done. Be of good heart, gentlemen. I think our small truths are nimble enough to defeat their enormous lumbering lies.'

'Chiffinch,' says Arlington. 'He was present when Prance withdrew his confession. He's a rogue, obviously, but he and Scroggs drink together. At the very least, Chiffinch won't be frightened of Scroggs and he'll be prepared to answer him back.'

'Will Scroggs believe him?' asks Aminta.

'It's a straightforward matter,' says Arlington. 'Did Prance retract his confession or not? Everyone knows he did – it was all over town that he'd done it. Scroggs will still want it all set out step by step, of course, but Chiffinch's role will be simply to nod his head when he's asked the question. It's not much to expect of him.'

'I'll explain what's needed,' I say.

The Page of the Bedchamber looks sideways at me. 'Why?' he says.

'Because, Mister Chiffinch, we may need a witness to the fact that Prance withdrew his allegations.'

'It's common knowledge.'

'Scroggs may demand proof.'

'Why was Prance taken from and then sent back to Little Ease if nothing had happened? Surely that's evidence enough? Richardson can tell Scroggs that.'

'But he wasn't there when the retraction happened and you were. As a lawyer, I can assure you that there is little that cannot be challenged in court. And if Scroggs is determined to convict, as I suspect he will be, then we need to ensure that there is no chance of the prosecution skipping round the facts, however well known. I just need you to confirm that you witnessed the retraction.'

'What's it to you if they hang? They won't be the first innocent men to die on the gallows. They won't be the last.'

'Because I believe in justice.'

Chiffinch looks at me and shakes his head sadly. 'Very well. I am willing to say that, but no more. I'm the King's servant – not Williamson's and certainly not yours.'

'Thank you, Mister Chiffinch,' I say. 'I am much obliged to you.'

'Well,' says Aminta, 'I've spoken to Mistress Tilden and Mistress Broadstreet. Both very respectable ladies, who will give a good account of themselves in court. They will say that Hill was with them all Saturday evening. He could have murdered nobody. They will also say that hiding a body in Doctor Godden's residence, as Bedloe and Prance will claim, would have been impossible. The room in question is not large and there were people coming and going the whole time. I've stressed to them that they should simply tell the truth and stick to it. Scroggs will try to make them say they are not entirely certain about things, but they must not be bullied and must simply reply that they are.'

'And Green?'

'His landlord and landlady are not the best witnesses – one hopelessly vague and the other with a cheerful inability to stop talking. But they will confirm his alibi, which is all they need to do. It would have been impossible for Green to have been in the places Prance says he was at the times he says he was. Berry was more difficult, but I think I've managed to establish which soldiers were on duty that week. The corporal in charge was most indignant about the accusation that they might have missed seeing a sedan chair leave the palace with Godfrey's body in it. They're men who are used to standing firm in the face of musket balls and cannon shot. I think Scroggs will have little joy if he tries to shift them from their position. How did you do?'

'Chiffinch will give evidence for Prance's retraction. Reluctantly, but he'll do it. So, that should shut off that line of argument.'

'Did you speak to Williamson?' ask Aminta.

'No. Arlington was right. If Sir Joseph's loyalties are, at best, unknown, then it's wise we tell him no more than he needs to know.'

'Well, we've done what we can. Hopefully the three men will manage without Williamson's help. The trial won't be until early next month. I would suggest we return to Essex – for a couple of weeks at least. There is no point in our remaining here.'

But I am delayed half an hour or so before we set out the following morning.

'I apologise for calling on you at your lodgings,' says Titus Oates, 'but the matter is of some importance. I have come alone so that we may speak freely.'

'I am, as ever, at your service, Doctor Oates.'

'Then I shall be brief, Sir John. First, I apologise if my men inconvenienced you or your constable. They considerably exceeded their instructions by trying to arrest him as they did. You were quite right to send them on their way.'

I try not to show too much surprise. The warrant Oates issued seemed clear enough, but perhaps he has conveniently forgotten that. 'I assume they have no intention of returning to Essex?' I ask.

'None at all, Sir John. You have my word on it. I would, however, still urge you to consider my proposition.'

'That I give evidence against Lord Petre in exchange for the Privy Council calling off the trial of Green, Berry and Hill?'

'Precisely. I could arrange for the charges to be dropped this afternoon and the men freed by tomorrow morning.'

I look at him. Could this really be the face that ordered Godfrey's death? Suddenly I have doubts. Just as Pembroke has his own modus operandi, so does Oates. He operates through the courts and is proving very effective at manipulating them. He has no need of clandestine seizures and stranglings. Still, it makes no difference to what I think of his proposal.

'I am sorry, but I must again decline your generous offer. All three are innocent. We shall be able to mount a very good defence.'

'Still, they will inevitably be found guilty. I do of course know that your wife and Mistress Hill have been active in talking to witnesses. All very good, sincere people. But you know that Scroggs will rip them to shreds. Of course he will. They will be left broken and humiliated. Not one word they have said will have counted for anything. Is it fair to put so many witnesses to so much trouble for nothing? You want the charges dropped because you say they are innocent. I want them dropped because we need to silence the real leaders of the plot. Men like Petre.'

'I am sure you can pay others to testify against Lord Petre.'

'Oh yes, another Bedloe or another Prance. But people are ceasing to believe Bedloe. You, on the other hand, with your reputation for honesty and integrity ... witnesses of your quality are hard to find for any money. Of course, I wouldn't consider for a moment offering you a financial reward. But you could save the lives of three men that you at least consider to be innocent and whom I regard as being scarcely worth the effort of hanging. Why follow a difficult road when there is another that is so easy and pleasant? Rarely have I seen so much mutual advantage.'

'What you mean,' I say, 'is that you know your case is weak and my denouncing Petre is your only hope.'

Oates shakes his head. I could have saved them so easily. But I have chosen otherwise.

'Then the three men will most certainly die. Or two of them will, anyway. You know Berry is reputed to be a Protestant? He chooses not to confess at the moment, but when he sees how things really stand, then he may. Perhaps he will even remember taking his instructions from Lord Petre. Then I shall have them all. Well, good day, Sir John. I wish you a speedy return to Essex. Please do give my best wishes to your constable.'

Chapter Twenty-Six

In which we discuss a murder

The journey back to Essex is easier. We have had a few days of respite from the snow and rain. It is cold, but the skies are clear and a brilliant blue. Travelling is still slow but the mud is now drying out and our horses are, as ever, uncomplaining.

'Are you travelling from London?' asks the landlord as he puts the bread and cold beef in front of us.

'Yes,' I say.

'Did you hear that they've caught the men who killed Sir Edmund Berry Godfrey?'

'They've arrested three men, certainly,' I say.

'Catholics?'

'Two of them are.'

'There you are, then. The sooner they hang the villains the better.'

'They'll need to try them first.'

'Just so long as they don't use false witnesses or legal trickery to get off.'

'It's more likely they'll use false witnesses and legal trickery to convict them,' I say.

The landlord nods. 'Quite right too,' he says.

A sudden flurry of snow delays our departure. But the fire inside the inn is warm and we can sit it out until the snow stops.

'Hanging Green, Berry and Hill will clearly prove popular,' I say.

'I am beginning to fear that could happen,' says Aminta. 'Scroggs may refuse to accept even Chiffinch's testimony of Prance's perjury.'

'Very well, let's consider the very worst case in which the defence witnesses are ridiculed and dismissed by Scroggs, and both Prance and Bedloe are allowed to give evidence,' I say. 'The prosecution must have at least two witnesses and the witnesses must agree with each other to some extent. But Prance and Bedloe don't. Bedloe accused Le Fevre, Walsh, Pritchard and a servant of Lord Bellasis of the murder. Prance says it was Gerald, Kelly, Green, Berry and Hill. Bedloe said Godfrey was decoyed to Somerset House at five o'clock on Saturday, stifled with a pillow and then strangled. Prance said it took place at nine, after a good supper. Green strangled him with a handkerchief, then wrung his neck right round, presumably breaking it in the process. As for the disposal of the body, Bedloe said it was taken to Primrose Hill on Monday. Prance said Wednesday. Bedloe says the body was taken in a sedan chair and then by coach to Primrose Hill. Prance says sedan chair to the Grecian Church and then horseback. And, although both claim to have been there on the Saturday evening, neither of them seems to have noticed the other, which is odd.'

'And none of that fits in with evidence from any other source,' says Aminta. 'Plenty of people saw Godfrey walking to and from Primrose Hill. Nobody mentioned anyone following him – except the man who saw Godfrey outside Somerset House, and he was far from certain. Nobody at Somerset House has come forward to say that they witnessed Godfrey's murder or the sham fight in the courtyard or that they noticed Godfrey's body lying for days in Doctor Godden's lodgings.'

'And everyone accused by both Bedloe and Prance, except Green, Berry and Hill, has conveniently vanished,' I say.

'So, where is Williamson's grain of truth in the middle of all of the lies?'

'Williamson could tell us, if he wanted to. But he doesn't.'

Clavershall West proves to be cold and damp, but at least nobody asks me to betray anyone. I hear nothing further from Arlington or Williamson. I hear nothing from Oates. His response to my putting his men in the stocks has been remarkably measured and pragmatic. It has not stopped him courting me as an ally, because on balance he needs me as an ally more than he needs revenge. This strange streak of pragmatism is an unexpected strength. There is also a stoical determination about him that I have only slowly come to appreciate. If rebuffed, he will try again and again, without much visible annoyance, until he gets to where he wants to be. In some ways a raving fanatic would be an easier opponent. If he has done a deal with Williamson, did he approach him in the same way? Did he offer Williamson, again and again, something he desperately wanted? Did he eventually succeed in winning him over? That Oates isn't the murderer doesn't mean that he hasn't bought Williamson.

A letter does arrive from Aminta's aunt, but it disappointingly contains mainly family gossip. The only reference to public affairs is that she tried to buy a Godfrey knife, but they had sold out. At least she doesn't say that the capital is about to rise against the King and supplant him with the Duke of Monmouth.

We travel up to town again early February, expecting the trial to start on the fifth but, having heard the men's not-guilty pleas, Scroggs agrees an adjournment, 'that the King's evidence might be the more ready'. The prisoners would, of course, have asked for an adjournment in vain, if they had needed more time to locate their own witnesses. The men are taken from the harsh, bright light of Westminster Hall, back down into their dungeon. A new date is set for the sixth, then for the tenth, but before we can all assemble again we receive some news from another quarter.

'I saw Betterton while I was out,' says Aminta, handing her cloak to our maid.

'Is he asking you to write another play?'

'If he is, he forgot to mention it. He had more important news. The King has dismissed Williamson.'

'Why?'

'He discovered Williamson was continuing to investigate the Queen behind his back. Williamson had given orders to search the Queen's apartment at Somerset House, without asking the King permission – I suppose he knew there was no chance the King would ever agree to it. The King apparently told Williamson that he marvelled at his effrontery in searching a royal palace. He added that he did not wish to be served by a man who feared anyone more than him.'

'Williamson and Oates seem in complete agreement again,' I say.

'That the Queen is some sort of threat? Even so, it's surprising Williamson hadn't learned from Oates's error. What does Williamson think is going on at Somerset House?'

'Something worth risking the King's anger to find out about,' I say. 'The King will have to take him back, even so. Arlington once sacked Williamson and had to reappoint him within a few days. Williamson knows too much about everything.'

'That was the old Williamson,' says Aminta. 'The one who had to be rescued from the Tower is less valuable.'

'Did Betterton know who is to be appointed in his place?'

'The Earl of Sunderland. A former ambassador and a gentleman of the bedchamber. He's sitting at Williamson's desk as we speak.'

'I know him. One of the rudest and most tactless men at court.'

'But the King still likes him better than Williamson.'

'What exactly did Williamson think he was doing, though?' I say.

'You've been a spy, you tell me.'

'You've been a spy yourself,' I say.

'Yes, but I never did anything as stupid as that.'

'When this is all over, I'll ask him,' I say.

'Well, you can't ask him now anyway. Betterton says he's already left town.'

'To avoid the trial? A guilty conscience?'

'Soon,' says Aminta, 'we'll know exactly how culpable he is.'

Chapter Twenty-Seven

In which we meet Lord Chief Justice Scroggs

Westminster Hall is packed. Even the jury box is full of people who clearly have no business there and who are threatened with fines of a hundred pounds each if they do not make way for the proper jurors. They leave with very bad grace but their purses intact.

The dense fog, which again shrouds London, has also found its way into places that it should not be. Looking up at the great hammer-beamed roof, I can see a brownish miasma swirling and half obscuring the upper part of the hall. A lyric poet might fancifully make out Godfrey's face staring down from it, but I have only a hard-headed writer of comedies beside me.

The prisoners are delivered in chains and in the same clothes that they have been wearing since they were arrested. But they seem happy enough with the general state of affairs. The witnesses that they had hoped to see are all there, mainly courtesy of Aminta and Mistress Hill. The men still believe that justice will triumph, and I still hope it will.

The court contains the very cream of the judiciary. Lord Chief Justice Scroggs is flanked by Mister Justice Dolben, Mister Justice Wild and Sir George Jeffreys, the newly appointed Recorder of London. Jeffreys is in his early thirties, smooth-faced and very pleased with himself. Sir William Jones, the Attorney General, will lead the prosecution. He has Solicitor General Winnington to assist him. Nobody at all will speak for the accused men, though they can speak for themselves if they are brave enough. The purpose of this hearing is not to consider whether they might be innocent, but to demonstrate publicly the many ways in which they are culpable. Acquittals at trials like this one are rare, but we are praying that this will be one of those memorable occasions. We have set in place everything that we can. And the men are, after all, not guilty of killing Godfrey. Williamson says so.

'I'm glad,' says Aminta, 'that I'm not up before Scroggs. He's a bit too full of himself and a bit too empty of other, nicer things.'

Scroggs is closer to sixty than to fifty, large and red-nosed. You only have to glance at him to guess rightly that he is one of the King's boon companions. He can drink anyone except Chiffinch under the table and the court knows it and respects him for it. He's waited a while to become Lord Chief Justice. He thought that he might perhaps be overlooked, but now he's here, exactly where he feels he should be. He surveys the hall with a proprietorial half-smile. This is not just his court. It is his stage, his theatre of justice. For the next few hours he will play the role of the genial and learned judge. The prisoners are his supporting actors, who will get a few lines when their time comes. He is already looking forward to the applause at the end, when he gives judgement.

Scroggs bows to the Attorney General, who bows back and then bows to the other judges, who bow in turn to the Attorney General's assistant, who bows to everyone. It is all very courteous and civilised. Who would not wish to be tried in a court in which people show so much respect for each other?

The jury are sworn in. The prisoners are asked if they have any objections. They do not. What would happen if they did? They have no idea. Nobody has explained. Best keep quiet. Scroggs smiles at them in a fatherly manner and invites the Attorney General to begin.

'May it please your Lordship,' he says, 'and you gentlemen of the jury, the prisoners who stand now at the bar are indicted for murder. Murder, as it is the first, so it is the greatest crime that is prohibited in the Second Table. It is a crime of so deep a stain that nothing can wash it away but the blood of the offender; and unless that be done, the land in which it is shed will continue to be polluted.'

I look at Green, Berry and Hill, the prisoners at the bar. They are frowning and wondering, as well they might, what the Second Table is and how it concerns them. The jury too are scratching their heads, and probably not for the last time.

The Attorney General turns to matters that are easier to understand without a copy of the Old Testament to hand. He is now outlining the main acts in the drama before us – Hill's alleged visit to Hartshorne Lane, to which Williamson referred, the decoying of Godfrey to Somerset House by Hill and Gerald, the murder, the concealment of the body in a small room and its transfer to Primrose Hill by sedan chair and horse.

'It would seem that Prance's version of events is to be preferred over Bedloe's,' says Aminta. 'That's helpful to know.'

'Then all the men have to do is to show that Prance perjured himself and we're home and dry,' I say. 'It would have been harder if they'd dropped Prance in favour of Bedloe and some new knight of the post.'

Oates is called. He really has come a long way since Ben dragged him into my dining room for me to try him for theft. He is like a magnificent ship, entering its home port at the end of a long but prosperous voyage, its black silk sails billowing and its rose-coloured flags flying gallantly. He swears his oath as if he were giving an Easter sermon before the King. Of course, what follows will be a string of lies – everyone including Scroggs knows that – but they will be well delivered and easy on the ear. The very best of lies. Oates catches sight of me for a moment and smiles. Very soon I'm going to regret turning down his thrice-made offer.

Oates makes no claim to have witnessed the murder himself. He restricts himself, wisely, to saying that Godfrey had confided in him his fear that the popish party would murder him. Oates is also pleased to confirm that Godfrey reported being dogged earlier that week, exactly as Prance had said he was. That seems to be that. Still, you couldn't have a trial of this importance without Oates putting in an appearance.

Another witness is called, who also says that Godfrey was in fear of his life. Some of the jurors are already yawning. So far there is nothing to trouble the prisoners. Anyone in London might have killed Sir Edmund Berry Godfrey. Then Prance's name is announced and for the first time there is almost complete silence in the hall.

I can tell at once that he is going to be a good witness – the sort of witness you'd like for your own client. He is self-assured but at the same time shows great respect for the judges and the court.

Everything he says seems carefully considered. He describes how he was approached by Gerald, Kelly and Green at the Plough Alehouse.

Jeffreys, the youngest of the judges present, has been lounging in his seat in a way that suggests he would rather be somewhere else, but he now looks up as if things have finally got interesting.

'Gerald and Kelly? Pray, who are they, Mister Prance? They are not in court today, I believe.'

'They are two priests, my Lord. Jesuits. And they said killing was no sin. It was a charitable act.'

'Where was it they said this?'

'They said it at the Plough, by the waterside.'

One or two of the jury nod to each other. The Plough is by the waterside, sure enough. Prance is telling the truth.

They move on to the twelfth of October. Was Godfrey dogged?

Prance is happy to oblige on this. 'On Saturday morning Mister Kelly came to give me notice that they were to go abroad to dog Sir Edmund. And afterwards they told me that Hill went to the house and asked for him.'

Hill has been growing more and more agitated during this account. He knows he needs to ask a question that will disprove Prance's account, but what should he ask?

'What time was that in the morning?' he blurts out from the dock.

'It was about nine or ten o'clock in the morning,' Prance replies very politely.

The jury nods. That's good enough for them. Not a moment's hesitation. Mister Prance knows his stuff. Jeffreys also sagely nods, as if Prance has introduced an important piece of evidence, and makes a brief note in a neat, clear hand.

Hill looks round the court. That question, in front of all these people, clearly took more effort and courage to ask than he ever knew he had, but it has got him nowhere. Nowhere at all. Was it the wrong question or was it the right question asked the wrong way or, worst of all, was it the wrong question asked the wrong way? How can he possibly tell which? He's never been in a place like this before, where everyone hates him and wants him dead.

But things have already moved on. Prance is describing how Hill and Gerald followed Godfrey all day, and how Godfrey was eventually lured into Somerset House, while he himself was dining at an inn with some companions. He continues to be a master of detail.

'What had you for dinner?' asks the Attorney General.

'We had a barrel of oysters and a dish of fish. I bought the fish myself.'

Again the jury look at each other. There's no problem with Prance's memory, then. And he paid for the fish. All of it. They'd like to go and have dinner with a man like that.

I too am impressed. I've seen Prance's testimony to the Privy Council and his evidence now matches it word for word. There are no hesitations today over whether he was buying or selling wood or the names of the priests. He has a pat answer for everything. Somebody has coached him well. Somebody who wants to make sure Scroggs can convict with a clear conscience.

There is something else the Attorney General apparently wishes to know. He is confident Prance will have the answer.

'I would now ask you a question,' he says, 'which, though it does not prove the persons guilty, yet it gives a great strength to the evidence. Do you know Mister Bedloe, Mister Prance?'

Prance looks vaguely round him. Bedloe raises a helpful hand and waggles his fingers.

'I do not know him,' says Prance apologetically. He clearly wishes he'd met him before. If only he'd known that would help us, he'd have gone out of his way to make Bedloe's acquaintance. But unfortunately he must tell the truth. He doesn't know Bedloe. Not even a bit. He's sorry but there it is.

'Had you ever any conference with him before you were committed to prison?'

I think Prance shudders slightly at the word 'prison', but he answers assuredly enough: 'Never in my life.'

The jury look at each other. Two independent witnesses then, who cannot have conferred.

Jeffreys smiles at the prisoners and invites them to cross-examine Prance. I wouldn't mind doing so myself. I might even mention his membership of the club at Primrose Hill, if only to throw him off his balance for a moment and make the jury wonder what else there might be in his past. But this time Hill fires a question that hits the target in the centre.

'My Lord, in the first place, I humbly pray that Mister Prance's evidence may not stand good against me, as being perjured by his own confession.'

Scroggs is suddenly alert to danger. He must have known this was a possibility but it seems to have caught him off-guard. 'Perjured? How?' he demands.

'I suppose, my Lord, that it is not unknown to you that he made an open confession before the King?'

Scroggs smiles genially. He is going to be helpful to the prisoner. 'Yes, he accused you *upon oath*. But afterwards, you say, he confessed it was not true – yet that confession that it was not true was *not upon oath*. How then is he guilty of perjury?'

The stone floor under Hill's feet has just given way. He thought he was on firm ground, but he wasn't. Has he just explained things the wrong way again?

'My Lord, if a man can swear a thing and afterwards deny it, he is certainly perjured?'

'Not if he has great horrors of conscience upon him and is full of fears, and the guilt of such a thing disorders his mind so as to make him go back to what he had before spoken upon oath – you can't say that man was perjured.'

Hill stands for a moment open-mouthed. By what legal sleight of hand has Prance been shown not to have committed perjury, when he clearly has?

Dolben kindly asks if Hill has any other questions.

Hill decides that the best thing is to ask Prance again what time he's claiming he visited Hartshorne Lane. Prance replies more politely than ever that it was nine or ten o'clock, but that he cannot be certain exactly. Scroggs nods approvingly. 'A man cannot be precise as to the hour.'

'My Lord,' says Hill, "tis all false that he says, and I deny every word of it, and I hope it shall not be good against me.'

Scroggs makes no commitment one way or the other. Instead he invites questions from Berry. Berry tries to disprove a remark, made in passing, that Prance had seen Berry at an alehouse, but merely establishes that all three accused men had possibly met Prance before. The Attorney General seizes on this, stating that the men had previously denied knowing him. There is an inconclusive discussion amongst the judges as to whether the prisoners did or didn't say that. The Attorney General for some reason chooses not to follow up his point. The jury is left feeling that somebody is covering something up and that it's probably the prisoners' fault. In the meantime Captain Richardson, from

Newgate, is summoned and is persuaded to say that Prance recanted his original accusation only because he was in fear of revenge by the papists. Hill is told firmly he now has the answer to his question. No more about that silly perjury, eh?

'It's not going very well, is it?' Aminta whispers to me.

'I've seen cases go better,' I say. 'But Chiffinch still has to give evidence. He won't be browbeaten by Scroggs. All he has to do is to confirm Prance did swear a proper oath before the King. And Prance should at least be asked whether the explanation for his denial is the one so kindly provided by Scroggs. The judge isn't here to give evidence.'

But Prance has been allowed to sidle away. Bedloe is up next. Bedloe strangely sticks to his story that Le Fevre, Walsh and Pritchard were the organisers of the murder, contrary to what Mister Prance has just told us. He adds that he was taken afterwards to view the body, and saw figures around it who might well have been the accused men. He certainly knew Berry well from previous visits to Somerset House and thought he had seen Green there.

Scroggs asks Green and Berry if that was true – would Bedloe have known them? They can scarcely deny that Bedloe might previously have seen them at the place where they habitually worked. So, they say 'yes'. Scroggs looks significantly at the jury and one or two of them make a note.

'It's still not going very well, is it?' asks Aminta. 'The sooner they call Chiffinch the better.'

Brown, the constable, gives evidence next. The body had been beaten, there was no sign of blood, no money had been taken. Scroggs reminds the jury, in the impartial way he has, that papists count theft as sin but not murder. And here we have a dead body that has not been robbed. Of course, it's not for him to tell the jury what to think.

'It must be very convenient for the papists to have only nine commandments,' says Aminta. 'I wonder why the Church of England insists on all ten.'

'It's a nice round number,' I say.

'I thought there must be a reason,' says Aminta.

Our friend Zachariah Skillarne is the next to be called. The Attorney General is particularly concerned about Godfrey's neck.

'Are you sure that his neck had been broken?'

'Yes, I am sure,' says Skillarne.

'Because some have been of the opinion that he hanged himself and that his relations, to save the estate, ran him through. I would desire to ask the surgeon what he thinks of it.'

'Sir, there was more done to his neck than ordinary suffocation or hanging.'

'We are all in agreement on that, at least,' says Aminta.

'It doesn't prove who killed Godfrey, of course, just that we have ruled out suicide. Nothing, except the plausible but perjured evidence of Prance and the blatant lies of Bedloe point in any way at all to the three men.'

But then such evidence comes.

'Are we about to be stabbed in the back?' asks Aminta.

'It would seem so,' I say. 'I thought we'd paid her quite well.'

'Somebody else has paid her better,' says Aminta.

Chapter Twenty-Eight

In which Lord Chief Justice Scroggs concludes and bows out

Few of the witnesses have looked as pleased with themselves as Elizabeth Curtis does. She's actually happy to be here. Finally, somebody is going to have to listen to her.

'Look upon the prisoners,' says the Attorney General, 'and tell my Lord and the jury whether you know them or not.'

'Green,' she says. 'I didn't know his name before, but I do now. He came to the house about a fortnight before the master died. He asked for Sir Edmund Berry Godfrey.'

'At what time of day was it?' asks the Attorney General, perhaps to save Hill the trouble.

'Morning,' she says. 'When I showed him in, he said "Good morning, sir" or something of the sort in English. That's how I recall what time of day it was. Then he looked over his shoulder at me and decided he'd better speak in French. At least, I think it was French. It was no language for a Christian, anyway. I couldn't understand him. Not a word, sir. Nobody could. Unless they were French. They might understand it, I suppose.'

She makes her ignorance of foreign languages sound like a virtue. Perhaps she recalls that a knowledge of French did Coleman no good at all.

'I never saw you before in my life,' says Green.

'Yes you have,' says Mistress Curtis.

There is a buzz around the great, echoing hall. There's not much doubt who the crowd believe and it's not Green.

'Are you sure?' asks the Attorney General.

'Of course I'm sure. I wouldn't say it if I wasn't, would I? And that man . . .' She points at Hill. 'That man was there on the Saturday morning that my master disappeared. He brought him a message.'

'Will you deny that?' Scroggs asks Hill.

'Yes, I do,' says Hill.

'Then you are wrong, Mister Hill,' says Mistress Curtis. 'I was in the parlour making the fire, sir, when Mister Hill called. I'd just carried in the master's breakfast, and so I showed Mister Hill in to him. But, a little later, I realised I had left my keys on the parlour table, so I came down again and noticed Hill was still there, so they must have had quite a long conversation. I couldn't say what, because I don't listen at doors. Unlike some people I could mention here but won't. Luckily for them. But I cannot believe Mister Hill can have forgotten his visit entirely.'

'Did you see him again?'

'Not until I caught sight of him in Newgate about a month ago. But he isn't the man who brought the note to my master on the Friday. That was somebody else entirely.'

'Was it one of the prisoners at the bar?'

'Oh no, sir. It was a very respectable gentleman. He stayed some time waiting for an answer but my master was unable to give him one.'

She frowns. She is trying to recall, just as I am still wondering, to whom the answer was sent. A common enough name, she said.

'Well, if it wasn't one of the prisoners who delivered the message, I don't think that it need concern us. But you are sure it was Hill on the Saturday morning?'

'He was wearing the same clothes that he is wearing now.'

'Have you ever shifted your clothes?' asks Scroggs.

'No, indeed I have not,' says Hill. 'But in Newgate she said she didn't recognise me.'

'Well, I do now,' says Mistress Curtis. 'And that's all there is to it.'

There is another hum in the room. This is the sort of evidence that they like. Plenty of circumstantial detail – the breakfast, the keys on the parlour table and above all the suspicious discussion in French. Certainly Mistress Curtis's refusal to be cowed in any way stands very much in her favour.

'What are we to make of all that?' asks Aminta. 'Has Curtis been got at?'

'Maybe Hill really was Saturday's messenger,' I say. 'But it still proves very little. It wasn't the message that killed Godfrey – not directly, anyway.'

'And Green?'

'There's no reason why he shouldn't have brought a message from Coleman earlier and indeed conversed with Godfrey in French if they thought Elizabeth Curtis was listening in. Somebody should have asked Green if he really does speak French. But, either way, it proves nothing about Godfrey's murder.'

'Let's hope the jury agrees with you.'

*

There is a short interlude, almost as if the court wishes to give us time to digest the information we have so far received. A man named Thomas Stringer is called to testify that Berry had issued an order that on the twelfth, thirteenth and fourteenth of October nobody was to be admitted to the Queen's apartments at Somerset House, which meant that Prance himself had been unable to gain admission. Stringer implies that this was in some way underhand and that it shows the body was being concealed there and that the order was made simply to keep people away. Berry cannot deny the order was issued – he merely says that it was not unusual.

'Who is that witness?' I ask.

'Stringer? I think he's Shaftesbury's steward,' says Aminta.

'Not an unbiased witness, then,' I say. 'But would the jury know that?'

'Not unless somebody tells them,' says Aminta. 'But it does sound as if the order was issued. Did Berry mention it to you?'

'No,' I say. 'But again, why should he?'

Stringer is sent on his way, presumably back to the Earl of Shaftesbury. In the meantime, the idea that a body might have been concealed by the Catholic Queen Consort hangs in the air. So does the idea that Berry has somehow withheld this evidence from the court, until tricked into confessing it. The jury already knows that Catholics do not regard murder as a sin. They clearly don't regard bearing false witness as a sin either.

Finally, the time has come to hear from the defence witnesses. They will not be sworn in, unlike the prosecution ones. Their evidence will not have the same status. They are very much here on sufferance.

Young Mary Tilden is the first. She testifies that Hill has been a servant of the family for seven or eight years. He was never out of the house after eight o'clock. She remembers clearly that on the night of the twelfth of October Hill was home all evening. She looks up at Scroggs, hoping to be released.

'What religion are you of?' Scroggs asks.

'Religion, sir?'

'Are you a papist, woman?'

She gives a nervous laugh. 'I know not whether I came here to make a profession of my faith,' she says.

'Are you a Roman Catholic? Yes or no?'

'Yes,' she says.

The jury exchange knowing glances. She tried to conceal it, but Scroggs has got her to admit it. You can't trust anything these Catholics say.

'I hope you didn't keep Mister Hill company *all night* after supper,' adds Jeffreys.

Mary Tilden looks from Jeffreys to Scroggs and back again. She is aware she is being mocked but she is not sure in what way. Is Jeffreys implying some improper relationship between her and Hill? She is confused and embarrassed but still does her best. 'No, I did not, sir – but he came in to wait at the table at supper, if that's what you mean. And I can say he was never abroad after eight at night.'

'You at least watched him until he went to bed then,' says Jeffreys, determined not to let his little joke go.

'I beg your pardon but if your Lordship saw the lodging you would say it were impossible for any to go in or out but that we must know. Our doors were never opened after supper.'

Scroggs mutters that, being a papist, she probably thinks she can say anything to a heretic. But she has made her point as clearly as anyone could.

'Well done, Mistress Tilden,' whispers Aminta beside me.

But then things fall apart. Prance intervenes that Hill could have obtained a key and gone out later. He happens to know there were plenty of spare keys. He is asked to clarify what time the body was moved. He says he knows that Hill went to fetch the horse at about ten or eleven.

Mistress Tilden is incensed at this string of lies. 'We had never been out of our lodgings – never after eight o'clock since we came to town.'

'Came to town? When were you out of town?' enquires Mister Justice Dolben.

'In October,' says Mary Tilden, turning toward her new inquisitor. Then she pauses. She can see that will invite other questions. Awkward questions.

'Nay now, Mistress,' says Dolben, 'now you have spoiled all, for in October this business was done. And you say you were not even in London then.'

It is in vain that Mistress Broadstreet intervenes to say that the family was out of town in September and returned at the very end of the month, just before Michaelmas Day. They were all there on the twelfth of October. Young Mistress Mary has simply got her dates mixed up. But it is too late. The jury can see the Catholics are up to their old tricks again.

Mistress Broadstreet is called to give evidence in her own right. At least she won't make silly mistakes about dates.

'Well, woman, what say you?' Scroggs demands.

Mistress Broadstreet takes a deep breath. 'We came to town upon a Monday. Michaelmas Day was the Sunday following. And from that time neither Hill nor the maid used to be abroad after eight o'clock. Hill always waited on us at supper and never went out after that. And the lodging was so little that nothing could be brought in but that we must know about it.'

The jury look at each other. That's pretty clear. They were there at the right time after all. Maybe it was just a slip of the tongue on Mary's part. Mistress Broadstreet seems very respectable and very sure of herself. And young girls are very unreliable. The men of the jury all know that.

Then things start to unravel for Mistress Broadstreet too.

'Your brother, Mistress Broadstreet,' says the Attorney General, 'he is a priest, is he not?'

'I have a brother whose name is Broadstreet,' she replies cautiously.

'And he is a priest, isn't he? Answer me, woman.'

'I hope I must not impeach my brother here. But about the other matter, I said on my oath that Lawrence Hill was with us all that evening and didn't go away until a few days after ...'

'Have you any more to say?' asks Scroggs, as if suddenly bored by this witness.

Mistress Broadstreet shakes her head and welcomes the opportunity to stand down.

So, there it is. They're all lying Catholics with priests in the family. The prisoners' first line of defence has had a massive hole smashed through the middle of it.

The second line unfortunately scarcely exists at all. Green calls his landlord, James Warrier, and his wife, Avis Warrier, to give evidence. Aminta has already told me not to expect much from them.

'I will say,' says James Warrier, 'that on the twelfth of October, Green was at my house, half an hour after seven, and he was not out of my house until ten.'

This is a good start, but then comes the cross-examination. How did he remember the date?

'I recollected my memory,' he says.

'But how?'

'By my work and everything exactly,' he replies.

'When did you remember this?'

'A pretty while ago.'

'But you still don't say how.'

'By my work.'

Captain Richardson intervenes to say that Warrier had previously said to him that nothing he could recall would do Green any good.

Warrier is able to answer that at least. 'Ah, but I did not then call it to memory,' he says.

'So, when did you call it to memory?' asks Scroggs.

'I did say, I could not do it then, as I have done since, in five or six days.' Warrier nods two or three times and looks up at Scroggs. Surely that's clear enough now?

The Lord Chief Justice makes one last attempt to establish which of them is sane. 'How could you recall it, Mister Warrier?'

'I can tell by a great many tokens. He was but fourteen or fifteen days in our house. But I never knew the man out after nine o'clock *in my life*.'

Scroggs turns to Green. 'Have you anybody else?' he asks. 'Anybody at all?'

Mistress Warrier quickly replaces her husband.

'She can't be any worse,' I say.

'She can,' whispers Aminta. 'Don't forget I spoke to her. The less she says the better.'

'I did not at all remember the day of the month at first nor the action. But my husband and I have since remembered,' she says with great confidence. 'We were desired by Mister and Mistress Green to eat fowl with them and my husband did command me the Sunday after to invite them to eat dinner with us. So, I went in the morning early, I think, and bought a dozen pigeons and put them in a pie and we had a loin of pork roasted as well. And when Mister Green was gone to the chapel Saturday in the afternoon, his wife came to me and said, "My husband is not well and when he comes home he will ask me to make him something of broth", and so away she went to market to buy something to make broth of. Well, while she was at market her husband came home and asked where his wife was. "Why Mister Green", said I, "she is gone to market". "What an old fool!" said he, "is this, to go out so late on such a night as this is! But I will go to the coffee house and drink a dish of coffee and pray tell my wife so". In the meantime, she – Mistress Green – returned and by the time she had been in a while, *Mister* Green came in and called to his wife for vittles. And she brings down some bread and cheese, and they stayed there a while till it was nine o'clock.'

'When was this?' asks Scroggs, when he can finally get a word in.

'It was the Saturday fortnight after Michaelmas Day.'

'The nineteenth of October?'

'Yes.'

'Sir Edmund was killed on the twelfth,' he says.

Mistress Warrier is stood down. Nobody feels it necessary to trick her into admitting she is a Catholic.

Berry calls Corporal William Collett and Troopers Nicholas Trollop, Nicholas Wright and Gabriel Hasket. They are large men in slightly faded red coats and buff-coloured breeches. White scarves are tied loosely and not inelegantly round their necks. Their polished boots ring on the stone floor as they march into position. They survey the motley collection of civilians in front of them and decide they've seen off better men than us.

Collett explains how Somerset House was guarded on the Wednesday night when the sedan chair supposedly left with Godfrey's body in it. He remembers it well because it was the day that the Queen went from Somerset House to Whitehall. The Queen, her ladies in waiting, her maids of honour, sweeping into the Strand in their coaches. He wouldn't have forgotten that. Trollop guarded the gate from seven until ten, Wright from ten until one, Hasket from one until four. The jury are scribbling furiously.

'And where did you place them?' asks Scroggs.

'To the strand-ward.'

'The gate they carried Sir Edmund out by?'

'There was no sedan came out in my time, sir,' says Wright.

'Nor in mine,' says Trollop. 'There was one went in, but none came out.'

'Was it an empty sedan that went in?' asks Scroggs.

'I suppose so, but we had no orders to keep any out.'

'If any sedan came out, would you have stopped it?' asks Scroggs.

'No, my Lord. We had no orders to stop any,' says Trollop.

Cannonballs may be whistling overhead, but the four soldiers know they are harmless. The enemy gunners' range is hopelessly wrong. They just have to stand firm and let them run out of ammunition.

Mister Justice Wild, who has played a relatively minor role so far, has a query though. 'Let me ask you but one question – did you go to drink or tipple in that time?'

Trollop looks straight ahead, his face completely expressionless. 'No, sir. Nor walk a pike's length off the place of sentry.'

'Is there not an alehouse close by?'

'Yes, but I did not drink one drop.'

'How can you possibly remember that, after all this time?'

'You are not the first to ask. I was twice before the committee.'

'We were all examined by the Commons committee long ago,' says Collett, stepping in as the only officer present, 'when it was fresh in our memories, sir. That's why we know now. We'll all tell you exactly the same.'

The other soldiers nod. Their stories will most certainly be identical to their corporal's story.

'What day of the month was it, Corporal?' asks Scroggs.

'Sixteenth, sir.'

'What day of the week?'

'Wednesday, sir.'

'Did you see Berry at all that evening?'

'No, sir. Nor on the Saturday before, sir.'

The soldiers are sent off, doubtless planning to make up for their total abstinence on the evening of the sixteenth of October.

But Berry has another excellent witness up his sleeve. Elizabeth Minshaw, the maid at Berry's house, testifies that on the sixteenth, the afternoon that the Queen left, he was playing bowls until dusk and then remained in the house all night – a fact that she knows because to get to his bedroom he had to pass through hers. He could have played no part that night in removing a body by sedan chair.

Mistress Hill feels that things have turned in the right direction and that this is the moment to go on to the attack. Why, she demands, did Prance withdraw his accusations before the King? Of course, Scroggs has given his view and Richardson has given his. But she wants to know what Prance has to say.

'It was because of my trade,' says Prance, quickly standing up, 'and fear of losing my employment from the Queen and the Catholics, which was most of my business.'

'I desire,' says Mistress Hill, 'that he may swear whether or not he was tortured.'

Torture has of course long since been outlawed, but Scroggs is not scandalised. 'Were you tortured?' he asks Prance in a matter-of-fact way.

'No, my Lord,' says Prance. 'Captain Richardson has used me as civilly as any man in England. All the time I have been there I have wanted for nothing.'

Except possibly a bed and blankets and a fire, but perhaps he has forgotten his time in Little Ease.

'He knows all these things to be false, as God is true,' says Mistress Hill. 'And you will see it declared hereafter, when it is too late.'

Glances are exchanged amongst the spectators. The words feel strangely prophetic. But Scroggs is unmoved.

'Do you think he would swear three men out of their lives for nothing?' he asks in a very reasonable manner.

Well, maybe not for nothing. He'll doubtless have been promised some share of the reward.

Mistress Hill remains unhappy. 'Well, I am dissatisfied,' she says. 'My witnesses were not rightly examined. They were modest, and the court laughed at them.'

But, fortunately, one witness remains to give evidence. I would not dare call him modest and it would be a brave man who laughed at him.

Most of the witnesses today would have rather not been here, but nobody shows that as clearly as William Chiffinch. His wrinkled face scowls at the court from under his black periwig and at Scroggs above all.

'You are William Chiffinch?' asks Scroggs. 'You are His Majesty's Page of the Bedchamber?'

'If you don't know that, Scroggs, your memory must be failing,' says Chiffinch. 'Do you wish to swear me in?'

'That won't be necessary,' says the Lord Chief Justice, undeterred. 'I think this court has only one question for you, Mister Chiffinch. Were you present when Mister Prance spoke to the King about his declaration?'

'Yes,' says Chiffinch. 'Is that all?'

'Mister Chiffinch,' says Jeffreys, 'can you tell us whether Mister Prance completely withdrew his earlier statement concerning the murder of Sir Edmund?'

'I can confirm that he did,' says Chiffinch. 'He revoked it utterly.'

'Did he say why?'

'He said that he had been persuaded to make the declaration against his will. He now wished to tell the truth. That did not seem unreasonable.'

'Perhaps you could clarify one other point for us. It has been alleged that Mister Prance was tortured. Can you shed any light on that?'

'He didn't mention it if he had been. I think most people probably would.'

'Was Mister Prance under oath when he spoke to the King?' asks Jeffreys.

'He swore on his life to His Majesty that what he said was true. I would have said that when a man does that before his rightful sovereign it was as solemn an affair as needs be and as binding on him as any other oath he might take in his entire life.'

Jeffreys turns to Scroggs and raises his eyebrows.

'But was the oath formally administered, Mister Chiffinch?' says Scroggs. 'Did he swear on a Bible, for example?'

'The King does not leave Bibles lying around for any fool to make his oath on.'

'So, he was no more sworn than you are?' says Scroggs.

'You are the lawyer, my Lord. Perhaps you would like to tell me?'

'Exactly. I am the lawyer. And you are not, Mister Chiffinch, and never shall be.'

'I have never had any desire to be one, my Lord. I have told you all I can. Prance's was a solemn oath, made freely, but not on a book of any sort. Is this at an end?'

'Unless any of the prisoners has a question for you.'

Scroggs looks at them. Mistress Hill seems to be about to put up her hand, but Scroggs quickly nods at Chiffinch, who turns on his heel and departs.

'Well, he did all he could,' says Aminta. 'He wasn't going to lie and say the King whipped out a Bible from beneath his robes and got Prance to place his right hand on the cover.'

'Scroggs would have found fault even with that,' I say. 'He'd have asked if Chiffinch could tell him the exact form of words used or something equally impossible to recall. He knows that Prance's evidence has to stand or the whole case collapses. That was the men's last chance and it has just walked out of the building with its feathers much ruffled.'

There is little left to do, but the Attorney General and the Solicitor General need to sum up for the Crown. They both make good speeches, but it is Scroggs, the man who will shortly decide which side has made the better case, who delivers the key speech for the prosecution. The jury, he tells us, should believe

Prance in every particular. 'There is not any one thing that is not backed up in one particular circumstance or other. And it is no argument against Mister Prance in the world that he should not be believed because he was a party to the murder, or because he afterwards denied what he first said. First, because you can have nobody to discover such a fact except one who was privy to it: so that we can have no evidence but what arises from a party to a crime. And in the next place, his denial, after he confessed it, to me does not sound as an act of falsehood but of fear. How short was his denial and how quick was his recantation!'

Scroggs points out, fairly, how insubstantial most of the case for the defence has been. He praises the soldiers but begs the jury to conclude that, in the darkness, they could be honestly mistaken about the sedan chair, even if they were sober. He hopes that we shall all soon be delivered from the delusions of popery and the tyranny of the Pope. He leaves the final decision entirely to the jury, in the certainty that they will do like honest men.

The jury retire. They take only slightly longer than my jury did in the inn at Clavershall West. The verdict is guilty. The following day all three are sentenced to hang. The court finally bursts into the long-awaited applause. Scroggs smiles modestly.

The curtain falls on the tragedy of Green, Berry and Hill.

Chapter Twenty-Nine

In which we have an audience with His Majesty

The judges have departed in their scarlet robes. The prisoners have been whisked away to live out their remaining hours in the twilight of Newgate. For the rest of us, getting out of Westminster Hall is a slow process, as the great crowd shuffles towards the ochre fog that is already flooding in through the massive, arched doorway.

'What now?' asks Aminta, above the coughing of Scroggs's departing audience.

'If the witnesses are to be believed,' I say, 'and I have no reason to think otherwise, then Green and Hill all have good alibis for the night of the twelfth of October, which is when Skillarne says Godfrey died. The soldiers say they saw nothing of Berry that night. Berry also has an alibi for Wednesday the sixteenth, when the body is supposed to have left the palace. In a court that based its conclusions on the evidence of witnesses, that should be enough. I am more inclined to doubt the testimony of the soldiers, at least when they say they took no strong drink all evening, but it would require a better man than Scroggs to get them to admit it. Still, if there was no murder at Somerset House, then we need not worry too much about how the body was taken out.'

'I think I do believe Mistress Curtis when she says that Hill was the messenger.'

'She was very certain. But that doesn't make him a murderer.'

'In that case, he might have admitted taking the message,' says Aminta. 'I mean, if he knew the message was harmless or, more likely, had no idea what the message was.'

'He wouldn't have had much time to think about his answer and knew Scroggs was seeking the worst possible interpretation on everything, just as Jeffreys did with Mistress Tilden. I can understand why he panicked and lied.'

'Chiffinch did his best,' says Aminta. 'Or, at least, as much as we could have expected him to do. He testified with reluctance, but Scroggs was obliged to accept everything he said.'

'Having listened to Chiffinch, no reasonable judge would claim that what Prance did wasn't perjury. Conversely, no reasonable court would have believed a word that Prance or Bedloe said, and it is their testimony that has convicted them. We have three innocent men who are about to be hanged.'

'Is there no hope at all?' asks Aminta.

'There is always hope. The King can still pardon them.'

'Then let us go and see the King.'

'Will he see us?' I ask.

'If we don't go, we'll never find out.'

The foggy walk to the King's apartments at Whitehall Palace could not be much shorter. Once through the wicket gate, we ask to be taken to Chiffinch.

'There was nothing to be done for them,' he says. 'But you knew that.'

'Thank you nevertheless for giving evidence, Mister Chiffinch,' says Aminta.

'I gave evidence as much against Scroggs as for the men,' he says. 'He's a drunken fool with no concern about anything but his own advancement. I should have liked to see them go free for that reason alone. I understand your desire to free them less than Scroggs's desire to convict, but doubtless you have your reasons.'

He looks at me as if trying to discover what I really think. What I really mean. In Chiffinch's world, saying what you really think is unusual and often dangerous. He's sure I wouldn't be stupid enough to do it.

'We hoped we could speak to His Majesty and beg him to pardon the men,' says Aminta.

'In spite of the court's verdict?' he says.

'Because of it, clearly,' I say.

'But all the same . . . What are three Catholics like that to you?'

'Berry is a Protestant,' I say. 'Apparently.'

Chiffinch finally smiles. 'You're wasting your time. He won't do it.'

'If it can be arranged, we'd like an audience nonetheless,' says Aminta.

'Much though he admires your plays, my Lady . . .'

'Then please remind His Majesty that my father, Sir Felix Clifford, and I served him loyally in Brussels twenty years ago,' says Aminta. 'And that my husband has also shed a certain amount of blood in his service.'

'He has a short memory,' says Chiffinch. 'Especially for debts. But I'll mention it by all means.'

*

We are kept waiting half an hour. The King has aged since I saw him last. His eyebrows remain as dark and thick as ever and his periwig is black and glossy. But there is much grey in his stubble, his eyes are more hollow and his cheeks more sunken. For the moment too, the cynical smile is missing from his lips. His expression suggests that Chiffinch has explained our mission and that the King doubts he can help us very much. His spaniels doubt it too. They lie at his feet and regard us with polite indifference.

Chiffinch stays in the room, a cross between a shrivelled cherub and guardian angel. He's seen a lot over the years. Nothing anyone says now is going to surprise him. Still, he may as well hear it, just in case.

The King begins by asking after Sir Felix. He hopes he's well. He asks Aminta what play she is working on. He promises to come and see it. Perhaps with the Queen. Perhaps with the Duchess of Portsmouth. Perhaps with somebody else. He enquires whether the winter has been a cold one in Essex. I say it has. He does not seem surprised.

'There is little I can do to help you over the matter of the three men, however,' he adds. 'I may as well tell you that now. I'm sorry, but there it is.'

'They are innocent, Your Majesty,' says Aminta.

'Why do you believe they did not kill Godfrey?' he asks. 'Scroggs says they did. He's Lord Chief Justice. He's paid to know these things.'

'The evidence rests entirely on Prance's information, which you yourself know to be untrue,' I say.

The King turns to his Page of the Bedchamber. 'Is that right, Mister Chiffinch? Is that what I know?'

'Prance is a rogue,' says Chiffinch. 'Almost as much of a rogue as my Lord Shaftesbury. Shaftesbury's man of business gave evidence, by the way, I assume at his master's bidding.'

'To what end?' asks the King.

'I think to remind the court that Her Majesty was present at Somerset House at the time when Godfrey was killed, and that her orders prevented the place being searched properly. Throw enough mud and it will stick.'

'So are the three men murderers, Mister Chiffinch? You clearly heard the evidence.'

'It doesn't matter what I think,' says Chiffinch. 'Scroggs declared them guilty. The court applauded him. So, there's no doubt what your subjects believe. There's no doubt what Parliament believes either. Or Doctor Oates. If you want to try to make them all think differently, you'll need to consider the consequences. I mean the usual ones.'

'And there you have it,' the King says. 'However innocent I thought the men were, my hands are tied. I dare not pardon any Catholic, lest Parliament suspects I do so because I too am secretly a Catholic. Which, purely for the record, I am not. My brother wished me to save Coleman. I couldn't do it. Not for any money. I probably won't be able to save Petre either. I won't let them touch the Duke. I won't let them touch the Queen. I won't let them touch the Duchess of Portsmouth. I'll try to keep them away from the Duchess of York if I can. And I'll bring down anyone who stands in my way. I am sorry for the three men, and for their families, but there it is. Have you tried appealing to Doctor Oates? He seems to have the power to do many things that I cannot.'

'I don't think he claims regal powers in addition to his episcopal ones,' I say. 'Anyway, when I last enquired, the price of his help was higher than I could afford.'

'Well, that's that, then. I hope you now feel that you have at least done your best.'

'Thank you, Your Majesty,' I say.

'Please give my warmest greetings to Sir Felix,' he says.

Chiffinch ushers us towards the door. We turn to thank him but he has already vanished. It's a trick that he has, never to be in any one place longer than he needs to be.

Elizabeth Curtis is waiting for us when we return to our lodgings. She has been there an hour, according to our own maid. She looks quite pleased with herself, but then most of the witnesses must be feeling relieved that their ordeal in front of Scroggs is over.

'I hope you didn't mind, sir, my giving evidence. Against Mister Hill, I mean. But it was the truth. He did bring the message in Saturday.'

'You are absolutely sure?' I ask.

'Yes,' she says. 'I thought it was him when I saw him at Newgate. But when I heard his voice, I was certain. That was him.'

'He denied it,' I say.

'Well, sir, we're all going to die, and no Christian fears death, but none of us wants to die next Monday, do we?'

'It doesn't mean he killed your master,' I say.

'Of course not, sir. I never said he did.'

There is a long pause.

'Is that all?' I ask.

'No sir. I wouldn't have come here just to say sorry. I mean, I'm not sorry, except that Mister Hill may hang and he seems a very pleasant gentleman. No, it was that I just remembered who the messenger on Friday was – or, at least, who sent him. The name was mentioned at the trial you see, several times, and I thought, yes, that's who it was. But my memory is so bad these days that

I decided I should come here straight away before I forgot all over again. It is a very common name, after all.'

'Which is?' I ask.

'Williamson,' she says. 'He was sent by Sir Joseph Williamson.'

The rumour that Williamson has left London proves to be correct. His servants seem strangely unable to say where he might be. Perhaps they are under strict instructions to be vague. I therefore go without delay to what was, until the day before yesterday, Williamson's office. I don't expect to find him there, but it is as good a place as any to learn what I should do next. Williamson's old staff are at least still in place. They make me welcome and show me into what was, for so very many years, Williamson's office.

The new occupant has as yet had little time to make changes. The Roman emperors are still there, each crowned with marble laurel wreaths. Williamson's desk still sits in the middle of it all, covered in papers.

Sunderland, now in possession of the desk, looks up. I introduce myself. He hasn't heard of me.

'So you were one of Williamson's agents?' he says.

'Not really,' I say. 'I worked for Arlington in the old days. And for John Thurloe before that – back in the fifties.'

'For the Republic?'

'Yes,' I say. 'Thurloe trained us well, though ultimately for the benefit of his royalist successor.'

'Ah,' he says.

Sunderland is much the same age as I am, but he is Secretary of State and I am merely a country magistrate. Whatever Thurloe taught me clearly hasn't done me much good.

'I congratulate you on your new appointment,' I say.

'An unexpected honour,' he says. 'And wholly unlooked for. I had not thought to rise so high.'

I do not doubt that he sees this post merely as a stepping stone to greater things. He is not noted for his modesty. And everyone says he has ability.

'I trust,' he adds, 'that you have not come here seeking work. If so, I have nothing for you at present. If you leave your name with one of the clerks, I can notify you if anything suitable becomes available.'

'I have work enough of my own,' I say.

'As a magistrate? Well, those duties are quite valuable in their own way. You should not feel, just because the tasks are repetitive and undemanding, that you are wasting your time. Far from it.'

'I rarely feel that, my Lord,' I say. 'But thank you anyway.'

'Good,' he says. 'Is there anything else I can do for you?'

'I had been hoping to speak to Sir Joseph about the Godfrey murder.'

'That would of course be impossible. The secrets of this department cannot be revealed to all and sundry.'

'He had me working on the case.'

'Did he? He said nothing about that to me, though he left quite quickly. He seemed annoyed he was being replaced by somebody more capable – and not before time. You can see the mess things are in.' He waves his arm at Titus and Vespasian. 'The earlier papers are put away in some sort of order, but the later ones might be anywhere. I found some correspondence relating to Prussian Pomerania filed under Domitian, if you can believe that! I shall institute a completely new system, based on logic and good sense. No dusty emperors. These marble busts can go to the storeroom.'

'I never quite understood why they were needed,' I say. 'The Roman numerals sufficed to indicate which cabinet was which. But Williamson liked them. There was more poetry in him than most people imagined.'

'Was there? Well, you will need to seek out Williamson if you have any questions about the work he asked you to do.'

'And where would I find him?'

'Is it an urgent matter?'

'Yes.'

'I think he was planning to leave London for a few days. Hopefully whatever you needed to ask will wait a week or two?'

'It will have to,' I say.

'You weren't expecting me to pay you for what you had done, I hope? Williamson had been quite prodigal with the very limited funds we have. He left some surprising orders for payment, that I shall have to honour. But I am sure there is nothing relating to what you say you have done.'

'No,' I say. 'I wasn't expecting to be paid. Many years of working for Arlington and Williamson have lowered my expectations, whatever I may have been promised.'

'Really? I would certainly not treat you in the same way. If we needed you. But, as I say, we don't.'

'No,' I say. 'I don't think you do.'

'I have no idea where Williamson is,' says Arlington. 'Why should he tell me? I'm nothing to him any more and he's nothing to me. I'd heard he'd gone to the country to stay with friends. Well, he has little enough to remain in London for, has he?'

'Sunderland seems competent as his replacement,' I say.

'When Sunderland was an ambassador, he upset everyone with whom he came in contact. He'll manage Parliament no better than Williamson. He'll certainly get no further with the Godfrey case – not that he'll be asked to, now they're going to hang three innocent men. Three should be enough even for Oates.'

'Chiffinch seemed less convinced of their innocence than we are,' I say. 'Though Chiffinch gives little away.'

'Chiffinch is the greatest cynic at the court. He thinks everyone is as crooked as he is. He takes it for granted that everyone is lying all the time.'

'Do you think he knows something that we don't?' I ask.

'Chiffinch always knows something we don't,' says Arlington. 'That's his job.'

I pay the men one final visit. We all know that we shall not be meeting again.

'You did your best, sir,' says Hill.

'I know that you did not kill Godfrey,' I say. 'And one day everyone will know that. The history books will record that you were innocent.'

'You think somebody will write a book about us, sir? That sounds unlikely.'

'Stranger things have happened,' I say.

'I doubt that history will remember us at all,' says Green. 'But you're right, sir. We killed nobody. I swear that to you as one who is about to meet his maker, none of us strangled Sir Edmund Berry Godfrey. When Saint Peter greets me at the famous Gates, he will not have murder set against me in his great book – other sins, of course, because we are all sinners, but not that.'

Berry nods. 'And the Duke will look after our families, sir. They will not starve. He has promised that.'

'Don't pity us, sir,' says Hill. 'We were convicted only because of our faith. We die as martyrs, even that old Protestant heretic Berry.'

And Berry permits himself a brief chuckle.

'There must still be something we can do,' I say.

'Not unless the King changes his mind or Williamson returns to London,' says Aminta. 'Now the King has dismissed him, he must be free to disclose whatever it was he previously wished to keep secret.'

'The execution date has been set for Monday,' I say, 'but there are often delays. As Oates predicted, there's a rumour they will hold off Berry's execution in the hope that he names other suspects in exchange for a pardon.'

'He won't do it,' says Aminta. 'Berry's an honest man.'

'Like Coleman,' I say.

There is no reprieve. The King does not change his mind. Williamson does not return. First Green and Hill are dragged to Tyburn and hanged. Then, a few days later, so is Berry. His final words are: 'As I am innocent, so receive my soul, O Lord Jesus Christ.' A shiver goes through the crowd, a realisation that they should have done something to stop this while they could, but they have left it too late. Still, what was there anyone could have done? Oates, Prance and Scroggs held all the cards. The rest of us could only look on as the cards were turned over by hands more skilful than our own.

The day after Berry dies, I hear that Williamson has finally returned.

'It will do the three men no good,' I say, 'but I would suggest nevertheless that we visit Sir Joseph.'

'Because he knows who really killed Godfrey?'

'I think so. We now know it was his messenger who visited Godfrey on the Friday night. So, it was to Williamson that Godfrey sent his message that he didn't know what to make of it.'

'Did Williamson know all along who the murderer was?'

'No, but I do think he had finally worked it out before he was dismissed. Perhaps before Christmas.'

'So, why didn't he tell you while it was possible to save the three men?'

'Because he still needed to protect somebody or something.'

'Who or what?'

'That's what I'd like to find out,' I say.

Chapter Thirty

In which Williamson asks us some questions

Williamson looks better than he did when I last saw him. His sacking by the King has relieved him of a burden. He glances up from a shiny new copy of *The Pilgrim's Progress* as we are shown into his sitting room by his maid. He puts his book down on a table and ushers us both into cushioned chairs. I think he knows this may take some time.

'Did you go to Berry's execution?' he asks.

I nod. 'I didn't attend the first two – Hill and Green. But it seemed right I should be there at the very end of this.'

'I thought I should go,' Williamson says. 'I arrived back two days ago. I could have gone. But then . . . it's not as if I would have been attending in any official capacity. Not any more. That's Sunderland now, and I wish him joy of it. Anyway, what difference could it make to anyone? I'd have just been one of the crowd, right at the back – unless I was willing to pay a fortune to somebody with a house overlooking the scaffold to let me have a seat at their window. Berry wouldn't have noticed me either way. Did he suffer much?'

'I think the hangman ensured his neck was broken straight away. Rather like Godfrey's.'

'That will have disappointed the crowd. They like it dragged out as long as possible.'

'Maybe not on this occasion. There was a lot of talk afterwards of his innocence.'

Williamson stares at the fire. I can almost tell what he's thinking. If the Catholics ever regained power, then many of us would die in the flames. Not even Coleman doubted that.

'Berry, innocent? It depends what you mean,' he says.

'You are,' I say, 'possibly the only man in the country who knows exactly what happened and who killed Godfrey. If you're not, you're still the only person I can ask.'

Williamson gets up and pokes the coals. He places the poker carefully back on the hearth, turns and looks at me.

'You know already,' he says. 'Just think about it. You have all of the facts, John. And you, my Lady. Just think. You'll find it's obvious.'

'The problem,' I say, 'is sorting out the relevant facts from the irrelevant ones.'

'Very well, let me help you. What was Godfrey's religion? Don't look so surprised. It's a perfectly reasonable question.'

'He was a member of the Church of England,' says Aminta. 'Is that in doubt?'

'Everything is always in doubt. You know that, my Lady. The King is punctilious in his observance of the rites of the Church of England. Yet I would question whether that is the religion he will die in. And the King is the head of the Church, while

Godfrey was merely a vestryman. So, both of you, what was Godfrey's religion? What evidence do we have?'

'As you remind us, he was an active member of Saint Martin's vestry,' says Aminta.

'And Oates became a Jesuit, but tells us he remained a Protestant throughout,' says Williamson.

'Very well,' I say, 'we also know he was a member of the Peyton Gang. A Green Ribbon man.'

'So, by inclination, an extreme Protestant?'

'Precisely. We must assume those were his sympathies,' I say.

'But he was also a friend of Edward Coleman. And he was a member of a Catholic club at Primrose Hill.'

'But there's no evidence he was actually a Catholic,' says Aminta.

'True. There is no evidence he ever became a Catholic. No more than that he was an extreme Protestant at heart. Even so, those two things together must have been uncomfortable for him. A member of an extreme Protestant club and a Catholic one. He cannot have been sincere in both respects.'

'No,' I say.

'How rich was he?' asks Williamson.

'He suffered a major loss when his godson Godfrey Harrison ran his business for him,' I say. 'But people seem to agree his finances had recovered lately. It's not entirely clear how.'

'You are aware that Coleman had funds from the French King for bribing English officials?'

'Coleman admitted doing something of the sort.'

'Are you saying that Godfrey took Oates's deposition to Coleman because Coleman was paying him to do it?' asks Aminta.

Williamson smiles. 'I am saying that any reasonable man looking at Godfrey's actions would have every cause to assume that's what happened. And he spoke of his fear that he would shortly be hanged? Does that not suggest that he thought he could be in trouble with the authorities?'

'Everyone who knew him agrees on that,' says Aminta. 'Mistress Gibbon says it. So do the servants. He feared he would be hanged.'

'By the authorities?'

'Presumably,' I say. 'Who else would do it?"

'Good. *Unless he had a very good reason for doing what he did*, then he would be hanged for treason. So, we are building up a picture of Sir Edmund in the days immediately before he disappeared. A Protestant and a Catholic. A loyal magistrate and a traitor who was in receipt of bribes from the French. Yet the treachery still feels odd, does it? After all, he was somebody who was punctilious in doing the right thing – think of the way he cleared his debts just before he died.'

'But,' I say, 'how does what you describe fit in with Godfrey's claim that Oates's deposition was his security, as he told people it was? It seems to be quite the reverse.'

Williamson smiles. 'I shall explain,' he says, 'or, rather, you will shortly see the answer yourself. Now, let us consider Godfrey's conduct on the day he supposedly died – please note, I say, supposedly. His manservant was anxious to accompany him. Such a thing would be perfectly normal. But Godfrey was adamant that he wished to go alone. Does that suggest to you he was about to do something that he was happy people knew about or something that he wished to cover up?'

'He undoubtedly wished his journey to remain secret,' says Aminta. 'There was no good reason for not taking Moor otherwise. Moor's subsequent journeys showed he was fit enough

to keep up with Godfrey. He was a clog on him in another sense
– that of preventing him doing something.'

'Precisely. Moor could be trusted with most things but not the
secret of his journey that morning. Nobody could be trusted with
that. Before Godfrey went out he received two visitors. One on
the Friday night and one on the Saturday morning. The one
on the Saturday morning was identified by Mistress Curtis as
Lawrence Hill. Can you think of any reason why Mistress Curtis
should have lied? Why she might have had a grudge against Hill?'

'No,' I say.

'Then we should assume that it was Hill and that the message
came from Somerset House. Shortly we shall have to decide why
that was.'

'And Mistress Curtis says the messenger on the Friday was
from you,' I say.

'She is correct. I always thought that the lowly Mistress Curtis
was the most intelligent of the servants. But again, I will explain
all of that in a moment,' says Williamson. 'Next, little was made
of it at the inquest, but have you considered the strange matter
of Godfrey's shirt?'

'It was very difficult to remove,' I say.

'Why? Think about it. Why was Godfrey so determined not
to give up his shirt?'

'His body was too stiff,' I say.

'Which means ... ? Come, you have lectured me on corpses
often enough. And you told Skillarne, who in turn wondered
about it enough to point it out to me when I visited him.'

But of course. That at least has been staring me in the face since
I first read the transcript of the inquest. It was stated quite clearly
that at the time of the inquest, the body was limp. But I missed
the significance of the shirt before the inquest had started.

'He can't have died on the Saturday night,' I say. 'The body was limp by the time the coroner examined it but still stiff when it was being undressed. And Brown described the body as being as stiff as clay when he came upon it the night before. A body remains stiff for up to thirty-six hours after death. Godfrey cannot have died until Wednesday at the earliest.'

'Exactly. So, he must have been kept alive somewhere between Saturday evening when he vanished and Wednesday when he was killed. Once again, we have to ask why?'

'Somebody wanted to question him,' I say.

'And the bruises?'

'The physicians could not agree on that. They thought it might be from a beating or that it could be due to the settling of blood.'

'Speaking as a layman, I'd say it's simpler to assume the marks are what they seemed to be, wouldn't you?'

'Very well. They beat him to get information, I suppose. Then they killed him, once they had it, because they couldn't risk releasing him.'

'No, they couldn't. Let us now consider a sequence of events. First, Oates approaches Godfrey. Next Godfrey and Coleman have a number of conversations. Letters are burnt. Next Coleman is arrested. His remaining letters are found with great ease – almost as if somebody had told the searchers where they were. They are evidence enough to condemn Coleman. Not even the Duke can save him. Shortly after, Godfrey is killed. Now do you see what happened?'

'Yes,' says Aminta.

'Yes,' I say. 'I don't quite see all of it. Who, for example, was your other investigator? But I think I now see most of it. And, yes, of course. That's why Godfrey died.'

The Final Chapter

In which we all provide some answers

'So,' I say, 'Godfrey was close to bankruptcy, when he was approached by Edward Coleman. Godfrey was a good choice as a man to bribe. He was the Court Justice, knew many influential people and was potentially able to supply information that would be of use to the French King in his dealings with King Charles.'

'That is precisely what happened,' says Williamson.

'How do you know?' I ask.

'Godfrey told me himself. He supplied Coleman with harmless snippets of gossip for some time and all was well. Then Coleman decided he wanted more for his money.'

'The Peyton Gang?' I say.

'Just so. Godfrey's masters needed to know how much of a danger they were to the Duke of York and other English Catholics. So, Coleman informed Godfrey it was time to deliver something more important and Godfrey obliged. Why shouldn't he? It wasn't exactly arduous work – he had only to find out where they met and then drink with them. He was never an extreme Protestant himself – but he was somebody that a group like the Peyton Gang would be comfortable recruiting, never suspecting for a moment that they were being infiltrated by an agent of the Duke of York.'

'He even owned a tavern in Hammersmith in which they could meet,' I say.

'So, Godfrey became part of the group of twelve on which Peyton relied. I doubt that it worried him that he was betraying any of their secrets. I think Godfrey disliked fanatics every bit as much as the King did. Godfrey's only problem was that I too was interested in Sir Robert Peyton. I already had a list of the members. When we swooped on the gang and deprived a number of them of their official positions, Godfrey was caught in the net.'

'So, you got him to change sides?' says Aminta.

'Exactly. In exchange for keeping his post as magistrate and not having to give up the much-needed bribes that Coleman was paying, Godfrey started to report to me on his dealings with the Duke's secretary and what was happening at Somerset House. I also got him to monitor the Catholics more generally.'

'So, you told Godfrey about the club at Primrose Hill and encouraged him to join it,' says Aminta. 'And the club members trusted him because he was Coleman's friend.'

'It gave us a further source of information,' says Williamson, 'about what they were saying in the city. Of course, knowing Godfrey was a friend of Coleman's, they held nothing back. In short, Godfrey became a fully fledged double agent. But the problem with double agents is, as you know only too well, that they can be uncertain which side they are really on. I think Godfrey sometimes had that problem. He had many acquaintances, but few close friends. He found friendship ... well, difficult. He was slightly overawed by the rich and articulate young secretary who was so keen to know him. Amidst all the deceit, I actually think there was something about the relationship that was genuine. And Coleman trusted him absolutely. He sent him on a mission to France last summer – Godfrey took messages to the French King's confessor and met other contacts there, all under the cover that he was travelling for pleasure. I was quite worried that we might not see him again, if the French saw through him, but he did return safely and gave me a very full report of his dealings with Père La Chaise. We discovered, for example, that Coleman was petitioning the French for funding for the Duke of York. Godfrey had a remarkable ability to ferret out facts.'

'Which meant,' says Aminta, 'that when Oates wanted to reveal his plot to somebody, Godfrey was the right man for you to direct him to. It had little to do with the fact that he was the Court Justice. He was already working for you and had the contacts to be able to investigate whether there was anything in the accusations.'

'I doubted there was any truth in them at all,' says Williamson, 'but it was worth checking.'

'So, when he took Oates's deposition to Coleman, it wasn't because he was a traitor – it was because you ordered him to?'

'Exactly so. I told Godfrey not to reveal what he was doing to anyone else – and especially not to Danby. Godfrey said it would look like treason. After all, he was still in receipt of Coleman's money. He feared that he would hang for it. He was a man who worried about things and that in turn worried me. I said I would ensure nobody ever accused him of being a traitor – nor did they.'

'And when Godfrey said that Oates's deposition was his security ...'

'He meant that my orders to him to reveal the deposition proved he was working for us, not against us. So, Godfrey went and spoke to the Duke's secretary – discussed it all at some length. Coleman wasn't too worried why he was doing it – it was the sort of gossipy intrigue that he enjoyed. Godfrey reported back to me that there was nothing in Oates's accusations whatsoever – it was complete fantasy. I was able to inform the King of that fact. We could let the Oates business run its course, and it was perfectly safe for the King to go off to Newmarket or wherever he fancied going. It was clear to me, however, that Coleman was increasingly a danger to everyone – directly to the Duke but indirectly to the King and the state itself. His correspondence with the French court was becoming wilder and wilder. He had to be stopped and it had to be shown that the King was taking firm action against such traitors. Coleman was worried enough about Oates that he was in the process of burning his extensive correspondence with the French, but he was doing it slowly and reluctantly. He loved rereading his own *bon mots* and La Chaise's delicious replies. Godfrey told me where the remaining letters were hidden – accidentally, I think, but he told me. So, when Coleman was arrested, my men quickly found what we were looking for. All very nicely done. It was clear Godfrey was an agent of the greatest value to us, so long as his role in Coleman's downfall was not suspected by the Catholics.'

'But it was,' I say.

'These things happen. Coleman told the Duke that the only person who knew about the letters was Godfrey. The Duke was obviously furious that his former secretary had been treated in such an arbitrary manner. In one sense, the Duke would have also been glad to see the back of him, but not like that. There was a hurried investigation held at Somerset House. The Duke concluded rightly that it was Godfrey who had betrayed Coleman. The Duke has a long memory for betrayals, but in this case he only needed to remember for a few days. I heard from somebody that things were looking bad and sent a messenger to Godfrey on the Friday night that there had been a meeting between the Duke and some of his people at Somerset House. I realise now that this troubled Godfrey a great deal, but at the time he just sent back a message that he didn't know what to make of it. Then, the following day, Hill was sent by the Duke of York to order Godfrey to report to Somerset House. Had I known that, I would have told Godfrey to go into hiding at once, but instead he dressed in his finest to go and meet the Duke and brazen it out. He never lacked courage. Then, quite suddenly it would seem, he decided that he would first go to the club in Primrose Hill to ask around and see if there were rumours that anyone had informed on him. At least, I can see no other explanation for his actions. Primrose Hill would have been a strange place for him to have gone for any other reason. There's nothing of interest there except fields and woods and the inn, and nothing of interest at the inn except the club. He changed into clothes more suited to the muddy fields and set out, with enough money in his pockets to bribe people generously if necessary. I don't know what he was told there but, by the early afternoon, he was clearly reassured enough to keep the appointment with the Duke.'

'So he went there quite willingly?' asks Aminta.

'As I say, my Lady, he had no sense of danger. It was the same with the Plague. He'd just charge into a pest house to arrest a thief, when nobody else would have dared. When he got to Somerset House, he was shown to the undercroft beneath the chapel. That didn't surprise him. He knew the meeting would be secret.'

'Is Somerset House the grain of truth in the tale?' I ask.

'One of the grains. There are others.'

'How do you know all this?'

'You've always accused me of having another investigator. He told me what I've just told you, though it took him some time to dig it all out. Once there and confronted by an angry Duke, Godfrey quickly realised his mistake, but it was too late. They interrogated him for four days, down in the crypt, by the light of wax candles brought in from the chapel. They beat him. I don't need a physician's opinion on the bruises. I know they beat him. They wanted to discover exactly what he had told me. The whole thing was nothing like Bedloe's account – that was clearly nonsense and invented just to get the money. Godfrey's dead body was never in Doctor Godden's lodgings. But the crypt was certainly a good place to keep a living man. Quiet as the grave down there. And they issued instructions from the Queen that nobody was to enter the palace, as you know from Stringer's evidence at the trial.'

'So that was another grain?'

'If you like. I am certain that the Queen was complicit. I was hoping to find written proof in her correspondence, but as you know I was prevented from doing so.'

'How much did Godfrey reveal?'

'Not a lot, I think. I've said he was a brave man. I'm fairly sure he would have died before he gave anything away. They would have got his pocket book, of course – we know he had it with him when he left the house but it wasn't on the body when it was found. Like Coleman's letters, much in the book may have condemned him, unless it was in code. Afterwards, there was no way they could let him go. None at all. I mean, he knew the Duke was involved in it. He'd have gone straight to me, to Scroggs or to

Danby and that would have been that. Nothing the King could have done would have saved the Duke then. Nothing. On the Wednesday, I think, they gave up on questioning and strangled him. Broke his neck in the process. They'd run out of time. Even in the crypt, somebody would have found him sooner or later. The order from the Queen couldn't have kept my agents out for ever. If the King hadn't stopped me searching Somerset House, I would have proved her part in it.'

'What would you have done then?'

'The Queen would have had to go, of course. Not to the Tower necessarily, but into exile. Back to Portugal. Or to Barbados maybe.'

'Had the King known your intentions, he would have stopped your operation straight away.'

'He's stopped it now.'

'How did they dispose of the body?'

'Not in a sedan chair, that's certain. The guards were telling the truth there, at least. Godfrey was cleaned up a bit after his beating – nicely polished shoes, though they should have also brushed the wax off his clothes. That was the day, as you'll also recall from the trial, that the Queen left Somerset House to go and greet the King. The soldiers reminded us of that and of the fact that the Queen never travels alone. Two or three carriages of maids and footmen and secretaries and ladies in waiting would have accompanied her. It was easy enough for another carriage to slip in behind them as the procession left Somerset House. A little way further on, it turned down a side street, then headed for Primrose Hill. The murderers knew that he'd visited it on Saturday. He'd told them that much. They knew there would be witnesses who would swear they'd seen him. What they didn't know was that he'd also been seen back in town afterwards

– that only really came out at the inquest. So they thought, if his body was found at Primrose Hill, it would look as if he'd gone there and stayed there – he'd never been close to Somerset House all day. The body presented problems for the men sent with it. As you know, it had already stiffened up by the time they reached Primrose Hill – more or less in the position it was in the carriage. That's why it looked so odd in the ditch, with the knees in the water and the clean shoes high and dry. It's also, as you've realised, why the clothes were so difficult to remove. They could just manage to get the coat off but the shirt had to be cut away.'

'Who took him there?' I ask.

'Green, Berry and Hill, of course. All loyal servants of the Duke and Duchess, trusted to keep quiet and capable of delivering a body to a ditch.'

'And they decided it would look better if Godfrey had been run through with his sword?' I say. 'So, this thing that puzzled us so much really was just the bad idea of three uneducated men, given a job that was beyond their ability and that must have terrified them.'

Williamson shakes his head. 'I think they were told to do it. Don't forget it was Godfrey's own sword. It was probably a coded message to me: my agent had nobody to blame for his death but himself. At least, that's how I took it.'

'So, you couldn't let that go unanswered,' I say.

'Certainly not. They weren't going to kill one of my people and get away with it.' Williamson pokes the fire again, more for dramatic effect than anything. The coals burst into flame. Williamson straightens up again with a much exaggerated grunt. 'Clearly I couldn't strike directly at the Duke, and the killers had gone long since.'

'But you could remove the accessories,' I say.

'It was obvious they didn't kill Godfrey – that was the two men calling themselves Gerald and Kelly – but they cleaned up after the killers. Green, Berry and Hill would do well enough.'

'And the actual killers, Gerald and Kelly?'

'Fled the same night. They would have been well on their way to France before the inquest even opened. But their three accomplices had nowhere to go, and anyway thought themselves safe because the Duke told them they would be. Initially it must have seemed a stroke of luck for them that everyone thought Godfrey died on Saturday – they all had alibis in place for that evening. Interestingly, if you remember from the trial, Berry claimed to have been playing bowls on the afternoon of the day Godfrey actually died, something nobody ever saw the need to check. In fact, that's when he and his friends were depositing Godfrey in a ditch. The three of them would have struggled if cross-examined over where they really were on Wednesday. Still, it was all the same in the end, because nobody believed them or their witnesses.'

'So, that's why you wanted them convicted, even though they hadn't killed Godfrey?' I say.

'Them or some larger fish. One or two of the more senior servants of the Duke who had helped plan the whole thing. A lot of people had a hand in it. But in the end it was them.'

'Your informant told you a great deal,' I say.

'Yes, he did.'

'So, why not produce him at the men's trials to say that? Why go through the farce of using Prance? Was it because your informant didn't want anyone to know he was reporting to you?'

'Exactly. And nor did I, if he was to carry on working for me, which it was vitally important that he did. I'm sorry I couldn't tell you who it was. I'm also sorry so much of your time was taken up with irrelevant evidence, but there wasn't much I could do about that either. The brothers feared that it was suicide and did everything they could to avoid that verdict, including bullying the servants into lying and trying to suppress any new piece of evidence, such as the missing shirt, that might cause the coroner to revisit a perfectly good murder verdict. They muddied the waters a good deal.'

'Since Godfrey was your agent,' I say, 'it explains why you knew by Saturday evening more or less what must have happened?'

'Yes. The brothers were already running around in a panic. Word reached us pretty quickly. We were in a position to put two and two together and we started to make enquiries then too. My people and the brothers both asking questions would have started tongues wagging. Bear in mind that, if we could have found out exactly where Godfrey was being held on the Saturday night, we could have saved him. It was worth trying. But the orders from the Queen meant we couldn't search Somerset House, even though that was one of the places we thought he might have been. I should have gone in anyway. Yes, I made mistakes. Like you, I had begun to think that it was probably suicide – that I'd simply put too much pressure on Godfrey and he'd cracked under the strain. I often didn't know quite what to make of him. But once I'd spoken to Skillarne and concluded that the death occurred on Wednesday, suicide was no longer a possible option, as you yourself also worked out. So, it was murder. Pembroke, Peyton and Oates all seemed to have motives, but there was a complete lack of evidence in each case. And, while any of them might have killed him in theory, I was convinced none of them would in practice have done it the way it had been done. I'd almost given up, then my other informant told me of the rumours that were circulating in Somerset House about Green, Berry and Hill undertaking an odd expedition for the Duke and about strange goings-on in the crypt. After that it all made sense. And I knew what I had to do.'

'Bedloe's invented evidence must have been a nuisance,' says Aminta.

'Exactly. I had enough genuine information by that stage to be certain nothing like that had happened and that he had just invented the names. But we were stuck with what he'd said, because Oates supported him.'

'So, you got Prance?' I say. 'And came up with a story that didn't entirely contradict Bedloe, but contained a grain or two of truth. In particular, the involvement of Green, Berry and Hill.'

'I think you suggested Prance's name to me some time ago – after your visit to Primrose Hill. I heard nothing more of him until he was denounced by one of his tenants and dragged before the Commons committee. Then I realised what we might use him for. He was, after all, a man of previous good character, who genuinely had a knowledge of Somerset House. We got Bedloe along to the House of Commons to identify him. We arrested Prance and told him what he needed to say.'

'So, when I got him to tell the truth . . .'

'It was very inconvenient indeed. That's when I realised I would have to stand you down if I was to get anywhere. I'm sorry about that. But Prance came round to the right way of thinking eventually. And, unlike Bedloe, he proved to be an excellent witness. But even if we had stuck to the plain unvarnished truth, Green, Berry and Hill would probably have been hanged as accessories both before and after the fact. They did actually assist both with summoning Godfrey to Somerset House before the murder and disposing of the body afterwards. Perhaps other things too. And they did nothing to stop the actual killers from escaping. There's no getting round any of that. Obviously Berry was quite right to say, before they hanged him, that he was innocent of the crimes they charged him with. They'd just charged him with the wrong things.'

'You imply they would have been hanged anyway,' I say, 'but, since the principals had fled, it would have been difficult to convict the accomplices. The principal must be convicted before there is anything that the accessory can be said to have aided.'

'You are right, that would have been another impediment if we had simply stuck to the truth,' says Williamson. 'But just because that is the law, it doesn't mean Scroggs wouldn't have found a way round it anyway.'

He's right. Once it had been decided the three men needed to die, for the good of the state, then there was no hope for them. Any judge would have done the same as Scroggs.

'Everything about the trial must have looked very unfair to you,' Williamson continues, 'and so it was. But the result was exactly what it should have been. Three of the men responsible for Godfrey's death have been convicted and hanged.'

'What you still haven't told me,' I say, 'is who your other investigator was. I thought it might be Lloyd, but I can't see him providing information on what was happening at Somerset House. I also thought at one stage that it might be Prance, but he has to be vastly more important than that for you to protect him so carefully.'

'Sadly, I can't tell you who he was,' says Williamson. 'I still have some loyalty to him. Shall I call for some wine? You have a cold walk back to your lodgings.'

'Chiffinch,' I say.

Williamson pauses, his hand on the bell rope. 'Why do you say that?'

'It's obvious. He has access to more information than anyone at court. He's trusted by the King and the Duke. He's as much at home at Somerset House as he is at Whitehall. And he's very good at getting people to talk. But you can't reveal him as your source because, right up to the moment you were sacked, he was helping you with your investigation into the actions of the Queen. The very thing that the King would eventually dismiss you for, but you were not to know that then. You thought you still needed Chiffinch for something very much bigger than a murder trial. Had he, rather than Prance, openly given evidence that he knew exactly what had happened to Godfrey, including the Duke of York's role in it, he would immediately have lost the King's trust and you would have lost your source of information.'

'Well, it makes no difference now. Sunderland has replaced me. He'll go along with anything the King says. He'll come to a bad end, but probably not soon enough.'

'I'm sure he'll continue to use Chiffinch,' says Aminta. 'You've done him a favour there.'

'I'm sure he will,' says Williamson. 'He won't find Kelly or Gerald, though. They'll be in Paris by now with different names. Maybe their real ones, maybe something else. It depends what the Jesuits want them to do next.'

'I really believed Green, Berry and Hill were innocent,' I say.

'And, in a way, they were,' says Williamson. 'They were as innocent as the day they were born. Utterly without malice or ill intent. Good men, who simply wanted to get on with their lives as quietly as possible. But they were unable to resist the orders of their masters that they should assist in the killing of Sir Edmund Berry Godfrey. That unfortunately made them murderers. Or accessories anyway. I suppose we shall never know the whole tale.

Not now Green, Berry and Hill are dead. People will continue to speculate, of course, but some stories are lost for ever. Well, there it is, John. I'll call for some wine, shall I?'

Journey's End

Was it morning or evening outside? Sometimes, down here where everything was blank stone lit by wax candles, he could just make out a church bell slowly tolling the hours, but the ten chimes he had just heard could signify one or the other equally well. It all depended on how long he slept after the last beating.

He'd certainly been here at least three days. The questioning had seemed endless. How much had he told Williamson? Why was he carrying so much money? What was the meaning of the strange code in his pocket book? They wouldn't tell him who they were, but he'd recognised the Duke of York, even with the cloak concealing the lower part of his face. He'd enjoy giving evidence against him.

But first he had to get out of this crypt and that meant sending a message to Williamson. He needed to find himself alone with one of his captors, so he could talk him into helping. Appeal to his reason and good sense. He knew he'd only get one chance – he'd have to choose carefully. But who was most likely to switch sides? The tall thin one or the old one or the stupid one? He heard the footsteps of somebody – just the one – outside. A key turned in the lock. It was the stupid one. The one who'd told him he was a Protestant. Yes, of course. Things had fallen out well.

'They told me to check that you were all right,' said the man, not unkindly.

'I wouldn't mind some food,' he said.

'I can only give you water. Unless you want to confess what you've done. Those are my orders.'

The man looked apologetic. He didn't like what he'd been asked to do. That was promising.

'You know they'll hang you for this? If I die, they'll hang you.'

'The Duke will protect us,' said the man.

Admitting the Duke of York was directly involved? He was surprised that even this one would make a mistake like that.

'Listen,' he said quickly, 'your Duke can't protect anyone. Not Edward Coleman, who as you know has already been arrested. And certainly not you. But I can protect you. I'll say you did me no harm and that you took a message from me to Secretary of State Williamson. The others will die, and deservedly, but you won't. Not if you do as I say.'

'And you want me to do what . . . ?'

'Go to Williamson and say that Sir Edmund Berry Godfrey is being held prisoner at Somerset House. That's all. He'll do the rest. You'll only be gone half an hour at the most. They'll never notice.' The man looked at him uncertainly. Was he going to help him? Godfrey had no idea. How could he tell? He took one of the three small gold coins from his pocket and proffered it to his jailer. 'Take it. There'll be more if you do as I say.'

The man allowed the money to drop lightly, almost unfelt, into his calloused palm and then closed a large fist round it. He nodded as if he understood. He turned and went back through the doorway. Again there was the sound of a key turning in the lock.

So, it was done. Mistress Gibbon was always telling him that he was not a good judge of character – his godson Godfrey Harrison, for example. But he knew that this time he'd made the right decision. The man he'd just entrusted with his life wouldn't let him down. Sir Edmund Berry Godfrey, magistrate and vestryman of Saint Martin-in-the-Fields, finally breathed a long sigh of relief.

The hours passed even more slowly now he knew help was on the way. Distantly the bells chimed twelve, then one, then two. But afternoon or nighttime?

Eventually he heard footsteps again outside. Several people were hurrying in his direction. The man had reached Williamson and Williamson had been as good as his word. It was going to be all right. However bleak things might have looked, however many bad choices he'd made over the past month – and, God knows, he'd made a few – he was actually going to get away with it.

He turned, with a confident smile on his face, towards the already opening door.

A Factual Note

Wat you have just read, and I cannot stress this strongly enough, is a fiction. But the real murder of Sir Edmund Berry Godfrey is one of the great unsolved cases in British criminal history. So, you may well wish to know to what extent I have stuck to the facts and to what extent I have allowed myself some artistic licence.

The short answer is that I told the truth mainly. ('There was things which he stretched, but mainly he told the truth', as somebody once said of a better writer than I am.)

The longer answer is as follows.

The crime remains, 350 years after Godfrey vanished, a mystery. That is not because people have failed to provide solutions, from the mundane to the highly imaginative. The first comprehensive account was that of Roger L'Estrange, sometimes called the first English journalist. In 1687, less than a decade after the murder, he produced *A Brief History of the Times*. It remains a good starting point for anyone seriously interested in the case. By then Charles II was dead, Oates discredited and the Catholic James II was on the throne. L'Estrange still had access to almost every witness who had given evidence at the inquest and the trials. They were interviewed at length. He concluded that Green, Berry and Hill were innocent, and that Godfrey had committed suicide. Roger North, in another early account, implied that Oates, Danby or Shaftesbury had commissioned the murder, but he was too cautious to say so openly.

Thereafter, writers have tended to fall into one of a number of camps.

Alan Marshall, a historian who has written extensively on the Popish Plot and the murder, supported the suicide-by-hanging theory, as did the psychologist Alexander Kennedy in a radio programme in the early 1950s. As a variant on this, Alfred Marks suggested that Godfrey did in fact stab himself to death rather than die by strangulation. Those that argue it was suicide stress Godfrey's mental state in the weeks leading up to his disappearance, his repeated predictions that he would hang, his brothers' and servants' fears that he had killed himself, the family history of mental illness, the previous occasions (notably during his university and legal studies) when he was obliged to give up his ambitions because of undisclosed medical problems, and the forensic evidence for death by strangulation. There are good arguments for saying that this is the simplest and most obvious solution.

A second theory, first put forward in a general way by the philosopher David Hume and then developed by J. G. Muddiman in 1924, was that Godfrey was killed by Philip Herbert, Earl of Pembroke. This was then taken up and developed into the most readable account of the case – John Dickson Carr's 1936 'true crime' book *The Murder of Sir Edmund Godfrey*. This argument is also convincing. Pembroke was notoriously violent. Godfrey (as I describe in the fictional account) had been on a grand jury that had indicted him for murder. The Earl was eventually found guilty by the House of Lords but was released having pleaded benefit of clergy (as members of the nobility could). He later went on to kill again. The injuries suffered by Godfrey before his hanging were almost identical to those inflicted by Pembroke on his other victims. According to this theory, Godfrey fled the country immediately after Pembroke's release, quite possibly fearing retribution – that he simply went on holiday would have been very unlike him. Some claim that the journey in question had in fact been during the previous year and therefore could have had nothing to do with Pembroke, but it is not essential to the Pembroke hypothesis that Godfrey did flee nor is it essential to my own plot. I have, for the purposes of this story, stuck with Muddiman and Carr on the date of the trip. If they are right about that, then it is not impossible that Godfrey did try to avoid Pembroke's revenge or (alternatively) that Coleman could have sent him to Europe as I describe. There are other clues pointing to Pembroke. Amongst the many stories that circulated after Godfrey's death, one was (as in the narrative) that his body had been found close to where Pembroke lived. One of the messengers who visited Godfrey could have been sent by Pembroke summoning him to a meeting. Pembroke possessed a carriage to transport the body and had loyal servants to help him. And Godfrey could have got wax on his clothes at Pembroke's residence, just as easily as he could in a Catholic chapel. Again, the theory is appealing because it is simple and straightforward, involving no complex plots. He was killed by a man known to be violent and whom he had offended deeply.

As a variation on this, Stephen Knight, writing in the 1980s, invokes the Peyton Gang in addition to Pembroke. Godfrey, as I say in the fictional account, was associated with the gang, which was actively plotting to restore Richard Cromwell as head of state. Later, he appeared to sympathise with the Catholics. That Peyton might have wanted revenge for that desertion is quite possible. Sir John Hall, in his *Four Famous Mysteries*, also tentatively suggests the Peyton Gang as possible perpetrators. Peyton and his supporters seem to me to be amongst the less likely killers, however, primarily because nobody appears to have blamed them at the time and no evidence has been put forward since that any of the gang members were involved. But it must be conceded that they undoubtedly had a motive.

J. P. Kenyon, the early modern historian and one of the leading experts on the Popish Plot, considers that the most likely explanation is that it was an unknown footpad with no previous connection to Godfrey, whose anonymity enabled him to escape all suspicion. This explains why the real killer was never caught. It also explains the delay in transporting Godfrey's body to Primrose Hill – working alone, he needed time to obtain a cart. The problem is why he went to all that effort but couldn't be bothered to take the money in Godfrey's pockets.

Few writers suggest that Godfrey's death was actually the direct result of a Catholic plot, but John Pollock puts this forward in his 1903 book, *The Popish Plot*. He claims the secret that Godfrey knew was that there had been a clandestine 'consult' of the Jesuits in 1678 and that he had to be killed to keep this quiet. The real killers were the more prominent men named by Bedloe, not Green, Berry and Hill, but the course of events was broadly as described by Miles Prance. Pollock cites the fact that Prance was relatively well treated by James II after he came to the throne, in spite of Prance's eventual conviction for perjury, suggesting that he was considered to have performed a valuable service in helping to shield the senior Catholics who had organised the murder.

North hinted at Oates as the killer, but few modern authorities have followed this up, although Sir James Fitzjames Stephen suggested it. The problem is that Oates personally seems to have been a coward and that (as I say in the narrative) he was always content to use judicial murder.

So far, so good, then. You will have noticed that, in my fictitious account, Sir John and Lady Grey give due consideration at some point to all of these possibilities – murder by the Jesuits because Godfrey knew too much about something, suicide, Pembroke's revenge, Oates and (in passing) the possible involvement of the Peyton Gang.

And yet, none of these possibilities seem to me to be particularly convincing. There are things that all of the previous writers (with the greatest respect) have failed to take into account.

First and foremost is the date of Godfrey's death. Forensic science was less well understood in the seventeenth century than it is now. People did know – and it was returned to over and over again during the inquest – that a stab wound after death would not bleed (or not much). But rigor mortis was poorly understood. Skillarne the surgeon actually gave evidence that 'the Bodies of Persons that are Hang'd, or Strangled, are always Limber; Whereas Bodies that Dye a Natural Death, are always Stiff, except in Apoplexies'. They would therefore have missed the significance of the evidence given by Mister Fisher who prepared the body for examination – Godfrey's corpse was so stiff that he could not remove the shirt and had to cut it off. But by the time the surgeons examined the body this was no longer so

– it was 'limber' again. The description of the attitude of the body when it was found in the ditch – and the constable reporting that it was as stiff as clay – also suggests that it had stiffened in an unnatural position by the Wednesday evening. These things together (if accurately reported in contemporary records) give us a fairly precise timing for Godfrey's death. Though affected by a number of factors, including temperature and the size of the body, rigor mortis usually sets in between one and six hours after death and disappears between twelve and thirty-six hours after death. If there was still rigor mortis when the body was found, and none by the time it was examined by the surgeons (quite shortly afterwards), it suggests that Godfrey was killed most likely on the Wednesday. He cannot possibly have died on the Saturday night.

Another fact that makes suicide difficult to believe is that Godfrey's neck was completely broken. Skillarne, who gave evidence at both the inquest and the trial, made it clear that this damage went beyond any normal hanging by suicide. The twentieth-century pathologist Keith Simpson (in response to the radio programme by Alexander Kennedy) thought that the description of the marks on Godfrey's throat suggested he could not have hanged himself – they were too low down – and that he must have been strangled with a ligature. Of course, there are (as I say) ways in which the neck might have been broken after death, but the likelihood has to be that he didn't hang himself.

There is also the question of Godfrey's stomach. Some writers say that there was no autopsy because the family objected. Others, including Skillarne at the trial of the three men, state clearly that there was one and that Godfrey's stomach was found to be completely empty. Was there an autopsy but a less thorough one than there might have been? It is one of the things we shall never know for certain, but it was certainly believed at the time that Godfrey had not eaten for days before his death, and this was mentioned by Doctor Lloyd at Godfrey's funeral. Of course, an empty stomach does not prove somebody has not eaten for days – the stomach empties in a few hours after a meal. Still, it supports the idea that Godfrey could have been imprisoned and starved before his death.

A further fact that has been largely discounted in the past is Coleman's role as an agent of the French court and the money he had at his command. It seems perfectly possible, to me at least, that Godfrey was in the pay of Coleman. Godfrey almost certainly needed money after his near bankruptcy. Coleman's peremptory command to attend on him ('one Clark would speak with him') supports the idea of an employer/employee relationship. I have no evidence that Godfrey was working as a double agent for Williamson, but it would certainly explain why Godfrey showed Oates's deposition to Coleman but was never accused of treason.

Another question that isn't really addressed by most of the studies is why Godfrey went to Primrose Hill. Plenty of witnesses saw him going there and some said that he had been seen there before. That he was part of the Catholic club that met at the White House (to which his body would later be taken) is as good a reason as I can find. Though I don't mention it in the book, Godfrey was a good friend of Richard Mulys, who was definitely a member of the club, and Godfrey openly expressed his fears of hanging with Mulys.

Williamson's role too needs to be looked at. He was never in the forefront of the investigations, oddly for somebody whose job was managing a spy network, but was always hovering in the background. Coleman gave himself up to Williamson, for example – not to Danby and certainly not to Oates. We know that Williamson never really believed in the Popish Plot or in Oates personally, in which history has proved him right. He was clearly well informed. We also know that he referred Oates to Godfrey. His eventual rift with the King and his subsequent sacking was over his search of Somerset House just before the trial of Green, Berry and Hill. What was he hoping to find? Or to cover up?

That Godfrey might have been working for Williamson, spying on the Duke of York and other Catholics, might explain a statement of Godfrey's that people have puzzled over. He said to a friend, Thomas Wynnel (though I attribute part of it to Mistress Gibbon in the fictional account): 'There is a design against the Duke of York and this will come to a dispute amongst them. You may live to see the end on't but I shall not. This much I tell you: I am master of a secret, a dangerous secret, and it will be fatal to me. My security in the business was Oates's deposition. Before Oates came to me he first declared it to a public minister; and then Oates came to me by that minister's direction. And then again, but no matter.' John Dickson Carr assumed that the minister in question was Danby and failed to get very far with explaining what Godfrey could have meant. The minister who had sent Oates to Godfrey was, however, Williamson. The dangerous secret could therefore have been that he was working for Williamson against a member of the royal family. The security was Williamson's instruction to him to let Coleman have Oates's deposition, which provided some sort of guarantee that Williamson would have to stand by him if the full facts became known. Or then again, he may have meant something entirely different, or Wynnel may have misquoted him, in whole or part. There is little in the Godfrey case that is completely clear and unambiguous.

The Queen too keeps a low profile but appears at critical points of the story. She, or her servants, did issue the instructions that nobody was to be admitted to Somerset House at exactly the time Godfrey's body may have been concealed there. She left Somerset House at a time when Godfrey's body is most likely to have been removed. Williamson obviously had his suspicions of her. I am not sure anyone else has ever identified the witness Mr Stringer as Shaftesbury's steward, but if I am right then his main purpose seems to have been to try to draw public attention to the Queen's involvement.

Chiffinch's contribution is notable mainly for being covered up. In the transcript of the trial he appears as 'Mr Chevins', who mutters a few innocuous words and departs. Those who were there confirmed he'd said a lot more, but it was evidently redacted in the official published version. What is certain is that, in 1679, Chiffinch was in receipt of secret service money. Payments to him continue after Williamson's time. Though it is unclear how much contact he had with Williamson (and his successors), he must have been doing something to justify the rewards.

Finally, nobody much questions why Green, Berry and Hill were selected by whoever told Prance what to say. They weren't mentioned by Bedloe. It is unlikely that they were chosen by Prance himself, unless he was more vindictive than he appears – the men were, after all, servants of his customers. Green, Berry and Hill were not even typical of the other victims of the Popish Plot, who tended to occupy more prominent positions in society. So who did decide to sacrifice them and why? The first part of the question is unknowable. But isn't the most likely answer to the second part that they actually were in some way involved in Godfrey's murder – perhaps, as I suggest, as accessories? It is even possible they were active participants in the murder – they would have been in the right place at the right time, with no alibis that we know of for the day in question. It is true that they all seem decent men, who just wanted to be left alone to get on with their lives. But the pressure on them from their employers would have been enormous. They were just unlucky to get caught up in something that was much bigger than they were. And it crushed them.

I hope that what I have said so far will at least convince you that my decision to declare Green, Berry and Hill guilty does not stem simply from a crime writer's desire to make the 'least likely suspect' the murderer. I am not suggesting that my solution should stand beside L'Estrange's, Hall's, Carr's, Marks's and Marshall's. But I do think that it is perfectly viable and fits all of the facts as known.

In terms of how I have told the story, I have stuck to the accepted dates and places as much as possible – departing from them only where the evidence seemed to justify it. In describing the trial of the three men, most of the time I have taken testimony verbatim from the court reports. I can justify the occasional deviation in a number of ways. First, undiluted seventeenth-century dialogue can be tedious and occasionally difficult to understand. The occasional paraphrase hurts nobody, especially where it clarifies for a modern audience what was meant. Second, what we have is what the clerk of the court recorded – which is not necessarily what the witnesses actually said. No version can hope to be completely true. Finally, the text was then, before publication, edited and approved by the Lord Chief Justice. This last fact probably explains why 'Mr Chevins' gets such a brief mention. I have no qualms about expanding it to what I think he may have actually said.

I must also admit to having misattributed statements – for example, giving Mister Mulys's words to Mistress Gibbon, as described above, in order to simplify the sometimes bewilderingly long list of witnesses. I have also allowed John Grey to learn some things in 1678 that would not be generally known until after L'Estrange's investigation some years later – but to do otherwise would be to deprive you, the reader, of relevant facts that you needed, to decide who the murderer was.

There are inevitably things I have missed out – the real story has too many characters, too many subplots for a work of fiction. Readers who know the Popish Plot well will look in vain for Tonge, Pickering, Wakeman or Ireland. The story that I was most sorry to leave out was that of Sam Atkins, Samuel Pepys's clerk. Since Pepys worked for the Duke of York, he and his own staff were targets for Oates and the other plotters. Bedloe claimed to have seen Sam Atkins amongst the murderers around Godfrey's body at Somerset House. Atkins protested his innocence but was thrown into jail. He was offered his freedom if he informed on Pepys. He very properly refused to do so, and endured many weeks in a cell as a result. Then he remembered what he had actually been doing on the night that he had been accused of being at Somerset House – he had been out on the Thames, until much later than he should have been, with a couple of young ladies and a few bottles of wine. It was the sort of conduct Pepys had reprimanded him for in the past, and it was therefore an embarrassing alibi to have to present, but Atkins was able to use it to good effect at his trial and was eventually released, without ever having said a word against his master. Pepys later helped Atkins in his subsequent career. It is a small tale of fortitude, heroism and virtue rewarded (with just enough vice added in to make it interesting). It deserves to be told, though in the end it provides no clues as to who killed Sir Edmund Berry Godfrey, hence its omission.

In short, this is a work of fiction, and I am allowed both to omit and to add as I see fit. Still, as I sit here in my study, on the anniversary of Berry's death, looking out at the first signs of spring in the garden, I think I can say that I have told the truth mainly and stretched things only where they really needed a bit of stretching.

Thanks

To David for his unfailing support over many years. To Krystyna and to Little, Brown for their continuing faith in the series. To Ann for reading the manuscript first and much else. To Howard for stepping brilliantly into the breach. To Trystan for being our fifth grandchild. And, last but not least, to the cardiology department at the Queen Alexandra Hospital Portsmouth, to whom I was rushed in an ambulance halfway through editing (but that, as they say, is another story).